Born in Hertfordshire in 1959, Dougie Brimson joined the RAF directly from school where he trained as a mechanical engineer. After serving for over eighteen years, and attaining the rank of sergeant, he left the forces in 1994 to forge a career as a writer.

Following the co-authorship of four non-fiction books examining the culture of football hooliganism, Dougie struck out on his own in 1998 and made the move into fiction with two books including the Lynda La Plante-inspired thriller, *The Crew*.

The following year, he returned to the issue of hooliganism with *Barmy Army*, a book which continues to cause controversy almost a year after publication.

He is currently writing another novel featuring characters from *The Crew* and has a burgeoning career as a television presenter and producer.

Dougie has been married to Tina for almost eighteen years and they have three children.

Billy's Log

The hilarious diary of one man's struggle with life, lager and the female race

Dougie Brimson

HEADLINE

First published in 2000
by HEADLINE BOOK PUBLISHING

10 9 8 7 6 5 4 3 2

ISBN 0 7472 6386 8

Typeset by Avon Dataset Ltd, Bidford-on-Avon, Warks

Printed and bound in Great Britain by
Mackays of Chatham plc, Chatham, Kent

HEADLINE BOOK PUBLISHING
A division of Hodder Headline
338 Euston Road
London NW1 3BH

www.headline.co.uk
www.hodderheadline.com

Dedication

For the lads who inspired this book.

Acknowledgements

With huge thanks to Tina,
Jacque and the girls at JEM.
Onwards and upwards!

This book was written on a
Pentium II computer supplied
by CTX Computers Europe Ltd
(01923 810800)

Chapter 1

The Wake

Friday 31 December 1999

16.30 p.m. – At home

Bollocks. If I wasn't depressed before, I sure am now. Why the bloody hell do I put myself through this every year? No one else I know keeps a diary, so why the hell do I? I mean, it's not as if I'm Richard Branson or David Beckham or that life is a constant whirl of parties and loose women. In fact, if the evidence of the last 365 days is anything to go by, my life is shite.

What really gets me is that I had such high hopes for 1999. I honestly believed that the two aims I set myself this time last year were achievable and for once, when I looked back, I'd be able to congratulate myself on a job well done. But no. Instead of a smug feeling of satisfaction, I have the all too familiar gut-wrenching ache of failure. I wouldn't mind so much if those ambitions were anything special. It wasn't as if I wanted to climb Everest or fly a Harrier jump jet. As a healthy, heterosexual male, is it really that unreasonable to want a bit of female company? And shouldn't everyone be looking for promotion at work?

But aside from a drunken fumble almost nine months ago, I've had sod all in the way of sex. And even that was more down to luck than judgement. After all, it's not every day that you bump into a drunken twenty-two-year-old Essex girl who's just found out her bloke is having it away with her best mate and has convinced herself that the most obvious way to teach them both a lesson is to have sex with the first available male she meets.

At least I *almost* got promotion. In fact I probably would have if that bastard Sean hadn't shown me his copy of *Maxim*. That's where the idea to photocopy my arse came from and I'm still convinced that bastard knew they'd put CCTV cameras in the copy room. Of course, it did briefly elevate me to comic genius status, which is something I suppose. Although things might have been different if anyone had twigged on to the fact that when I said I was taking a picture of my chocky starfish to see if my piles had cleared up or not, I was actually telling the truth rather than taking the piss. The high-ups on the top floor weren't impressed, that's for sure. I knew I should have gone to plan B, and told them that what I had actually been doing was using my initiative to save the company time and money. After all, a quick flash of their copier works out a damn site cheaper than a day on the sick.

Mind you, much as I'm pissed off about it, 1999 wasn't all bad. The trip to Wembley and winning promotion with the Hornets was one of the best days ever. And I did discover the delights of *Sabrina The Teenage Witch*, although I guess I really should be more concerned about that than gratified.

The other big plus of 1999 was that I finally got rid of the flat-mate from hell. I still can't work out what I was thinking of, letting my spare room to an Australian minge magnet. Did I really think, or hope, that his formidable sexual prowess would in some way rub off on me? If so, I must have been bloody raving. Listening to some antipodean stud rogering his way through the entire female population of south Hertfordshire may be strangely arousing at first, but after the sixth consecutive night, it becomes a major pain. And walking into the kitchen to find a different semi-clad female eating their way through the contents of your fridge each morning does tend to make you feel frighteningly inferior. In the end, it was a bloody relief when immigration tracked him down and sent him on his way, although I still feel slightly guilty about that. How was I to know that he wasn't here legally? If he'd told me, I wouldn't have tried to register him as a tenant for the Council Tax. Still, it's an ill wind. You don't appreciate your own space until some other bastard invades it.

But really, aside from those rare glimpses of happiness, the plain truth is that, once again, the highs of last year were well outnumbered by the lows and it's becoming increasingly clear, even to me, that things can't go on like this. Not for much longer anyway. For a start, there were far too many references to hangovers, take-aways and wind-ups at my expense and at twenty-nine going on thirty, that's not good. In fact, it's bloody terrible.

Of course, I could blame Maria for all this, and indeed have on numerous occasions. It's true that nothing's been the same since we split almost two years ago now and, if I'm honest, I settled into this rut because it was easier to do that than not do it. But blaming her isn't fair. Not after all this time. I don't even miss her that much, I just miss the sex.

But I can't rely on good fortune supplying me with a rampant Essex girl again and, in truth, I can't hang about for it either. I'm in this rut because I'm lazy. Pure and simple. And at the moment I can't see any kind of future except more of the same and that has to change. The problem is, where do I start? And how?

Oh well, whatever it is, it'll have to wait. It's New Year's Eve and tomorrow will be a whole new century. Maybe change is on the horizon, who knows? At least I have a party to go to tonight. The delights of my old mate Budweiser beckon.

Chapter 2

January

Tuesday 4 January

10.15 a.m. – At home

Bloody hell, I feel rough. No, not rough, worse than rough. So rough in fact, that I can't even think of a word to describe how rough I feel.

Why does a hangover feel a thousand times worse when you close your eyes? I've been asleep for hours without even the remotest hint of a problem but now that I'm awake, every time my eyelids drop, the noise in my head increases and the throbbing feeling from my bladder becomes increasingly urgent. I wonder if, rather than sit here, I should just get up and go to the toilet. Then again, rather than move, I could just wet myself. I live on my own so no one would ever know. And I'll need a shower later on anyway. But if I do that, I'll have to wash the chair and the carpet. Not an attractive idea.

Unusually, my stomach feels all right. There must be a reason for that, although it escapes me at the moment. Mind you, much the same can be said for everything else that's happened recently.

I think I need to go back to bed. Looking at this screen isn't doing me any favours at all. Mind you, after three days on the piss I don't know why I'm surprised by that.

11.15 a.m. – At home

I've given up on bed. Every time I begin to drift off, the bloody phone rings and, by the time I get up, it stops. I can't even find out who it is because the number has been withheld. Although it can only be someone who has not been with me. Otherwise, they would also be suffering a thousand slow and painful deaths. Much like they will do anyway if they don't sod off.

13.30 p.m. – At home

If there is a god, I have obviously pissed him off somehow because he is focusing every single ounce of vengeance on me. Not only have I found a message on the machine telling me I have to be at the old man's by 7.00 p.m. tonight to meet the latest in a long line of women, but I finally caught the phone to find Kev ordering me to meet him and the lads at the Red Lion in an hour. Why can't people just leave me alone to suffer alone and in silence?

Still, at least I know why my stomach isn't giving me grief, although finding that on the doorstep when I picked up my milk wasn't pleasant. Maybe if I leave it long enough, someone else will clean it up for me.

14.45 p.m. – At home

By all accounts I excelled myself last night. Not only did I get totally bombed, but I was thrown out of the pub by Terry when first I tried to pull his daughter, then his wife and then dropped my trousers and urinated up the bar. As a result, I have been banned from the Red Lion for ever. Something Kev and all my other so-called friends were well aware of, as they were all waiting for me to turn up just so that they could witness the obviously amusing spectacle of one of their mates being physically ejected by a maniac of a landlord.

At least the walk home has made me feel a bit better.

15.30 p.m. – At home

Now that I've just about sobered up, it's beginning to dawn on me that maybe being banned from the Red Lion isn't going to be so bad. It could, in fact, turn out to be a blessing in disguise.

After all, as I was reading through my diary the other day, it was worrying how much time, not to mention money, I've been spending in there. And it's hardly the most social place in Watford. Apart from Terry's wife and daughter, who aren't exactly lookers anyway, the only other woman who ever dares enter is Alice the old cleaner. Things are bad, but they're not that bad. So maybe this could turn out to be the kick up the arse I've been needing. The thing which forces me out of this crater that has become my life.

Who am I trying to kid? I'm gutted.

16.05 p.m. – At home

Kev has just rung and told me that after the threat of a boycott by every single one of the lads, Terry has relented and will allow me back in if I get down there right now and grovel to him.

I am quite touched by this show of unity, even though I know full well that they would never have carried out their threat. After all, it took us years to mould the Red Lion into the pub we wanted. No way would we all go through that again.

Wednesday 5 January

11.25 a.m. – At home

Last night I proved that I really do have no shame. Terry, who has christened me 'thrush' for some reason, made me kneel on the floor in the middle of the pub and proclaim him as the Almighty before forcing me to drink the most foul-smelling concoction he could conjure up. God knows what was in it, but it cost me £10 and now I feel worse than ever.

Still, it's good to be back and it could be much worse – I could be back at work today.

I've also found a short, sharp message on the answer machine from the old man. He must have rung last night, although I hardly think 'where are you you bastard?' is the best thing to say to your son so early in the new year. Then again, he is going through a very strange phase at the moment. I'd best nip round there later.

16.15 p.m. – At home

Dad's just rung again. He's on his way round. This must be important.

19.30 p.m. – At home

As expected, when the old man turned up, he was not alone. He was with a woman. Well, I say a woman, compared to him, she was a girl. Kathy. And she was stunning. How the bloody hell does he do it? What on earth makes a blonde-haired page three lookalike want to go out with an overaged no-hoper with next to no hair? On second thoughts, I don't really want to know. She is, though, just the latest in a string of females that have passed though his grubby hands since he walked out on Mum. Indeed, it is fair to say that, since the split, he has been like the proverbial dog with two dicks. But this latest one – well, jackpot is the word that springs to mind.

His reason for turning up was to tell me that he's moving. Not just to another part of the South, but to Telford. He's found himself a new job doing what he spent a lifetime doing before he was made redundant and ended up driving a van. However, part of the deal is that he has to move to the Midlands and so he's off. But if he expected me to be sad, then he was disappointed. I'm glad. Not for him, but for me. Because, sadly, I am one of an increasing number of people of my age who have a parent who shames them. Not on the odd occasion, but all the time.

It's bad enough that he's able to attract women younger than me into his sordid world, but ever since he left Mum, he treats me as if I'm his best mate. He just doesn't understand that I don't want him as a mate, I need him as a dad. Primarily because I'd like him to teach me how the bloody hell he can attract all these women. After all, isn't that's what dads are supposed to do?

I've actually had nightmares in the past where he turns up at work and begins chatting up the younger birds at work and one of them ends up as my mum.

The tragedy is, of course, that he is simply me thirty years from now. I know that and he knows that I know that. If a consequence of him moving Telford is that I will be reminded of it less often, then I'll pack his bags for him right now.

22.30 p.m. – At home

By a sheer fluke, tonight I stumbled on something which could turn out to have a major impact on my life. I read a few years ago that the late-night supermarket was one of the best places to pull and, as a result, began to haunt the local Somerfield's every Thursday night. Unfortunately, all the single and available women in Watford seem to have been doing their shopping on Wednesday night at Sainsbury's instead. The place was bloody heaving with them and it was all I could do to concentrate on the job in hand.

I've always had an odd fixation with women in supermarkets and I'm not really sure what it's about. It could be the unkempt, natural look and the fact that they tend to wear either loose jumpers or tight, skimpy sports gear when they go grocery shopping, which does make for some enticing sights when they bend over. I've seen more flashes of cleavage tonight than I have for many a moon.

Then again, it could just be that the low temperatures in the freezer section, which thankfully is remarkably large in Sainsbury's, do tend to have a rapid and rather startling effect on the female breast which I find oddly arousing. The only downside is that the sudden appearance of a pair of Scammel wheel nuts does reveal the amount of sag present. And not even the best looking bird can really carry off droopy tits.

Whatever it is, I reckon Sainsbury's will be seeing much more of me in the future. Oh yes indeed. And coming on the back of Dad's impending departure, maybe things are looking up.

Thursday 6 January

06.30 a.m. – At home

A terrible night. Of the worst possible kind. I was in the middle of an exceedingly dirty dream involving Kathy, me and a bottle of warm baby oil when my dad walked in and started to get undressed. Thankfully, even my subconscious realised that this was a perversion too far and shocked me back to life. I don't even want to think what would have happened had I not woken up.

However, being awake at four thirty and unable to get back to sleep, my thoughts have returned to the ongoing trauma that is my life. Because reading my diary the other day has shaken me a little.

The stupid thing is, if I'm honest with myself (something which has been strangely lacking over the last few years), I know exactly what the problem is. I suppose I've always known. It's because, like my old man before me, I always take the path of least resistance and let things happen *to* me rather than making them happen *for* me. And because of that, as my diary proved only too clearly, almost everything I do is a habit which has crept up and taken residence in the ritual that is my existence. That would be great if I actually enjoyed myself, but I don't. Not really. I'm stuck in a job that bores me shitless, have a group of so-called mates who treat me as a cross between a stooge, a bank and a taxi, and spend every other Saturday watching a sport which more often than not depresses the hell out of me and takes most of my money into the bargain. In fact, it's fair to say that my life carries on without me half the time and I just walk along behind it taking all the shit other people throw at me.

I've let myself become a serial victim because it's easier to do that and go with the flow than it would be to do anything which might bring about a change. That would require effort. The one thing I've never really put into anything.

Of course this inbred idleness is also the main reason why I'm on my own. And that's the thing that's really getting me down because it's beginning to dawn on me that at the root of my problems is the fact that I'm just fed up with being single. Not just because I want someone to look after me and who I can look after, but because I'm lonely. If I'm not in the pub, at work or at football, I'm here, at home. And more often than not, with no one except Sky Sports or Talk Radio for company. If nothing else, that's frighteningly sad.

Now I'm depressed again. And to add insult to injury, I've got bloody work today.

09.30 a.m. – At work

Normally, on my daily train journey into London, if I wasn't getting shoved around by bastard commuters, or working out how I could smack the obligatory arsehole with the hissing Walkman, or the mobile phone with the jolly tune which goes off every twenty seconds, I'd spend my time imagining what I'd do if I had five minutes alone with the stunning redhead who gets on at Harrow. Aside from Geri Halliwell, she is my perfect woman. However, not even the sight of her looking as gorgeous as ever could shake me from my mood this morning.

The fact is that unless I do something about it, my future is going to be a sad and lonely one. That is not an attractive idea.

10.45 a.m. – At work

Bollocks. I've just been told that our current leader and drinking partner Dave has been sacked and we are to have a new boss as from Monday. Hardly surprising given events at the Christmas party. After all, it's one thing having the managing director's wife walk in when you've got some bird performing oral sex on you in the ladies' toilets. But when that young bird is her seventeen-year-old daughter . . ., well, that's something else. I think they call it legend.

Of course, the women have banded together as only women can and have now labelled him a kid fiddler which is a bit strong. She was seventeen after all and extremely fit if I remember right, although I think I'll keep that opinion to myself. I've seen the women in this mood before and it'll only take one word from some poor male to set them off. They'll just rip into their chosen victim like a pack of wild animals and calm will only return once they've satisfied their blood lust. And I'm quite happy to let someone else suffer that fate.

One thing I have noticed, though: it's strange how unattractive women can be when they're pissed off. Especially if it's with you.

14.30 p.m. – At work

Dave was waiting for us in the pub and, after buying us all a beer, announced that he is to appeal against his dismissal on the grounds that he thought she was giving him his Christmas bonus. Knowing him, he probably isn't joking either.

19.30 p.m. – At home

A hectic and fraught day. Not only have I had all Dave's work to deal with, but I've also had to make sure my own is up to date.

I've also been giving a lot of thought to my future, but having decided that I have to do something, I still don't know what to do or, for that matter, where to start. I guess I can only make that decision when I know what it is I actually want. Because the only thing I'm sure of at the moment is that what I've got just isn't it.

I need help. And the only person I can talk to is Lou. She might be my sister, and admitting to her that I'm going nowhere might well be the lowest point of my life so far, but the sad fact is she's all I've got. There is no one else.

22.20 p.m. – At home

Lou was no bloody help at all. In fact the only advice she could offer was to go and get pissed to cheer myself up. Although tempted, that's probably the very last thing I want or need.

Ray, on the other hand, was more sympathetic. He might be my brother-in-law, but he obviously recognises a kindred sprit because, as I was getting in the car, he came after me and told me that no matter what happens, I should always think positively. Although I suspect that this is actually good advice, at the moment I can't really see what I have to think positively about. Today was no different from any other day. In fact it was worse because I know that, if I hadn't pulled the photocopier stunt, I'd already have been offered Dave's job.

Maybe Lou's idea was better after all.

23.45 p.m. – At home

As I was soaking in the bath, the thought struck me that Ray is right. It's all very well moaning, but nothing is ever going to change until I shake off this sad bastard mentality and get on with things. What's more, seeing Ray and Lou tonight has made me realise what it is I actually want.

Much as I've been trying to kid myself, I'm never going to be one of these perfectly content thirty-somethings who lead a full, active and flawlessly single life. Mostly because the majority of people who live like that base it on the full, active and flawlessly single life they had when they were twenty-nine. I'm twenty-nine, and my life sucks. It's like a bloody punchline. And not a particularly funny one at that. More importantly, it's not what I want. I want what Ray and Lou have: home, wife and kids. It's certainly what I wanted with Maria and I'm starting to realise that, when we split, I kind of accepted that my chance had gone. The fact is that it hasn't. It's there waiting for me and it always has been. But, as with most things, I've been spending my life waiting and hoping for someone to come along instead of going out there and looking for them. And I guess that's the key, that's what has to change. And the only person who can force that change is me. But where the bloody hell do I start?

After all, if I'm brutally frank, I've never been that successful with women although I have always suspected that much of the blame for that lies with porn. Years of exposure to two-dimensional flesh has conditioned me into believing that every woman under twenty-five is actually a rampant sex machine who is constantly gagging for it and that only women who are either a size 10 (or a top-heavy 12) and look like a lap-dancer on heat are worthy of sleeping with. This is obviously bollocks which begs the question: why have I fallen for it for so long?

And so I suppose what I have to do is stop wasting my time thinking like that and consciously lower my sights a little. From now on, lust has to give way to reality and I need to look for a woman who might not be top-shelf magazine material, but who could certainly do a job for me. Who knows, maybe what I'm after is right under my nose and I haven't even noticed.

But even though making this decision is a major, and positive, step for me, I'd be lying if I said I wasn't a little gutted. I mean, you set yourself goals and work to achieve them, but I have to face it, it looks like I'll never get to sleep with Geri Halliwell after all, which is a bit of a bastard. Then again, as my dad is fond of saying, 'they're all the same when they're lying down and the lights are out', so maybe it isn't all bad.

I wonder if I have grounds for legal action against the publishers of *Escort*?

Friday 7 January

07.00 a.m. – At home

Nothing like a kick in the teeth to start the day. Thanks to bloody MTV, I've just received a stark reminder that my ultimate dream will always remain just that, a dream. There really should be a law against scantily clad women bouncing around asking you what you want, what you really, really want this early in the morning. Especially when you already know that you can't have it.

09.50 a.m. – At work

Ginger was on the train this morning, but it was different. If anything, she looked even more stunning than normal, but instead of an overwhelming sense of lust, I just felt cheated. It was as if she knew I had given up on her and was making a special effort to take the piss. In fact, I'm sure she even gave me a knowing smile, just to taunt me.

16.30 p.m. – At work

Shit. This morning, the staff in the sales department were called together and told that, as from Monday morning, our new boss will be a woman. Not any old woman either, but one of the power dressing mid-thirties, man-hating fascists who terrify me so much. She's coming from the Mitcham office, which is another bad sign as, from my experience of visiting the place, the whole town is full of arseholes.

There's no doubt that this is going to have a major impact on me and my fellow males because, although we have always been in the minority in this department, thanks to the influence of Dave, our former and admittedly sexist boss, we've always held the upper hand in this particular battle of the sexes. As a result, aside from the odd cryptic comment, any attempt at anti-male rhetoric from the female ranks has been quickly quashed. The women, of course, have become used to this and therefore the office has always had a kind of 'laddy' ambience.

But now, not only have our numbers been depleted by the loss of our leader, the entire fabric on which the sexual politics of the office have been based for years is about to be ripped from under us. Already, the women are salivating at the prospect of having one of their own cracking the whip and the day has been spent fending off remarks such as 'now you lot will get yours' from grinning females. This change in their mood is almost scary. I could almost hear the testosterone running for cover.

I think, to paraphrase Winston Churchill's 'we will fight them on the beaches . . .' speech, we are in the shit. Big time.

21.30 p.m. – At home

Word at the usual end-of-week piss-up was that our new boss is called Julia. Worst of all is that, according to Kev, she asked for a transfer because she recently caught her old man rogering her best mate. Something that is sure to make her sympathetic toward the few males who she will have total control over. Including me.

How much of this is true, of course, is difficult to fathom.

Usually, Kev's information is a potent mixture of half-truth, total bollocks and wind-up. In this case, I'd happily settle for that.

Saturday 8 January

21.30 p.m. – At home

Thanks to Watford's pathetic early exit in the FA Cup, we had no game today so I spent the afternoon with Lou and the kids. Something which always cheers me up but suddenly seems to have taken on added significance. For the first time, I actually began to wonder what it would be like if I wasn't able to leave them and come home when I got bored. I don't think it'd be too shabby to be honest but then again, they are five and eight which is long past the nappies and bodily fluid stage.

I've also just rung Mum in New York, largely as a result of my subconscious 'experience' with Dad and Kathy the other night which is still worrying me slightly. As usual, she's happy as Larry and who wouldn't be living out there?

I also had a chat with Kenny, but for someone who single-handedly rebuilt my mum's self-confidence after Dad dumped her for the first in a seemingly never-ending conveyer belt of bimbos, he is a boring bastard. Then again, you can't put a price on your mum's happiness and if she loves him, that's all that matters. He is loaded as well which helps, although I could have done without having him remind me that I'm knocking on thirty, single and I was spending Saturday night phoning my mum. He does have a point.

Sunday 9 January

22.30 p.m. – At home

I've always hated Sundays. I still can't understand why on earth I haven't wised up to the fact that I'm too old, too fat and too crap to play football with a group of yobs whose idea of training is to spend Saturday night drinking low-alcohol lager instead of Special Brew and smoking Silk Cut Lights instead of roll-ups. Add to that the fact that I was sub again, and so ended up running the line for an hour before being sent on to have the shit kicked out of me by everyone I had flagged offside in the first half and it isn't hard to imagine why my enthusiasm for playing the great game is on the slide.

As if that wasn't bad enough, I limped back to the flat to find a message on my answerphone telling me that my darling sister, who was supposed to be supplying me with dinner today, has gone down with flu and so their Sunday feast will now consist of a bag full of Big Macs and chicken nuggets. Hardly the most attractive offer given that I have that at least three times a week anyway.

The result of this is that the whole afternoon, and most of the evening, was spent in the pub on my own watching Sky Sports and reading the papers. What's worse, the only food I've had is three bags of crisps and a handful of cheese cubes the barmaid begrudgingly dumped on the bar.

And now I face a long, restless night as I await my fate at the hands of a new boss. Mind you, if this indigestion doesn't stop soon, I know where I'll be spending most of it.

Monday 10 January

10.30 a.m. – At work

The dreaded Julia hasn't surfaced yet. As a result, the office is awash with the rumour that Dave has been reinstated. A rumour that I know is total bollocks because, in a moment of madness, I started it. Bizarrely, the effect since the 'story' broke has been startling. The lads have grasped this ray of hope with both hands, while the women have become almost resigned to the fact that fate has, once again, kicked them in the teeth. Normally, I would feel some degree of sympathy towards them but, in this instance, I don't. The truth of the matter is that if they find out it was me who denied them the simple pleasure of a half-hour's one-upmanship, I will become their number one target.

14.30 p.m. – At work

Well, she's here. A typical career bird straight off the production line: thirty-fiveish, two-piece grey trouser suit, dyed auburn hair and a face which carries an expression which can only be described as a cross between hostility and arrogance. I've always had this suspicion that when birds like her go home, they spend their evenings wearing leather and indulging in sexual practices which more often than not involve the domination of some poor male.

Her figure's a bit iffy as well: decent top half but the arse is dropping a bit. I would, as the saying goes, but that is hardly a recommendation.

18.30 p.m. – At home

A strange day, fraught with uncertainty and fear. In the end, the fascist female didn't even so much as look at me all day but I have been told that I have to see her in the morning to discuss 'ideas'. What that really means is that she's going to change everything just for the sake of changing it and I'll be doing all the work while she takes the credit. Top.

Tuesday 11 January

19.30 p.m. – At home

Not a bad day as it happens. My meeting with the fascist didn't go too badly, although I suspect that this had more to do with the fact that I spent most of the time imagining her in a latex cat suit rather than listening to what she was telling me. I really must deal with this fear of power dressers. I'm sure it's not true. At least not in the majority of cases anyway.

To be fair, her expected hatred of all things male has not materialised because it is clear that she simply dislikes everyone. I suspect that this is an attempt to remain aloof from the minions but it has backfired badly. The women, who were looking upon her as a potential saviour, now regard her as a traitor to her sex. The blokes are just relieved.

On the way home, my thoughts returned to the small matter of my future and, for once, the women at work have turned out to be quite useful. As there is no chance that any of them would ever go out with me, I've decided to use them to try to work out what kind of woman I should be looking for. I've never really gone in for all this 'when it happens, you'll know' bollocks. After all, under that golden rule, I could end up living with anything just because we 'connect', to use a well worn 'birdism'. And I can't have – and don't want – that, so I'll need to work out where the boundaries of what is, and what isn't, acceptable to me actually lie.

So, as from tomorrow, I'm going to begin placing them into specific groups depending on their appearance, age and dress sense. The difficult bit has been sorting out the groups, but so far I've come up with:

Obviously out of reach
Prick teaser
Fit as fuck
Perfect
Plain but could scrub up
Frumpy clothes but acceptable features

Plump but still quite fit
Plain but beyond help
Tubby but presentable
Pig (includes fat or lardy)
Grumpy, frumpy or bland looking
Bitch or hard-faced
Oldie (any female between 35 and 40)
Goldie (forty-plus)
Geezer bird (or lesbian)

Clearly, in terms of my target sector, we are talking upper mid-range here but, all in all, it seems a pretty sound set-up to me.

Wednesday 12 January

11.30 a.m. – At work

Work on the segregation of my female colleagues has begun with, I have to say, some success. Amazingly, it has also made things much easier on the work front. For, once I've categorised an individual and no longer regard them as acceptable, my whole approach to them has become more relaxed. I even spent thirty minutes alone with Janet from the post room and never imagined her naked once. That is quite an achievement for me, although it has to be said that, at her age, it wasn't the most enjoyable vision anyway.

15.00 p.m. – At work

Sean has just paid me a visit and I now know why I have been saddled with the nickname 'Thrush'. Apparently, when I get pissed I become an irritating cunt.

Nice to know that you can count on your mates for support in troubled times.

18.45 p.m. – At home

Another good day spent studying the female form although, in my defence, this time it was to work out which ones weren't actually worth studying at all. Bizarrely, out of all the women at work, only seven fall within what I have begun to accept is my target range. This has helped me begin to form a mental picture of the type of woman I should go hunting for. It needs a bit of fine tuning, but at least I'm getting there.

Sadly, of the seven I did select, four are married and two are engaged. This left only Katie, who has just split up from her bloke. The problem is, before him, she used to go out with Sean which immediately renders her unattractive. After all, I wouldn't want to touch anything he's been near.

Oh well, the lech fest that is Wednesday night at Sainsbury's beckons. After a day of studying the female form and, for the most part, discounting it, I am looking forward to this.

22.00 p.m. – At home

Holy shit, I can't believe it. Two and a half hours in a supermarket. In the end I only left because my Pepperoni pizza had defrosted and was bringing tears to the eyes of everyone within five yards. I don't know if it's the shared experience of shopping, the surreal location or simply the anonymity which is the attraction, but it is clear from the number of furtive glances, innocent smiles and cryptic comments that many of my fellow shoppers were also there on the hunt. It was like a nightclub without the music.

As ever, the freezer section was *the* place to be with a truly massive nipple count. If I didn't know better, I'd swear that Sainsbury's had actually dropped the setting on the cabinets. I've certainly never known any supermarket to be that cold before.

God I love breasts. They're just so wonderful.

Thursday 13 January

14.00 p.m. – At work

Following the euphoria of last night, it's been back to earth with a bump. A pile of work appeared on my desk overnight which, I suspect, was put there by some arsehole working late who could not be bothered to do it themselves.

I've also heard a disturbing rumour that Julia has apparently been asking about property prices in Watford. This does not bode well. There are two empty flats in my building and the last thing I want is my boss living near me. She might start to think we're mates, which would never do as it would stop the lads coming round. Then again, being as most of the time they drink me dry, it might not be such a bad thing after all.

On the plus side, Sean has just rung and informed me that we are off out with Kev tonight. Given my new-found interest in the female form, will the women of Watford be safe? Probably.

Friday 14 January

11.00 a.m. – At work

A strange night last night because, for once, I didn't arrive home pissed. Instead, I went to bed feeling not a little ashamed and hugely embarrassed.

It all started when I turned up at O'Neill's to find Kev and Sean already drinking double shots of vodka. As usual, the application of the former Soviet Union's finest export had turned the two of them into a pain in the arse, and they had already upset more than one female – not to mention their accompanying boyfriends. Of course, once I arrived they got even louder because they adopted that old 'safety in numbers' mentality. This meant that I spent the entire evening dying of shame as they made crude and sexist comments to anything with breasts, while all the time trying to stop them getting a good kicking. Something which, by the time it came to head for home, I would cheerfully have done myself.

More importantly, because I had to keep an eye on them, I couldn't have much to drink myself and so, without the effects of alcohol to cloud my awareness, witnessed at first hand what a bunch of obnoxious pricks my mates are.

What really pisses me off is that last night was just another in a long line of examples where I have ended up being their fall guy. They spent the night embarrassing everyone within hearing distance, especially me, and then expected me to get them home. Which of course, like a mug, I did. I even had to pay for the cab, and will I see that money again? Will I bollocks.

I'd like to think that I don't behave like that when I get pissed, but I have a sneaky feeling that I do. And if that's the case, is it any wonder that I'm still single? Come to that, is it any wonder the rest of them are either?

21.15 p.m. – At home

Amazingly, I feel more cheerful than I did this morning. Something I suspect has much to do with the four bottles of Budweiser I had after work and the fact we've got Liverpool at home tomorrow. I love lager. It has so many redeeming features.

Those bastards never apologised for last night though, or paid me back for the taxi. Why aren't I surprised?

Saturday 15 January

11.30 p.m. – At home

Just got in after what was, to say the least, an eventful day. Top game despite losing 3–2 but we did have loads of laughs although, as usual, most of them were at my expense. There must be a reason why things happen to me, maybe I'm paying the price for something I did in a previous life or something, but it really is starting to get on my tits. I mean, every game I've ever been to, someone shouts 'get your tits out' to the teenage cheerleaders who dance around on the pitch at half-time. And has anything ever happened to them? Has it bollocks. Yet the first time I ever do it, I get physically assaulted by some deranged old bag who had to be pulled off me by Sean. How the fuck was I supposed to know that two of them were her grand-daughters?

Still, the lads will get bored with taking the piss after a few days, they usually do.

Sunday 16 January

15.30 p.m. – At home

Just for a change, I've been giving some more thought to my search for a partner. And sadly, those thoughts have not been good ones.

I have suddenly realised that while I've been hanging around waiting for some eighteen-year-old Geri Halliwell lookalike to fall at my feet, all the real women my own age have been getting on with things. By now, most of them will be either involved with someone and so are out of bounds, or they are divorced with kids and so are bitter and twisted men-haters. That means that my choice is limited to what's left, which is either second best or second hand. Neither of which option fills me with much joy because it means that I'm going to end up with either some ugly slapper who no one else wanted or someone else's reject. And then I'll grow old spending every day being reminded what a failure I am and grow into a bitter and twisted old git. Bloody great.

Monday 17 January

12.20 p.m. – At work

As expected, the cheerleader related piss-taking has abated as lunchtime approaches. Lads are so fickle. They know it's my round first, so they also know that if they wind me up too much, I won't go to the pub which means that one of them will have to stump up. I guarantee that once that lager is on the table, they'll start again.

15.30 p.m. – At work

I was wrong. My own indiscretion was forgotten as other more important matters have gripped our attention. Just before lunch, word broke that we are to have a new female in the office as from next Friday. Although we are surrounded by women all day, it is hard to describe the enormity of this announcement, but the feeling is almost identical to the one you get when you hear that your club is about to sign a foreign striker. You've never heard of him, never seen him, but word is that he's the dog's bollocks. It's anticipation mixed with hope. Of course in this case, we don't need her to knock in thirty goals a season, we don't even need her to be good at her job. We just want her to be single, look top and be one of those rare women who prefer the company of blokes to other birds. Something which cannot be said about any of the ones we already have.

21.30 p.m. – At home

Got in late tonight after an extra session in the pub. Never have I known such expectation among the lads yet it is a dangerous thing. I know what a kick in the nuts it can be to have your hopes and dreams dashed and if she turns up and is just a clone of one of the other women, the mood will plummet to one of sombre despair.

Thankfully, I don't share their mood. I would guess that's to do with the fact that I have begun to regard the women at work as no more than examples rather than prospects. Is this a step forward or a step backward I wonder?

Tuesday 18 January

22.00 p.m. – At home

An eventful day today. I arrived for work and was immediately dispatched to Mitcham for a sales conference. Julia was supposed to go with me but was called away at the last minute and, much to my delight, I was instead accompanied by the vision that is Liz from marketing. She might not be what you would call classically stunning, but this is a woman who radiates sex. I've seen it a thousand times, blokes just can't help it. Christ, I can't. You just have to turn and look at her whenever she walks past. God only knows what she's like when she's up for it. It must be bloody frightening.

Of course, being so desirable, it was almost impossible not to imagine her naked, so in the end I gave up and did just that. I have to say that it was bloody marvellous as well.

Sadly, my new-found awareness of women has yet to impact on my conversational skills. Something I've always had a problem with thanks to the old 'I want to see you naked' fixation which was certainly the problem today. Indeed, judging by the look of relief on Liz's face when we parted, I can only imagine that today has confirmed for her the generally held opinion that I'm a complete tosser whose entire life revolves around work and football.

But I am getting over that and now I have to get over this. Of course, the ideal thing would be to talk to my dad or other blokes, but I know that neither of those things will happen. First off, of the very few times I have ever discussed anything like this with my old man, his simple advice was 'make 'em laugh', which might be easy for Jim Davidson but is fucking hard for someone like me who can't tell a joke to save his life. And secondly, no bloke would ever ask their mates for advice about anything like this because blokes are twats. We don't talk about problems, we get pissed and hope they go away.

If I had the bottle, the bloke to ask is Ray's brother Steve. He might be as skinny as a rake and look like Curly Watts from *Coronation Street*, but he sure as shit can talk to birds. They bloody love him, even though, more often than not, all he does is take the piss out of them. I've seen him surrounded by women all laughing like drains as he slags them off. Yet if I even attempted to say anything like the same things, they'd batter me senseless and then call the Old Bill to have me locked up. What the fuck is that all about?

But of course, I'll never ask Steve or anyone else because if I did, it'd be like admitting I was crap. And no bloke, never mind me, will ever do that, even though I obviously am. But if I'm going to be the lean, mean fanny-hunting machine I want to be, I have to sort this out and fast. It's not going to be easy though.

Wednesday 19 January

11.20 a.m. – At work

Barry from marketing has just sent me an e-mail and demanded to know what I did to Liz yesterday. By all accounts, she has come into work singing my praises because for once she spent a day with a bloke who did not spend the entire time trying to get inside her underwear. As that was exactly what I had been doing, at least mentally, I am somewhat perplexed.

The danger, of course, is that Barry, who is well known as being both a Chelsea fan and a wanker – although it could be argued that the two are one and the same – is winding me up. It would not be the first time there has been an inter-departmental spoof such as this and, for all I know, the entire company could be in on the gag and are waiting for me to bite. If that is the case, I have absolutely no confidence in any of my so-called mates warning me because the only time they ever become concerned about embarrassment is when it happens to them. On the other hand, ridiculous as it sounds, there is always the chance that he is telling the truth and, if I play my cards right, I could be in line for the shag of a lifetime.

15.20 p.m. – At work

Rather than risk making myself look a prick, I bit the bullet and rang Lou. As my sister, she is duty bound to offer guidance and she came up trumps. Her advice is simply to go up to Liz and apologise for acting like a boring twat all day. If it is a wind-up, I won't lose face and if it isn't, I might get a date out of it. Either way, I can't lose. The downside is that, in return for her wisdom, I have to take the kids swimming on Sunday afternoon. Something she knows I hate because it'll mean missing the match on Sky. But at least I'll get a decent Sunday dinner out of it which is something.

19.10 p.m. – At home

I can't believe it. For once, my abject fear of embarrassment at the hands of a woman, coupled with my ability to lie in the face of adversity, has not only saved me from a fate worse than death, it has possibly earnt me a date with the horniest looking woman I (almost) know. Having decided to defy my inbred cowardice and take Lou's advice, I actually bumped into Liz as I was on my way to see her. For some reason I cannot fathom, I did something I've never done with a woman before and instantly went on the offensive. In a voice that belied my terror, I followed Lou's advice but added that someone had told me that she thought I was a knob of the first order and I wasn't exactly thrilled to be with her. However, that was no excuse for my behaviour and I was bang out of order. At this, *she* apologised profusely and told me that she had never said any such thing. She even offered to go for a drink one night if I fancied it.

Unbelievably, in a voice that was so cool I amazed myself, I didn't accept on the spot but said something like 'yeah, that'd be great' and then made my excuses and left. I don't care if she meant it or not. For me, that was a major result. More significantly, I have learnt a valuable lesson. In the battle for lust, bullshit, if applied sparingly, is astonishingly effective. And if I can get away with it with someone like Liz, I can get away with it anywhere.

22.30 p.m. – At home

Just got back from Sainsbury's where, once again, available women outnumbered single blokes by about ten to one. After three weeks, faces are becoming more familiar and a few women even said hello.

Somewhat bizarrely, I became embroiled in an odd conversation with two blokes about the merits of Mr Ben's mild curry sauce. It was only after about ten minutes that I realised they were obviously a gay couple having a domestic, so I made my excuses and left them to it.

Sadly, the nipple count was lower than usual tonight which was a bit of a downer although it was pissing down so everyone was wearing coats. On the plus side, I can't even begin to imagine what a delight that place will be in August.

I am still undecided about how to progress with Liz. My gut instinct, driven as it is by both desperation and lust, is to dive in and go for it. But I know that if I do that I will fuck it up, because that's what I always do. The alternative is to play it cool for a while and casually slide in there in a week or so. Funny thing is, if I'd have found myself in this position yesterday, I'd already have fallen flat on my face by now and would be sitting here licking my wounds. But having discovered that dishonesty is actually the best policy, things are different. And as playing it cool goes totally against my obviously flawed better judgement, I guess that's what I'll do. Nothing ventured, nothing gained as they say.

Thursday 20 January

21.10 p.m. – At home

A strange day today. Word is out that I am the one male in the entire building that Liz does not regard as pond life and the lads are on my case. According to Phil in accounts, it is my duty to exploit this, sleep with her and then give everyone else a full and highly detailed report. Not only because they are desperate to hear what she is actually like in bed, but also because one of the frequent discussions among the marketing lads centres on the noises she makes when she orgasms. Opinions vary from groaner to screamer, but they are desperate to have this resolved. Indeed, there is even money on the table.

This is, of course, puts added pressure on me. Leaving aside the small matter of getting her into bed in the first place, how can I be expected to do the deed without, at some point in the proceeding, forming a mental picture of the entire marketing department cheering me on?

Friday 21 January

09.20 a.m. – At work

Just the way to start the day. A bad night's sleep followed by a cancelled train and a late arrival at work where, inevitably, the first person I bump into is Julia.

Unfortunately, I did not get the bollocking I expected but was instead given the news that she has found a flat in Watford and has even made an offer on it. Soon, not only will we be neighbours, but we'll be able to travel to and from work together.

Thankfully, what she doesn't know is that the address she gave me is on the other side of town from where I live which means that it would be easier for her to use the tube into Baker Street than share the proper train with me.

Something to be grateful for I suppose.

But has this woman no sense of decency? Doesn't she realise what an impact this is going to have on me?

09.52 a.m. – At work

Things must be slowing up. It took all of thirty-two minutes for the first piss-take to arrive; the mail lad has just dropped me off a Jiffy bag with an apple inside and a note saying 'for teacher'. The fact that no name was included is significant for it marks the start of what will almost certainly become a long-term piss-take.

11.45 a.m. – At work

If I ever get the chance to put a curse on someone, I'm going to stick it on the twat who invented funmail. Thanks to him, some arsehole has set up billy@teacherspet.com and circulated a memo to the entire staff informing them that I will not be able to come to the pub after work because I have detention.

12.15 p.m. – At work

If I ever get the chance to grant three wishes to someone, I'm going to stick it on the star who invented funmail. Thanks to him, and the comedy genius who set up billy@teacherspet.com, Liz has just rung me to find out what it's all about. During what was a remarkably relaxed conversation, she dropped in at least two hints about me taking her out, both of which I avoided. Playing it cool is obviously working but it's bloody hard work. If anything, she sounds even dirtier on the phone. So much so that I felt a stirring in my loins just talking to her. God only knows what actual physical combat must be like.

14.30 p.m. – At work

I cannot begin to imagine what the people at this firm will ever do if I leave. I've just spent an hour in the pub where I was the only topic of conversation. First I had to endure a stream of jokes about schoolgirls, swots and spanking and then I had another grilling about Liz.

Now, apparently, if I don't do the deed, I will be letting down my entire sex. As sex has consistently let me down ever since I passed puberty, I hardly think that's fair.

16.10 p.m. – At work

Yee hah! Just bumped into Liz on my way back from the mail room and, before I knew it, we were arranging to meet for a quick drink after work tonight. This is an astonishing development. Fuck me, I have a date! And with a stunner. I'd best keep that very, very quiet.

20.45 p.m. – At home

As a bloke, there are some things you just don't want to hear on a first date. 'I have to be home by ten because of the babysitter', 'my ex-boyfriend is really jealous' or 'is it in?' are three that spring to mind. But one I never expected to hear was 'I wasn't really surprised when I found out you were gay.' It would be bad enough in any normal circumstance, but when it comes from a woman who can give a grown man an erection just by licking her lips, it is a major body blow. As if that wasn't bad enough, by the time my brain had actually absorbed what she had said, she had gone on to something else and I didn't even deny it. I just sat there like Forrest Gump while she went on and on about what wankers men were. After an hour of this, she scribbled her phone number on a bit of paper, got up, kissed me on the cheek and left me sitting there in stunned silence.

I still haven't got to grips with the enormity of this one sentence. It has so many different implications. The most important of which is who told her, because it has 'wind-up' written all over it.

However, rather than go mental, ring her up and set her right, I have decided to take my time before I decide what to do. After all, I need to come out of this on top otherwise I'll be a laughing stock for months.

Saturday 22 January

18.20 p.m. – At home

A strange day today – not only did the lads unexpectedly lose at Bradford, but I've spent most of it thinking about the bizarre events of last night.

As I see it, I have a few things in my favour. First, although she thinks I'm a faggot, I did take her out and I do have her phone number. Second, from the few details I actually remember, I have picked up a few bits of information about women and what they actually want from blokes which is valuable stuff. Third, if I come clean, she'll feel bad and at least I should get another date out of it. On the negative side, as it stands, I have no chance of a shag or even a good grope. And she did humiliate me, albeit unintentionally.

Whatever happens, I have to get it sorted and fast. Whoever set me up must know we went out Friday and so come Monday morning it will be all over the building. Pound to a pinch of shit, they'll be desperate to tell everyone else as soon as they walk through the door.

It will, however, have to wait. I'm off out with the lads from the football club tonight to say our collective goodbyes to Mark the goalie who has decided to follow his dream and move to Spain. That means lots of lager, passive smoking and possibly a curry. Thank God we've not got a game in the morning, although I must remember that I have to go swimming in the afternoon.

Now there's a thought, maybe I should ask the lads for advice? Let's see, you take out a horny-looking bird but she thinks you're gay. How should I set her right? Yeah, I can see them giving that a compassionate airing over the veggie pilau.

Sunday 23 January

11.30 a.m. – At home

Liz was right the other night: blokes are wankers. All of them. I like a practical joke as much as the next geezer but when they end up with you rushing to casualty in a blind panic, that's when things have gone a bit over the top.

It's my own fault. Red wine always gives me a killer headache which is why I never drink it. And I should have stuck to that golden rule when Mark produced two bottles of the stuff and poured them out for everyone to use as his goodbye toast. If I'd done that, I'd never have experienced the terrifying spectacle of what appeared to be blood coming out of my knob when I went for a slash this morning. Nor would I have flipped out and rushed down to the casualty department only to be handed a piece of paper by an extremely annoyed receptionist telling me that my urine wasn't laced with anything more serious than totally harmless bright red cold water dye.

She then told me that, late last night, a fax had arrived at the front desk explaining exactly what had happened and giving a list of the victims' names, as well as a full apology to the staff. For what it was worth, I was number six.

Mark, of course, has vanished off the face of the earth. And a good thing too. I'm not a violent man, but most of the others are. And while I'm sure there's a funny side to this, it'll be a bloody long time before I see it.

I have to admit though, it was bloody clever. I wonder how I can use it on the lads at work?

22.00 p.m. – At home

Much as I love Joe and Katie, I hate taking them swimming. Especially on Sundays. It's bad enough that my local pool resembles a life-size version of Mousetrap, what with all the slides, water shoots and all the other bollocks they've put in. Most of which seem to have been specially designed actually to discourage you from trying to move along under your own steam, which kind of defeats the whole object. But add in the accompanying sound-track of Boyzone, Steps and bloody S Club 7 being played far louder than it should have been and the place becomes like a hell on earth.

And it's even worse on Sundays because it turns into a refugee centre for divorced dads. Each one of them trying to keep their offspring amused until they can take them to McDonald's and then dump them back on their mothers.

But today was even worse than normal. It was a bloody nightmare. Not only had a small red stain appeared on the front of my white Calvin Klein boxers – no doubt as a result of a less than whole-hearted shake after my last leak – but as I was having a quick slash, there was still a trace of red dye evident. And so I spent the entire time swimming around with my testicles clenched together, terrified that even a tiny leak would leave a long trail of red in the water behind me. Something which would almost certainly have instilled a degree of alarm into even the most tolerant of swimmers. By the time I got out, my entire groin was throbbing.

As if that wasn't bad enough, when my usual post-swim slash released yet more pink urine, a guy standing behind me freaked out and began giving me shit about sexually transmitted diseases and basic hygiene. In the end, one of the pretty boy attendants came over and I was forced to explain everything to him in front of an increasingly hostile, and thanks to the bright spark who came up with the idea for communal changing areas, mixed, crowd. I don't know if they believed me or not, but at least I gave them a bloody good laugh. Thank God no one I knew was there. I can't even begin to imagine what the bastards at work could make out of this one.

The one saving grace was that, when I took them home, Sunday dinner was waiting for us, which almost made the whole experience worthwhile. And judging by the smiles on both their faces when we arrived, I got the impression that my sister and her husband may not have entirely wasted their kid-free afternoon. I hope she washed her hands before she peeled my spuds.

At least the kids enjoyed themselves. I suppose watching your uncle lose what remains of his dignity in front of your eyes must have a certain appeal. Even when you're eight.

22.30 p.m. – At home

Decided to bite the bullet and rang Liz to set her straight rather than wait. Sadly, she was out which means I'm going to have to move fast in the morning.

Monday 24 January

09.30 a.m. – At work

A stream of messages from billy@teacherspet.com greeted my arrival at work but, thankfully, as yet there has been no mention of my apparent homosexuality. I have also spoken to Liz and asked to meet her in half an hour for a quick chat. God knows what she thinks I want to talk about, but she was very keen. Must be a girlie thing I guess.

10.30 a.m. – At work

Met Liz and broke the bad news that I am no more of a back door bandit than she is. Sadly, I got the impression that she was more angry than embarrassed which hasn't exactly done me any favours in the confidence department. After all, it confirms my fear that if she hadn't thought I was gay, she'd never have come within a million miles of me.

Although I'm more than a little pissed off about that, I can kind of see her point. After all, it can't be easy having to deal with the lustful attentions of every male she works with. The thought of having at least one bloke who had no sexual interest in her at all must have appealed. I remember reading somewhere that's why a lot of good-looking birds have an empathy with gays.

The irony is that, because my only concern was setting her right, I wasn't even thinking of her in any sexual way at all. But nevertheless, the second I broke the news, I felt the barriers go up, which is a bit of a downer. Anyway, after that, all I could do was give her my number and tell her to call me if she ever wants a chat. Remarkably mature of me but probably completely pointless.

At least I know who set us up, Barry the wanker. Thank fuck he's off sick today. I just hope it's nothing trivial. I wonder if he drinks red wine?

18.10 p.m. – At home

Spent the day feeling bad about Liz and plotting the downfall of Barry the Chelsea wanker. Even the endless stream of teacher's pet jokes and the sight of Ginger on the train home did not lift my spirits. This evening will be spent watching Sky Sports and hoping like fuck that Liz rings me up. Not so that I can chat her up, but so that I can try and cheer her up. And myself come to that.

23.50 p.m. – At home

I can't sleep. This thing with Liz is getting to me. It's a situation I've never been in before and I have no idea how to handle it.

The truth is that, despite what happened, I enjoyed her company the other night and thought we got on OK. It certainly made a change to have some intelligent conversation that didn't involve lager, football or fanny.

But if her reaction to me today taught me one thing, it's that my reluctantly adopted life of slobbery means that I have about as much chance of scoring with her as I have of scoring at Old Trafford. It pains me to say that, but it's true. Yet if I can accept that I have no chance with her sexually, surely she should be able to accept that the fact I'm not gay doesn't mean we can't be mates. Because I actually think we could. It would certainly do me the world of good to have someone else to talk to and socialise with away from the lads. Who knows? She might even be able to help me break out of this rut and introduce me to a whole new circle of people. She only lives in Camden, that's no distance from me.

Besides, I've never really had a proper mate who's female,

although I've always imagined that they can get seriously complicated. I mean, how do you react if you're out with your (female) mate and some wanker comes over and starts trying to pull her. Do you get jealous or what?

I need to try and speak with her about all this. And I'd also like to know why she wasn't surprised when Barry told her I was gay. That is strangely worrying.

Tuesday 25 January

19.45 p.m. – At home

At last the teacher's pet jokes have dried up and, what with Barry still being off, it was quite a quiet day. I managed to bump into Liz as well, which was quite handy because she was much more cheerful and relaxed than yesterday. Maybe I should call her and put my cards on the table? Then again, maybe not. It could be asking for another knock-back and one a week is about as much as I want.

Aside from that, Ginger was on the train both to and from work which was a pleasant distraction. If anything, that woman gets sexier by the day. It's just not fair.

Wednesday 26 January

09.30 a.m. – At work

Just made work in time today, which was a relief because Julia was on the prowl with a face that would kill at ten paces. Maybe the batteries on her vibrator ran out last night.

More importantly, there is a message on my voicemail from Liz; she wants me to call. She sounds annoyed so I'll leave that until later.

09.50 a.m. – At work

Liz has just rung again but my fears were unfounded. She was only calling me to tell me that Barry the wanker is back and she has set him straight in the best possible way. In front of the whole office, she told him that rather than embarrass her, I let her go along with the stupid idea that I was gay which, according to her, makes me more of a gentleman than he could ever be. Coming from the woman who is the sexual fantasy of the majority of males in the building, that must have been cringing to watch never mind experience. Top bird.

18.15 p.m. – At home

Aside from the episode with Liz, today was major boring. Julia never thawed out at all, which cast a dark cloud over the entire workforce. Thank God for Sainsbury's.

22.30 p.m. – At home

It's no wonder that some of the supermarket chains have started having single-only nights because, after tonight, I'm becoming increasingly convinced that in these odd and confused times, shopping has replaced the pub and the club as *the* place to pull. It's not even the end of January and it's bloody freezing outside, yet there were still women walking around Sainsbury's dressed as if they were on their way to Stringfellow's. It's surely only a matter of time before they start blacking out the windows and installing cubicles.

When I think about it, it's bloody obvious why this has come about. Thanks to the emergence of the nightmare that is 'girl-power', most pubs have become inhabited by packs of overly aggressive females desperate to prove that they've thrown off the shackles of sexism by behaving just like . . . blokes. Try and chat up one of them, and not only do you risk abuse and ridicule from the rest, but also the chance that she could drink you under the table. Not attractive.

In a supermarket, not only are you sober, but you can actually have a conversation. Which must also explain why cooking, which has always been boring as fuck because every single person on the planet hates doing it for themselves, has suddenly become so interesting. It's the ideal icebreaker.

The problem for me is how to take advantage of that. I've never been that good in the kitchen, although I have got past the stage of using my smoke alarm as a timer. Maybe the time has come to brush up on my culinary skills. Especially if it could help me snare something like the brunette I followed around tonight. Dark haired, slim and definitely in the fit as fuck category.

Thursday 27 January

15.15 p.m. – At work

I've done something which only a few short weeks ago, I would have thought impossible. I've just rung Liz and asked her if she'd like to meet up for a quick drink after work to make up for the misunderstanding of the other night. Astonishingly, she said yes, and now I'm shitting myself.

This is a whole new experience for me, taking out a bird I already suspect in advance that I've got no chance with. Still, I suppose it takes all that pressure out of the situation although I hope she doesn't start telling me she fancies any of my mates. If she does, I'm out of there. That would be a kick in the nuts too far.

16.50 p.m. – At work

Bollocks. Word is out that I'm having a drink with Liz. It can only have come from her end because I haven't told a soul. The upshot is that I now have Mike threatening to follow us and make a full report in the morning, while Sean has started a sweep to see how long it is before she dumps me. Sometimes the people in this office are so juvenile. Mind you, if I had the nerve, I'd have a fiver on about ten minutes.

22.10 p.m. – At home

My thoughts about Liz proved to be correct. In fact, I think she knew what I was going to say because, before I could start, she made it quite clear that she isn't looking to become involved in any kind of relationship other than a platonic one. Which not only saved me the trouble and embarrassment of explaining my own position, but was as broad a hint that I have no chance with her as I'm ever likely to get.

The fact that sex wasn't on the agenda was, and is, strangely reassuring as it instantly removed all the usual terror of rejection which overwhelms me whenever I'm on the pull. As a result, I relaxed, she relaxed, and we just talked.

I was, however, more than a little stunned when she explained her reasons for thinking I was gay. And apparently, she is not the only woman at work to have thought this, which makes it even worse. Because, according to her, I am a runt. This is the term the females at work apply to the person among a group of lads who not only appears to spend most of the time in a state of perpetual shame at the antics of the others, but who also looks ill-at-ease in their company. Couple this to the fact that she'd never seen me with a woman and hey presto!

Although shocked to discover that once again my mates are causing me grief, albeit unwittingly, the more I think about what she said, the more I'm starting to consider the possibility that she might have a point. Not about the gay thing, but about the lads. Even I've begun to notice that I don't feel the same buzz about a night out with them any more. In fact on most occasions lately, the only feeling I've had as I've been getting ready to go out is one of impending doom. More often than not, with some justification. Maybe all I've needed is someone to point out what I already knew. That I've suddenly become a reluctant and half-hearted lad. Christ, that's something I never thought I'd say.

On a more positive note, if nothing else, tonight I proved to myself that I am capable of spending a pleasant and totally embarrassment-free evening alone with an attractive woman. And for me, that's a huge step forward. I'll settle for that right now.

Friday 28 January

10.15 a.m. – At work

Once again, I am in the shit. Not for any of the usual things, but for apparently breaking one of the unwritten rules of lad-dom. The rule which states quite clearly that if you've had any kind of sexual experience with anyone other than a wife or girlfriend, you are duty bound to tell every gory detail to everyone else.

I am in this position because last night I took out a bird who is not only sex personified, but who regards every other male in the building as vermin. And so, using typical lad logic, it follows that I must have had a result.

While normally I would lie like a dog and tell everyone that she went like a train, the plain fact is that nothing happened and, because I like her, I can't and won't lie about that. The problem is that no one believes me and the more I deny it, the worse they get.

Quite how everyone has come to this conclusion escapes me. I mean, I am the bloke for whom the phrase 'you sad bastard' was invented. And it is fair to say that my contribution to these sordid debates has, over the last few years, been negligible. Yet still they insist I must have done the deed. It is now at the stage where the marketing lads are convinced that I could actually settle the orgasm bet but am holding out for a bribe.

The more I actually think about this, the more convinced I am that Liz is right: blokes are wankers.

12.00 p.m. – At work

The lads are still on at me and I am still denying everything. The trouble now is, that each time someone says something, I can't help smiling at the irony of my situation. Which inevitably makes them worse, and more abusive.

I have, however, decided not to get in contact with Liz and try for a repeat. Instead, I'll play it cool and wait for her to get in touch with me. After all, I don't want to seem desperate.

16.25 p.m. – At work

Still not heard from Liz, which is a bit worrying as it's getting near knocking-off time. I've decided to stick to my guns though and play it cool. Everything else I've done lately has seemed to work so why not stick with this? It's not as if a weekend of sexual frenzy is at stake.

Not surprisingly, the lads have still got the hump with me and their mood was made worse when they heard that the new bird isn't starting till next Friday now. The one saving grace is that I have found out that Julia has had an offer on a flat in Watford turned down.

16.50 p.m. – At work

My 'play-it-cool' tactic has paid off. I've just had an e-mail from Liz thanking me for last night and asking if we can do it again one night next week. My response was rapid and to the affirmative. I also checked that she has my number and told her to ring over the weekend if she's at a loose end. Excellent!

23.10 p.m. – At home

The lads were a bit subdued in the pub after work tonight. They're obviously still pissed off with me so I slipped out early and headed home. To be honest, I'm shagged out. It's been a mad week what with one thing and another, and as we haven't a game tomorrow thanks to our pathetically early FA cup exit, I think tomorrow will be spent blobbing out.

Saturday 29 January

19.20 p.m. – At home

I've done fuck-all today except play FIFA 2000 on the Playstation and eat crap. But I feel all the better for it.

However, thanks to a call from Sean, I've decided that a quick pint is not such a bad idea after all.

Sunday 30 January

18.45 p.m. – At home

Once again, Sean has caused me grief. I don't know why I ever go out with him, he's a bloody walking nightmare. Thanks to him, I got wrecked last night and ended up drinking rum & black which is bloody fatal because, as usual, I ended up projecting purple vomit. This time over my new Ben Sherman shirt, which is ruined.

As if that wasn't bad enough, I turned up for the game this morning to find out I had actually been picked to play. By half-time, I felt like death on legs. Then, when I jumped for a header in the second half, their number nine elbowed me in the gut and I threw up what was left inside my beer gut all over him. He was not pleased, as the ache in my jaw will testify although lucky for him, the ref saw the funny side. He was too busy laughing to send him off.

Monday 31 January

15.20 p.m. – At work

A bad day. My head, stomach and jaw all hurt, Julia keeps giving me odd looks and the blokes have still got the arsehole, so no one is speaking to me. As if that isn't bad enough, Liz isn't in today so I can't even ask her if she wants to come out and play tonight. I need my bed.

Chapter 3

February

Tuesday 1 February

11.20 a.m. – At work

I always enjoy the day after a hangover. Each time it happens, it's my own little victory over the demon drink. My stomach is, admittedly, still a bit iffy and the jaw aches a bit but I can live with that because at least my head is clear. And I know from experience that the first pint of Budweiser I have at lunchtime really will taste like nectar. The only downside is that I've had to spend all of this morning sorting out the mess I created yesterday. What was I on?

13.30 p.m. – At work

Damn. I had to miss lunchtime thanks to a pile of work dumped on me by Julia, so I had to make do with a bag of crisps and a diet coke. As a result, my taste buds are screaming for lager and I know that if I don't get one soon, my stomach will join in with the complaining. It always happens like that.

15.25 p.m. – At work

Weird. Mike has just been in to see Julia. He doesn't normally come down here, in fact I can't recall him ever doing so. And he didn't come over to talk to me either.

17.00 p.m. – At work

Bollocks. If only my body could have held out for ten more minutes, I could have got over the road in time but now I'm starting to feel like shit again which means that when I do have a pint, it'll taste crap. I also know, from bitter experience, that the next stage is a major headache and another bout of spewing. Luckily, the worst should kick in after I get home.

20.30 p.m. – At home

As expected, I feel like shit again. The fact that I'm so familiar with the timetable of my hangovers is a bit of a worry. You would have thought that I'd have learnt a lesson by now. Then again, it is a comfort to know that, by morning, I'll be fit and well again.

Wednesday 2 February

12.50 p.m. – At home

I felt like shit when I woke up, so called in sick. Luckily Julia was late so I spoke to Sarah and told her to pass on a message. The thought of her fantastic, nineteen-year-old breasts cheered me up for a while and so I turned to my beloved Playstation and FIFA 2000 for comfort.

Only when I lost 7–2 to a Manchester United side made up entirely of reserve goalkeepers did I realise I wasn't on top form so I settled into the delights of Richard and Judy instead.

It amazes me that women want to go out to work when, through the simple act of getting married and having kids, they can legitimately stay at home and watch daytime TV.

15.45 p.m. – At home

Just had a call from Julia making sure I'm all right. She sounded remarkably concerned and so I laid it on a bit thick. Although when she started talking about doctors and sicknotes, I said I'd probably be in tomorrow as I've got loads of work to do. A bit sucky-uppy, but it keeps her happy. Besides, I do feel better and tonight is Sainsbury's night, which should cure all my ills. A good lech never did anyone any harm.

17.20 p.m. – At home

Liz has just rung to tell me I'm a stupid twat. Somehow she's found out about my hangover and damaged jaw and said that, at my age, I should have known better. After telling her that because she's just a girlie she doesn't understand anything about blokes, I mentioned that I'll need weaning back on to lager after my enforced layoff and she's promised to see what she can do later on this week.

I'm glad she rang and I do sense that something good is happening. It's nothing sexual, she made that quite clear, but it feels right, I suppose. I've certainly never felt anything like this about any of the lads I've known. Friendship among blokes seems to revolve around ritual abuse and how much embarrassment we can cause each other.

22.10 p.m. – At home

Sainsbury's was, for once, a bit of a downer. Not because the ratio of bird to bloke was low or as a result of a low nipple count, but because of a bloody vegetarian.

I was talking to this tidy sort dressed from head to foot in black Adidas about the two-for-one offer on Magnums, the world's greatest ice cream, when this skinny tosser walks up and tries to start a discussion with us about the rights and wrongs of eating meat. Considering my trolley was full of steak, pork strips and chicken breasts, while hers was a healthy mix of pasta, vegetables and rice, I was obviously on a bit of a loser. And so rather than rise to the bait and end up looking a twat, I made my excuses and moved on. A little embarrassed but certainly a lot wiser.

I shan't make that mistake again. Maybe I need to add a new category to my list: carnivore.

I've never trusted veggies anyway. They all have this holier than thou attitude that gets right on my tits. Now I have an extra reason to hate them. I could have been in there.

Thursday 3 February

10.10 a.m. – At work

Got into work to find my desk piled high with work and a note from Julia telling me she wants to see me. Have had to put this off because she is late in again. Shit, if I had her time-keeping she'd have given me the sack by now.

11.25 a.m. – At work

Just had my meeting with an extremely happy Julia who only wanted to tell me that her revised offer on the flat in Watford has been accepted. Not good.

Still, on the plus side, she did confirm that the new bird will start tomorrow. News that is sure to please the lads who, to a man, still have the hump with me over my failure to deliver anything on Liz.

11.50 a.m. – At work

Just received an e-mailed get well card from Liz with a message asking if I want to start my lager re-training after work tonight. Mailed her back and said only if she's buying.

22.35 p.m. – At home

A top evening of lager, laughs and some surprisingly interesting conversation. I learnt a lot tonight including the fact that the resentment aimed at her from the less attractive females at work can be especially brutal. More so, in fact, than the lustful attentions of some of the sadder males. As she talked, I got the impression that she has been looking for someone to confide in about this and, for some reason, I guess I'm it. God knows why. It can't be because we have that much in common other than the fact that we're both single.

No matter, call it ally or soul mate, it seems we get on, we enjoy each other's company and, thanks to either fate or Barry the wanker, we have been thrown together. And that's all that matters.

Friday 4 February

15.10 p.m. – At work

Thankfully, my fellow males' low opinion of me has been all but forgotten this morning following the arrival of the new girl. It turns out, however, that she isn't a girl at all: she's in her late forties, tall, slim and very pretty in a mature Lesley Ash kind of way. Rumour is that she's just divorced her old man and her kids have left home so she's getting herself back out into the world.

Having hoped for an eighteen-year-old page three clone, this unexpected development made for a lively lunchtime debate about the attraction of older women. General opinion being that our new colleague is easy on the eye but too old to be lusted after. However, as expected, three rapidly consumed pints of lager coupled with Kev's observations on the long-term effects gravity has on breasts soon turned the discussion into the usual 'who has the best tits in the office' argument. Sarah won. As usual.

16.45 p.m. – At work

The older woman debate has resurfaced and looks set to run and run. Sean has suddenly announced that, when they were at school, he used to fancy Kev's mum, a statement quickly endorsed by Mike who said, and I quote, 'I always wanted to give your mum one.' Kev was not best pleased to find out that some of his mates spent their adolescence masturbating while fantasising about his mum and has gone into a major sulk.

As they are all a couple of years younger than me, I didn't have the pleasure of knowing their mums when I was at school, but having got to know Kev's mum since, have to admit that she is still something of a looker so must indeed have been stunning when she was younger. However, for me, it was Tom's mum who did it. There was something about her that got me every time and, I have to say, she still does it now. As Tom is a major-league psycho who delights in taking the piss out of everyone when we all go to football, I'd best keep that to myself.

Although delighted that my own mum did not feature in their conversation, a mental picture of Sean having sex with the woman who gave birth to me has suddenly appeared in my subconscious. It is not attractive!

Saturday 5 February

10.05 a.m. – At home

Last night was one of those heavy post-work, Friday night sessions which happens all too regularly. For once, Kev refused to come out with us as the revelations of lunchtime were proving too much for him to handle but the older woman debate continued to dominate proceedings. That was until Sally turned up. As usual, she put the dampers on the whole evening at a single stroke when I asked her if she ever fancied older men. She said that, to her, *we* are older men and the chances of her fancying any of us is zero. Bloody eighteen-year-olds.

The strange thing is, the idea of an older woman has suddenly become quite intriguing. Maybe, after twenty-nine years and barely a flicker on the stud-o-meter of life, I had been looking at it all wrong. Maybe I'm one of those blokes who goes for older women. The type who needs mothering rather than lusting? And if I am, what's wrong with that? I've always had this suspicion that romance is wasted on the majority of young birds and, in any case, just what constitutes an older woman? I'm twenty-nine so, in those terms, does old mean anything over forty? or even forty-five? To be honest, I can't see me lusting after anything over fifty although Helen Mirren is getting on a bit and she's bloody stunning. And now I think of it, I have always had a soft spot for Fern Britton, although I don't know how old she is. I need to give this some serious thought when I have some spare time. After all, as Sean said, 'Many a good tune is played on an old fiddle.' And even a quiet hum would do me at the moment.

21.15 p.m. – At home

I obviously opened my big mouth last night because today was a living nightmare. Not only did I feel shit, but when Tom walked into the pre-match pub the first thing he did was look at me and shout, in a voice which even the people outside could hear, 'Oi!, Ellis you pervert, what's this about you fancying my mum?'

This led on to a period of piss-taking which went beyond either pub or terrace humour and descended to the level of mockery. The fact that Tom is the loudest person I know meant that his abuse of me let both Mike and Sean, the two people who started it all, off the hook. Not that this stopped them from joining in of course.

It was so bad that at half-time, when I was queuing for a slash, people I barely knew were asking me about it. Some old boy even told me there was a proper name for fancying your mum, as if it were some kind of disease. Mind you, he soon shut up when I threatened to give him a slap, although I then felt the need to point out that it wasn't my *own* mum that I fancied but someone else's. I now know that this is hardly the best dialogue to come out with on a Saturday afternoon while having a slash during the half-time interval of an English league fixture. During the second half, people were pointing at me.

After the game, it continued. The fact that the team had played crap and lost again made it even worse because the lads' abuse of me gave them something else to think about and something else for me to hate the players for. If they'd been any good no one would care about me but, no, they were shit and I was in the shit.

My afternoon was brought to an abrupt halt when Tom took me to one side and quietly offered to set me up on a date with his mum if I fancied it. Not being one to hurt his feelings, rather than simply tell him to eff-off, I merely said no thanks, to which he replied 'Ah, but you thought about it didn't you, you perv, or you'd have told me to eff-off!' – much to the merriment of the entire pub, who all knew that he was setting me up. At this point, my brain, overcome with lager and after suffering hours of verbal abuse, took control of the situation and issued the immortal line 'I've already had her once and she was crap.' Which succeeded in getting me a punch in the face.

Which is why I'm sitting here with a cold flannel on my face waiting for *Match of the Day*.

Sunday 6 February

11.00 a.m. – At home

I'm sure there's a medical reason for it, but at the moment, I can't work out how a gut full of Budweiser and a simple punch in the face can possibly cause every inch of my body to be throbbing with pain. At least a check in the mirror has confirmed that my nose isn't swollen too much. Although it doesn't look pretty.

11.30 a.m. – At home

I've just had a call which clearly came from the touchline of the game I should be playing in at this very moment. In between the swearing, I gathered that the lads are two men light and it's all my fault. Given that I've missed turning up for only one game in the last two seasons, have been substitute for most of those and the only thing I have in common with David Beckham is that we live in Hertfordshire, I suspect this has more to do with mine being the only phone number they have at the moment rather than the facts. Still, what's a bit more abuse on top of everything else.

I can't even be arsed to get up to go for the papers because I don't want to see anyone and I certainly don't want to read about fucking football. I'll just sit here, thinking about my life and how shit it is. Billy Ellis, twenty-sodding-nine, single, sad, bored and battered. What a bloody catch if you'll excuse the pun (battered, catch . . . oh bollocks).

11.50 a.m. – At home

I've been thinking about calling in sick tomorrow, but that would just give the bastards more time to prepare their slagging fest. Best to face it and get it out the way.

15.00 p.m. – At home

Just got in after what I can only describe as yet another bloody farce. I finally went out to get the papers but, in the newsagents, caught sight of a top-shelf soft-porn mag dedicated to women over forty. Given recent events, not to mention interest, I simply had to have it but didn't want to get it in Patel's, as I'm in there every day and the last thing I need at the moment is more gossip. The only alternative was to jump in the car and head for the other side of town in search of a suitable supplier. Why do so many bloody women work in newsagents on Sundays? Haven't they anything better to do? I ended up having to drive almost twenty bloody miles before I could finally purchase a copy of *Forty & Fab* from a shop with a male assistant. Even he was vaguely familiar but by then I was past caring. Knowing my luck he'll be Mike's uncle or something. Then again, Mike's not even Asian and he lives in Rickmansworth not Enfield.

Jesus, why oh why is it so difficult to buy porn? I've nothing to be ashamed of. It's healthy to be interested in sex and this is, after all, in the name of research. My future love life could be at stake here.

Of course, driving home, curiosity got the better of me and, rather than wait until I got home before I took a peek, I tore off the plastic coating as I was driving along. The woman on the front certainly seemed fit enough and so when I pulled up at a set of traffic lights, I flicked open the pages to look at who, or what, was in the middle. As I'm staring down at what looks like acres of naked flesh, I realised that between me and the kerb had appeared a cyclist. Not any cyclist of course, but a woman. Her steely gaze – almost certainly hardened by years of sexual frustration, feminism and anti-male soap operas – alternating between me and the open pages of *Forty & Fab*. The look of anger on her face soon turned to one of disgust and then she started shouting abuse at me while I sank ever deeper into my seat, desperately willing the lights to change but knowing that the traffic flow at that particular junction meant that I could have been there for ever. The only person smiling during the whole sordid event was Mary from Belfast. She looked totally at ease with the fact that she was totally naked, legs akimbo and in a car on the A41 just outside Watford. Lucky her.

By the time I reached the sanctuary of home, I half expected the police to be waiting outside, which would just about have set things off nicely. After all, how many reports of perverts reading soft-porn in full view of the general public can they get on a Sunday afternoon?

20.30 p.m. – At home

Thanks to the events of this evening, I already know that tomorrow is almost certain to enter the top ten worst days of my life.

Just before four o'clock, Kev arrived, unannounced as usual, to take in the delights of the Sunday game on Sky Sports. Being a mere junior accountant on twenty-seven thousand a year, he can't afford a satellite dish of his own so, despite the twenty-minute drive from his house, he prefers to come round to my flat and watch mine. I wouldn't mind if he ever brought any beer round but it's only right I supply that as well. After all, I earn around three grand a year less than him and have a bigger mortgage to boot. So I can obviously afford to keep him beered up.

As we listened to Andy Gray talking his usual pre-match bollocks, the only reference he made to the events of the last two days was 'How's your nose you prat?' before the two of us watched Arsenal and Liverpool play the game in a style that is only ever seen at our place when the televisions are on in the executive lounges.

At half-time, as usual, he headed for the bog and the fridge in that order. Returning with my last six pack of Budweiser in one hand and the brand new bag of peanuts I'd been saving in the other. And then it happened.

As soon as I saw him reach down for the papers, I knew I was in the shit. Everything slowed down like it does when you're about to have a car crash or you realise the angry looking bloke approaching you is the boyfriend of the girl you've just asked to dance. As he lifted up the *News of the World*, there, right underneath, was my fresh copy of *Forty & Fab*. There was a pause and then he bent down and picked it up, holding it outstretched between his thumb and forefinger. I don't know if the strangled cry of 'What the fuck is this?' was one of genuine shock or simple elation, but no matter. As I desperately tried to feign indifference, he spent the entire second half devouring the numerous photographs and commenting loudly on everything from the number of stretchmarks to the appalling wallpaper, and then had the nerve to ask if he could take it home with him! What could I say to that?

And so now, I haven't even got it to look at, so am none the wiser and £3.75 out of pocket. But the fact that I had it in the first place was enough. It means that I face unimaginable horror in the morning. I am considering not only calling in sick, but resigning from work and changing football clubs.

Monday 7 February

07.50 a.m. – At home

I have a feeling of impending doom. In fact, I don't think I'd be this nervous if I found out my girlfriend was pregnant as I was waiting to take my driving test.

Today is going to be hell. And my face still hurts.

09.10 a.m. – At work

Inevitably, after a nightmare journey into work which involved a signal failure and a twat with a mobile phone who insisted on talking at full volume about what he did this weekend – as if anyone else in the carriage gave a shit – I have arrived at the office to be greeted by Kev's handiwork.

First, I had to endure a series of sniggers from the receptionist, and then arrived at my desk to find an extremely unglamorous picture of Mary from Belfast stuck to my PC screen. Something which has obviously gone down well with the women in the office judging by the laughter.

God knows what else he has planned. But, knowing him, this latest episode of humiliation is going to be dragged out for days. Wonderful.

10.15 a.m. – At work

I've just received an e-mail from billy@isapervert.com asking me what the opposite of paedophilia is. Despite my best efforts at remaining aloof, I could not help but laugh. Whoever my tormentor is, they are certainly inventive.

23.00 p.m. – At home

Hard day today but not all bad. The new girl, Sue, was obviously told about my apparent fixation with older women at some point, for when I bumped into her on my way to the mail room, she gave me a grin and a broad wink which, if anything, made her look even more attractive. Maybe I really am on to something.

By the time I left work, the level of piss-taking had died off a bit, although this was largely due to rumours that one of the older blokes in accounts was arrested for kerb crawling over the weekend. It's an ill wind as they say.

I also called the folks tonight to let them know I'm still alive. Lou was watching *Coronation Street* so cut me off quick and still hasn't rung back and Dad told me that Kathy had left him but he now had a new bird anyway so doesn't really care.

I wonder if there is actually anything sadder than finding out your dad has a better sex life than you do?

Tuesday 8 February

09.10 a.m. – At work

I was collared by a remarkably cheerful and friendly Julia on my way in and given the extremely bad news that, because her new flat was vacant, she'll be able to move in next weekend. She then started asking me about pubs, clubs and the best place to do her shopping. God knows why she's started asking me all this: I can think of at least six other people from this company who live in the Watford area.

Maybe she was waiting for me to offer my help with the move. If so, she'll be waiting until hell freezes over. As her number two, I might have no choice about spending time with her at work, but I'm sure as shit not going to socialise with her away from it. Not only do I resent her for taking a job that should have been mine, but she and her type still scare the shit out of me.

Besides, coming on top of the *Forty & Fab* episode, being caught fraternising with the boss is the last thing I need or want.

10.35 a.m. – At work

My bloody e-mail has just delivered a scanned-in photo from *Forty & Fab* with my head superimposed on to the body of some sad, scruffy but obviously aroused bloke loitering in the background of a picture in which an extremely wrinkled and unattractive woman is posing in a way she really shouldn't be.

Although I have to admit that it's a work of genius, a click onto the 'reply to all' button has revealed that almost everyone in the company outside of the management have received a copy. And thanks to the anonymity of hotmail, I have no chance of finding out who the guilty party is. I could make a bloody good guess though.

11.55 a.m. – At work

In the last hour, I've had seventeen phone calls and three visits. Each wanting to know more detail about the photo and my rumoured craving for older flesh. Although I denied everything, it has to be said that the arrival of Sue at my desk almost bordered on the suggestive. I had no idea that any woman could say 'Billy, you naughty boy' in such an obscene tone. Clearly, at some point I am going to have to pursue this. Although I think I'll leave it until the fuss has died down a bit, and I've worked out a way I can try it on without anyone else ever finding out.

Thankfully, Julia wasn't on the list. I don't want her getting ideas like that.

14.20 p.m. – At work

Liz has just been down. Aside from wanting to take the piss as a result of my most recent humiliation, she requested my company for a post-work pint or three. An offer I readily accepted.

Hopefully, the fact that I was the reason for her all too rare appearance in this office will have gone some way towards rebuilding my credibility. I'll ask the other lads once they've scraped their tongues off the carpet.

14.55 p.m. – At work

If anything, Liz's visit seems to have attracted even more interest in me and my sex life because I am now coming under pressure to reveal the true nature of my relationship with her. Not just from the lads either, but also from her fellow females who are clearly intrigued by the very notion that something is going on which they do not know about. Indeed, I have been getting some very odd looks from Sue.

Clearly, this is not going to go away until they have something to chew over and so I have decided to take the only sensible course of action. Smile, but say nothing. It drives them mad.

16.15 p.m. – At work

I've just spent ten minutes in Julia's office during which time she did nothing but talk complete bollocks about how her solicitors are costing a fortune. Not that I took much notice. I was too busy staring at her PC screen which was displaying the offending photograph image of me in glorious digital colour.

At least she didn't laugh. Well, not until after I'd left the office anyway. Although when it gets to the stage where your boss is taking the piss, that's when it goes from funny to problem. Because this could well fuck me up in the future. After all, I've just missed out on promotion because of a bloody photocopier, this could well turn out to be just as damaging.

16.35 p.m. – At work

I have just mailed the lads and registered my displeasure at the fact that yesterday's stunt has been discovered by my boss.

Although showing any sign of anger at a wind-up would usually be asking for trouble, I am hoping that the word 'boss', and the implications that go along with it, will ensure that there is no repeat. After all, this company may be a bit slack in some areas, but one thing they are strict on is using dodgy e-mail accounts and downloading unsolicited files. That's sacking territory.

23.45 p.m. – At home

I told Liz about the rumour mill at work tonight, but she already knew and so we have also made a joint decision to let them get on with it. If nothing else, it should be fun. There is also the added bonus that not only will such a tactic give me a bit of cred, and finally lay to rest the suspicion that I am gay, but if everyone thinks we're a couple, it should reduce the amount of lechery she receives. Even my mates know better than to have squalid fantasies about a mate's bird.

The other thing we discussed tonight was the thorny subject of relationships. Astonishingly, the topic was raised not by her, but me. We had moved from the pub to a curry house when, without thinking, I simply asked why she hasn't got a bloke in tow. A question which obviously shocked her a bit because after a pause, she simply said that she doesn't really know. She then went into this long speech about reaching twenty-five and wanting to meet someone who was after more than a feel of her tits. Although I can well understand the male fixation with tits, especially when they are as well proportioned as hers, I am starting to consider the idea that she isn't really any different from me. We're both looking for someone who is more interested in what we're like on the inside than what we look like on the outside. The difference of course, is that she's stunning, and I'm a tub of lard.

Yet for entirely unrelated reasons, neither of us are anywhere near finding someone. And while I have a sneaky feeling that, given a chance, we could actually be good for each other, the fact is that at the moment, there seems to be absolutely no sexual chemistry between us. But to be honest, I'm quite happy with that for now. It's about time something good happened to me.

Wednesday 9 February

11.30 a.m. – At work

Responses to yesterday's mail have been coming thick and fast and all are of the 'yeah, that's bang out of order that is' variety. As the first few came from my immediate circle of mates, I have no doubt that at least one of them is responsible and will have been busy deleting files and mail accounts all morning.

15.15 p.m. – At work

Thanks to the delights of an irate customer, I forfeited lunch today trying to trace their lost order. However, while normally missing out on my daily dose of America's finest export would have been a major pain in the arse, today it was a joy. For I got to spend a very enjoyable hour alone in the office with Sue.

Time spent with Liz has obviously helped my confidence with women. For although I had the odd flashback from within the pages of *Forty & Fab*, my conversation with her felt remarkably relaxed. Something which until only recently, would have been all but impossible.

To be fair, even though she is (much) older than me, she has remained fairly immune to the ravages of both time and two sons and, if anything, looks even better close up. Not sexier, just better. Like many women of her age, there is a confident, almost motherly glow about her. And she has fabulous legs which is always a good selling point.

The only downside is that she has a slight trace of facial hair. Very fine admittedly, and not in the five o'clock shadow league of my granny, but it's there nevertheless. I know this is the norm in women of a certain age, but to be honest, it leaves me cold. I haven't had much chance to caress the flesh of a women lately, but when I do, I'd rather it felt like silk, not corduroy.

16.00 p.m. – At work

I've been trying, without success, to work out how I can try my luck with Sue. However, thinking about that has also made me consider how and when I make the leap from simply chatting, to chatting up. Something I have always had a major problem with.

The thing is, the whole pulling thing seems to be totally different from when I last enjoyed any success. For a start, when I listen to the girls in the office discussing their weekends, it's like hearing a tape of us ten years ago. In fact, it's worse. Because when we used to boast about getting shitfaced and shagged, we all knew it was bollocks. When this lot talk about it, it's true! But what I can't work out is whether or not this laddism has filtered through to all the women of my age. If, as I suspect, it's infected only a proportion, how do you tell who is and who isn't a ladette? Where does geezer-bird end and feminine charm begin?

What this means in real terms, of course, is that there's even more scope to experience what has always been my ultimate terror: rejection, the best contraception known to man. And, in the case of Sue, that rejection would be both major, and public.

I suppose that's why dating agencies have sprung up everywhere. They get around the first contact phase and go straight into the face to face. I reckon I could cope with that, but the very idea of joining something just to find a bird, isn't only sad, it's a bit scary. After all, when we signed up on Mike's behalf last year, they didn't even check to see if we were actually him. And if they can fuck up with three lads having a laugh, God knows what horrors they could set me up with. Knowing my luck, it'd be Mike.

But at some point, I'm going to have to take a risk and face up to this. Otherwise, I'll never get anywhere. Of course, I could always ask Liz for advice. I'm sure she'd point me in the right direction. But that would mean coming clean about a lot of very personal things and, although I feel more comfortable with her than any other woman I know, I don't know if I'm ready to make that step yet. That's heavy stuff.

22.15 p.m. – At home

As I was leaving for Sainsbury's, the old man turned up and introduced me to his latest conquest. Unlike the gorgeous Kathy, this one is a pig of the first order. I'm no catch, that's for sure, but she looks like Paul Gascoigne in a dress. God knows where they met but, wherever it is, I need to find out so that I can avoid it.

Sadly, by the time they managed to take the hint that I was going out and pissed off, my shopping time was limited to actually shopping rather than leching.

Thursday 10 February

09.20 a.m. – At work

I've been so preoccupied with everything else lately that I've only just realised that Monday is that most hated of days on the singles calendar, Valentine's Day. I'm not a violent person, but if ever I meet the wanker who thought that one up, I'm going to batter them senseless.

It's all right if you're a good-looking bird or a popular bloke, you're bound to get loads of cards telling you how great you are and how much everyone fancies you. But if you're plain, fat, ugly or just boring, which kind of describes me to a tee, then you might as well hang a sign around your neck telling people you're a sad, lonely bastard.

And, as if that isn't bad enough, as sure as shit smells, someone somewhere is plotting to do something to embarrass me in front of everyone else. I know that, because they always do it. And when I find out who it is, they are dead. I just hope that whatever they come up with this time isn't as bad as last year. It was two months before I could look Sandra from the sandwich bar across the road in the eye again. Whoever it was must have known that the bloke who worked with her was her husband when they sent those flowers and that message. I'd never even thought of her naked until then. I do now though, every time I see her.

12.50 p.m. – At work

Spent most of the morning with Sue taking her through the tedious subject of unpaid invoices. Ordinarily, this would have been a mind-numbingly boring time but being in close proximity to those legs made it well worthwhile and for some reason, as we talked, she leant in close a lot and each time she did so, the top she was wearing fell forward revealing a glimpse of both her bra and a very ample and inviting cleavage. I don't think she noticed I was copping an eyeful but if she did she certainly didn't seem to mind. If anything, I could have sworn the slight smile on her face became even more inviting. It was very nice though.

15.25 p.m. – At work

In my new spirit of confidence, I have decided to go on a Valentine's Day offensive. At lunchtime, I purchased a remarkably cheap-looking pack of cards and these will be sent to every ugly woman at work, each with cryptic messages suggesting it came from either Sean, Kev, Mike or even Barry the wanker. They are, after all, the four people at the top of my hit list.

23.30 p.m. – At home

Trouble is on the horizon. I bumped into Liz as I left work and we went for a quick drink which turned into a long session. Somehow, we got on to the subject of blind dates and when I said I had never been on one, she immediately offered to set that right. Apparently she has a friend who she thinks would be perfect for me and, despite my protests, the deal is done and she won't budge. I don't know if I'm excited by the prospect of this or not. Well, I do; I'm not. I'm bloody terrified. She could be a right donkey with the personality to match for all I know. Then again, she could be a stunner and when I turn up, she could think she's drawn the short straw.

The more I think about it, the more I can feel all the old insecurities returning. The very idea of sitting with a woman I don't even know and trying to stimulate interesting conversation is beyond frightening. All I can imagine is two people sitting there in embarrassed silence. Each one trying to work out how the hell they can get the hell out of there. Oh God.

Friday 11 February

12.30 p.m. – At work

Thank Christ the morning is almost over. I've spent the entire time trying to avoid answering the phone just in case Liz was on the other end with news of my impending date. Thankfully, she hasn't rung yet so maybe she's forgotten.

On the plus side, I have caught Sue looking at me a few times from across the office. I'm sure she's eyeing me up. To be honest, as each day passes, she is looking increasingly attractive and, the more I think about it, the more sure I am that if I tried, I could get in there. The problem is, if I'm wrong and I did try it on only to get blown out, I would never live it down. Correction, I'd never be able to live it down. Is it worth the risk I wonder? Maybe, maybe not. I still have a problem imagining what it would be like to actually have sex with someone who's at least ten, if not fifteen, years older than me. Then again, I have a problem imagining what it would be like to have sex full stop. But it would take an awful lot of bottle to take a punt at Sue and, at the moment, I haven't got that bottle. And although she's got great legs and a tidy cleavage, there's still the hairy face to consider.

14.15 p.m. – At work

The deed is done. My cards have all gone in the internal post. To avoid them being traced back to me, I even went to the trouble of slipping them into the mail box in personnel while all the women were gossiping about last night's *EastEnders*. I was going to send one to Julia on Kev's behalf. But that's a bit too close to home.

15.10 p.m. – At work

Julia has just emerged from her lair and informed us all that a memo has come down on high warning of dire repercussions should the mail system be clogged up with Valentine's pranks. Oops.

15.30 p.m. – At work

Julia's announcement prompted renewed concerns about my standing with the high-ups. And because I daren't attract any more attention, I've just been back to personnel and recovered all my cards. Cowardly I know, but better safe than sorry.

When I got back, Mike was in with Julia again. I can't think what that's about. Maybe I should just ask him. Or her.

15.45 p.m. – At work

Bollocks. Liz has just rung and the blind date is arranged for tomorrow night. Her friend's called Fiona, she's twenty-six and we're meeting at a restaurant in Camden at eight o'clock.

Although I'm terrified at the prospect, I have grudgingly decided to accept whatever lies in store. It was inevitable that at some point I would have to go out on a date, and at least this way I don't have to go through the chatting up stage. I guess all I can do is go through with it and put it down to experience.

16.10 p.m. – At work

Just rung Liz to try and extract more information about this bird Fiona, but all she said was that I'll really like her. I'd like to know how she can say that considering that, up until a few weeks ago, she had me down as a faggot.

16.30 p.m. – At work

Just rung Liz to apologise for being a twat and then came clean and explained that I haven't been on a proper date, never mind a blind one, for almost two years. That's why I'm so apprehensive.

She just told me to relax because Fiona is great and we'll have a good time. I think I'll be the judge of that.

23.45 p.m. – At home

Had a few with the lads after work and then we all headed up for a few more in the Red Lion.

During the journey, I asked Mike about his visits to Julia but he was very evasive. I'm beginning to suspect that something's going on. Christ, maybe he fancies her! Now that would be a turn-up for the books.

Despite this possible revelation, my mind wasn't really on the job in hand and so, when they decided to hit a club, I left them to it. I have more pressing matters on my mind, and they involve a little thing called fate and a woman I've never met.

Saturday 12 February

08.30 a.m. – At home

Hardly slept a wink last night thanks to my incredible apprehension. I haven't felt like this since the England–Argentina game during France 98.

09.30 a.m. – At home

Needed to hear a human voice and so rang the only person I knew would be up, Lou. After a chat about Dad's new bird, the kids came on and as usual cheered me up with this week's exciting instalment of their happy, hectic and totally stress-free lives. In fact they made me laugh so much, I let my guard down and offered to take them swimming again tomorrow. I must stop doing that.

Mind you, at least I know now why the old man is with the old tug: according to Lou, she's a very rich widow. I wonder why she was dressed like a bag lady when she came round here then?

18.00 p.m. – At home

A crap game today: 1–1 with poxy Leicester. I suppose a point is better than nothing, but only just.

Worryingly, the rest of the lads spent the entire afternoon talking about anything and everything except work. A clear and dangerously ominous sign that they've got something planned for me on Monday. But more importantly, I am beginning to feel incredibly nervous about tonight and I know that feeling will increase over the next two hours.

I don't really know what I'm expecting, to be honest. There are so many possible permutations. What if she takes an instant dislike to me? Or I to her? I've even considered the remote possibility that she thinks I'm great and asks me back to her place. But what if she's a pig? Do I go or do I turn her down? And if I turn her down, how do I do that without hurting her feelings? Fucking hell, this is ridiculous. I have to chill out.

At least I know what I'm wearing. It took about an hour, but I've finally settled on my lucky Pepe shirt and my new chinos. Smart, but casual.

19.00 p.m. – At home

Time to go. I've decided to act the gentleman and simply go with the flow. Whatever happens, happens. End of story.

23.50 p.m. – At home

Well if that was a typical example of a blind date, all I can say is: never again. To be honest, it's hard to think of what exactly was the low point. After all, there were so many. It started OK, she was certainly pretty enough (slim, dark hair, nice jugs), but as the evening moved along, I began to have a sneaky feeling that we were being watched. This was confirmed when she went to the toilet and I was immediately joined by another woman who hissed venomously that if I did anything to upset her friend, I would be history. She then returned to her table where, I noticed, she was in the company of what I can only describe as a coven.

I was still recovering from this verbal assault when Fiona returned only to launch into a long and totally unprovoked attack on males in general. When she came out with the immortal line that 'men are all the same, the only reason they look different is so that women can tell them apart', I suddenly realised that here was a woman on a major rebound. Then, as I was silently whispering a curse in Liz's direction, a couple entered the restaurant, the male half of which, judging by the shriek from the coven, was Fiona's ex-boyfriend. At this point, the whole evening becomes a bit of a blur. I know there was a fight, and that my lucky shirt became covered in vegetable curry. Then the police came and an irate waiter, his perfect Indian accent now replaced with perfect East End English, threatened to batter me senseless unless I settled the bill. When I protested that none of this was my fault, he was joined by another irate waiter and so I paid up. To the tune of £53.72. By the time I had sorted all that out, Fiona and the coven had vanished leaving me to deal with the ex-boyfriend. And as his new girlfriend had pissed off after taking exception to watching him being bollocked by the police for causing trouble with his ex-girlfriend, he was not best pleased. Luckily, the irate waiters got me out the back door before he could actually get hold of me and, after walking around Camden covered in curry for about half hour, I went back to my car and drove home. A bit wiser, a lot poorer and having definitely decided never to go through that experience again. Liz owes me, big time.

Sunday 13 February

20.45 p.m. – At home

After the trials of last night, I had kind of hoped today would be better but, if anything, it was worse. After letting the lads down last week, I was again consigned to my familiar role of both substitute and linesman and spent the entire ninety minutes running the line despite the fact that we were 3–0 down by half-time and eventually lost 5–1. Coming on top of last night, this obvious show of animosity was not what I needed and so I gave the post-match pub a miss and headed for Lou's.

But on the way, I took the long overdue decision to call a halt to my footballing career. I certainly don't enjoy it any more, so what's the point? It's not as if the social life is that great. On the rare occasions we actually all go out together, much of the entertainment seems to revolve around slagging each other off. Well fuck it. I get enough of that at work and in The Red Lion.

Thankfully, Lou managed to cheer me up and even though her highly infectious laughter resulted from a brief resumé of my blind date experience, by the time I left with the kids I felt a lot better. However, my weekend of purgatory was far from over, because at the pool, I bumped into Dad's old bird, Kathy.

In any normal circumstance, being almost naked with a female like her is the stuff of wet dreams. But when you're with your niece and nephew and in the company of about a hundred other people, many of whom are teenage boys, it's a nightmare. Of all the times I have been embarrassed in my life, I don't think anything will ever come close to the sight of a fourteen-year-old spotty youth climbing out of a swimming pool with a red face and an erection. The fact that Kathy merely glanced at him and murmured 'that's nice' before continuing her chat with me made it even worse. I actually felt my penis shrinking as she was talking.

Thankfully, Katie came to my assistance when she announced the urgent need for the toilet and, by the time I returned, Kathy had left. Easy as it is to imagine her giving me pleasure of the most sordid kind, the physical act of having sex with someone after my own dad is too sick to even contemplate. Still, at least I know what he saw in her.

When I got home, there were four messages on the answerphone from Liz. Much as I want to talk to her, I'm not going to return her call. I'm still pissed off about last night and, hopefully, with each second that passes, she's feeling a bit worse. It serves her right.

21.10 p.m. – At home

Liz has just rung again and left another message. This time, rather than simply asking me to call, she left a long message explaining that Fiona called her this morning, told her what happened and that she's really sorry. For a second, I debated whether or not to pick up the phone but decided against it. I'll let her sweat until tomorrow.

Monday 14 February

09.20 a.m. – At work

Liz has just been down and, during a whirlwind visit, wished me a happy Valentine's Day and then hurled abuse at me for not returning her calls before telling me to me to meet her for lunch. By the time I got round to speaking, she'd pissed off.

09.30 a.m. – At work

Shit, bollocks, fuck, wank and damn. The mail has just been delivered and there are three cards in my in-tray. This is bad. From years of working in mixed offices and knowing my female colleagues' opinions of me as I do, it's 99.9 per cent certain that all three will be bogus and the bastards who sent them will be watching and waiting to see how I react. The obvious thing to do would be to throw them in the bin. But there's always the chance, however remote, that they are genuine which could, potentially, open up all kinds of possibilities. Then again, seeing as in all the time I've ever been here, I've never had one genuine card, the chances of that happening are remote.

Despite Julia's warning, a glance down the office confirms that, as usual, every female in the place has been deluged with cards. Sarah has proven particularly popular this year although, given that her breasts have grown even larger over the last twelve months, that's hardly surprising. Even Sue has a little pile of cards, which is quite nice really. Shows that someone else apart from me has had unclean thoughts about her.

10.00 a.m. – At work

Just had a call from Liz asking me if I'd got her card yet. Judging by the laugh, I imagine that she thought I was taking the piss when I asked which one was hers and so I explained my predicament which merely drew the usual abuse, more laughter and the news that hers is the one in the yellow envelope.

Having opened it and perched it on the end of my desk like some trophy, I am now left with two white envelopes staring up at me from my in-tray. I think I'll leave them until later. Much later.

But now I feel guilty for not getting a card for Liz. Although considering she's made it quite clear that she doesn't want to be the object of my affections, why should I have? And on which point, why did she buy me one? Christ almighty, is nothing involving women straightforward?

10.35 a.m. – At work

Well, at least I can hazard a bloody good guess as to why Mike has been coming down here now. Julia has just called me into her office and during one of the most embarrassing episodes of my entire desperate life, thanked me for sending her a Valentine's card.

God knows what she expected me to say but the only thing I could come up with was some bollocks about me being 'that kind of bloke' and 'what with her being new, I didn't want her to feel left out'. At this point, my brain finally caught up with the situation and I tried to change the subject by asking her about her new flat. Something which not only started her off on another moan about solicitors and removal men, but which also attracted an invite to 'come round and see it one night'.

Although tempted to see which room she's turned into her dungeon, I would rather slit my own throat.

As for Mike, he's dead.

11.40 a.m. – At work

There is indeed, a god. The person I suspect is behind so much of the trial and tribulation in my life has finally got his comeuppance. Mike has just called and told me that Kev is spitting bullets because the ugly bird from personnel has just been up to see him and confirm their date on Friday night. Apparently, someone has set him up and he thinks that someone is me.

Tempted as I am to claim the credit, the pile of cards in my drawer proves I am not responsible. I'd love to know who is though. If only to shake their hand.

While I had him on the phone, I thanked Mike for pulling the stunt with Julia. Inevitably, he denied it, although when I suggested that I might begin to spread a rumour that he's actually been trying to pull her himself, he spun some bollocks about her asking him all about me and what I do away from work. He's such a twat.

12.35 p.m. – At work

Sue has just walked over and nervously thanked me for her card. She also said that, although she's very flattered, she doesn't think it would be a good idea if we went out together. It isn't the age difference, apparently, but the fact that we work together. It could make things uncomfortable.

I don't know whether to laugh or cry. Still, thanks to the bastard who sent it on my behalf, at least I didn't have to go through the embarrassing process of actually asking her myself.

14.45 p.m. – At work

An interesting lunch with Liz, although I didn't have to tell her about Sue and Julia because she already knew. Are there no bloody secrets in our company?

More importantly, when Fiona had rung her on Sunday, she had obviously neglected to mention a few of the details which have now been well and truly filled in. Especially the bit about me having to pay the bill. Hopefully, a cheque for £53.72 and a replacement shirt will be heading my way fairly soon.

21.30 p.m. – At home

I've fucking well done it again. Walked right into something that is certain to rain shit down on me for weeks to come.

I don't even know how it happened. One minute I was walking out of work and the next I'm standing in a bar with Sue ordering a Budweiser and a white wine while she, having found out about Kev and the ugly bird and put two and two together, was apologising for embarrassing me about the card. It was all perfectly innocent, not an unclean thought had entered my head.

And then, my whole world fell apart. Again. First, as I'm sitting down, she knocks her drink right into my lap. And then, just as I'm about to leap up and let out a scream, the door opens and in walks Barry the Chelsea wanker and some of the lads from marketing. Of course, they saw us straight away and judging by the delighted expressions on their faces, immediately drew the obvious conclusions. And so what do I do? Nothing, that's what. Instinct rooted me to the spot because I knew that if I'd stood up with the front of my trousers soaking wet, their lives would have been complete. And mine would have been a nightmare.

But of course, Sue, not having such in-depth knowledge of the average lad's mind, dives into her bag, grabs a packet of tissues and proceeds to dab away at my groin. Ordinarily, this was something I would have been more than happy to experience but in this instance, sitting across an almost empty bar from a group of lads who all still have the arsehole with me, it was probably the very last thing on earth I would ever want. Even in my panic-ridden state, I could think of at least four one-liners to suit.

What made it worse was that, by the time she'd finished apologising, again, and then bought herself another drink, she had to gulp it down and shoot off home. Leaving me to sit there alone until Barry and his cronies got bored with taking the piss out of me and fucked off. What a bastard. And to add insult to injury, I arrived home to find, surprise surprise, not one Valentine's card on the mat.

Tuesday 15 February

08.45 a.m. – At work

Came to work early today to make sure I'm here before news of last night hits.

This also gave me time to open the two cards left over from yesterday. One of them came from Sean, who had not only filled it with a series of abusive one-liners, he'd also signed it, while the other contains a drawing of a heart with only a question mark beside it. That could have come from anybody. Male or female. To be honest, I'm past caring. I bloody hate Valentine's Day. As if I haven't got enough to worry about.

09.10 a.m. – At work

Liz has just called and in the most sarcastic voice I have ever heard, told me that I'm a bastard. Word is that I was seen out on the town last night with another woman. I have some explaining to do at lunchtime.

Just what I need. On top of everything else, now even the women are taking the piss.

09.35 a.m. – At work

Sue has just been over and offered to pay for cleaning my trousers. For some reason, I had to laugh.

10.10 a.m. – At work

Great, now billy@isapervert.com has returned.

10.30 a.m. – At work

A stream of messages has arrived from various lads congratulating me on my choice of women and enquiring how I got on last night. Wankers the lot of them.

14.10 p.m. – At work

Didn't fancy the pub, so spent lunchtime with Liz instead. After telling her about last night, something which, ironically enough, almost made her wet herself, we spent the rest of our lunch-hour talking bollocks. Basic stuff like when we left home and why, what music we like and if we could legally kill one person, who would it be. Rubbish really, but good fun. It cheered me up anyway, which was just what I needed.

22.30 p.m. – At home

Today was rougher than normal, although I don't really know why. Maybe the last few days have started to catch up with me. They have been pretty hard going.

I know it's daft, but the thing that keeps jumping into my head is the sight of last night's empty doormat. It was really bloody depressing. Mostly, I suppose, because it seems to sum up my life pretty well.

Wednesday 16 February

09.40 a.m. – At work

I had a terrible night last night. I just couldn't sleep, so in the end gave up and had a soak in the bath.

For some reason, my mind keeps returning to my shite life and what's been going on lately. The thing is, after reading my diary, my plan was to change things for the better, but if anything they've actually got worse. Since New Year, I've had the blind date from hell, been turned down by a bird old enough to be my mum (even though I didn't even ask her out) and have resorted to buying oldie porn and hanging around a supermarket hoping to get lucky. As if that lot wasn't bad enough, I've been punched in the face twice, almost been poisoned and missed out on promotion. Again. And on top of that I've got mates, if you can call them that, who seem to spend their entire lives working out new ways to piss me off. And 2000 is only six weeks old! Fuck knows what the rest of it has in store.

The only good thing going on at the moment is Liz. Christ, without her to talk to I don't know if I could carry on.

11.10 a.m. – At work

I don't know what the bloody hell is up with Julia. She keeps asking me about things to do in Watford and what I do when I'm not at work. And she's got this really annoying habit of twirling her hair as she speaks.

Bloody woman. Doesn't she know I'm in the middle of a crisis.

12.00 p.m. – At work

Holy fuck. The thought has just struck me that when Mike told me that Julia had been asking about me that other day, he might have been telling the truth. Could all this small talk actually be a hint that she wants me to ask her out?

Shit, now what do I do? I can't ask him, that would show I was interested in my boss and word would be around the lads like wildfire. And I can't ask her: what if I'm completely wrong and walk into a wind-up?

15.00 p.m. – At work

I don't know what the fuck is wrong with me but I really needed to talk to someone at lunchtime. Sadly, Liz was busy so I ended up walking down Charing Cross Road on my own. It hasn't helped.

The only thing I am sure of is that I can't ask Julia out. Not just because I'm not sure what the response would be, but because she's my boss. And she still scares the shit out of me.

22.00 p.m. – At home

Well, at least one good thing has happened today, although in truth, I'm not sure how or why. One minute I was standing in the fresh fruit section asking some piece with dyed red hair the best way to cook courgettes and the next I was asking her if she fancied a quick coffee. Unbelievably, she said yes and after hurtling round to buy only the bare essentials, we were soon chatting over a steaming cappuccino. Her name is Michelle, although she prefers Mitch and she manages one of the women's clothes shops in the big mall in town. More importantly, she asked for my number and has promised to call.

A few weeks ago, I would never have even dared imagine such a thing. I mean me, giving my number to a bird I've only just met. Maybe things aren't so bad after all.

Thursday 17 February

14.40 p.m. – At work

Spent lunchtime with Liz and finally told her all about my Wednesday nights at Sainsbury's and especially last night. Amazingly, rather than take the piss, she simply told me that she prefers her local launderette which not only has a café inside but also nice, comfy armchairs to while away the time between washes. I've never heard of such a thing but having only just spent £350 on a new Hotpoint, I'm buggered if I'm going to find out either. Mind you, at least I'd get the chance to get a look at Liz's underwear.

Although still quite pleased with myself after last night, I'm a little bit disconcerted to hear that a woman as gorgeous as Liz has to resort to meeting available blokes while she does her washing. What the fuck is happening these days?

Friday 18 February

10.50 a.m. – At work

Sean has just called to ask if I'm going to the game tomorrow. After a sigh, I told him that same thing I tell him the Friday before every away game; to fuck off. They have done this ever since I announced I was stopping doing away games two seasons ago and now treat me as if I'm some fair-weather scarfer rather than someone who hasn't missed a home game in seven years and has been a season ticket holder for the last five. It's beginning to piss me off a bit.

14.15 p.m. – At work

Although I didn't really fancy it, I'm glad I went. Because for once, the lunchtime pub was the scene of someone else's misfortune.

After I'd got the first lot of beers in, Sean suddenly announced that he'd heard a rumour that Kev was seen out in the company of the ugly bird from personnel last night. Despite his pathetic denials, this led on to speculation that Kev had actually sent her the Valentine's Card himself and had tried to blame it on one of us in case we found out he actually fancied her. In the end, he came clean, but only on the date, not on the conspiracy theory. And his defence that he took advantage of the situation because she was, 'gagging for it', seems fair enough although some of the more lurid claims he made after that did seem a bit perverse.

This led on to a discussion about all the other cards sent, and it seems I was not the only one on the receiving end. Although in the case of Mike and Sean, the women who received cards on their behalf simply told them to sod off and die.

Despite a subtle line in questioning, I was unable to gain any information about any other cards, so the anonymous one I received remains a mystery. Which does beg the question, what's the bloody point?

21.50 p.m. – At home

Met up with Liz for a quick drink after work. She's off out tonight with a load of her mates and asked me if I wanted to go. Although tempted, I told her that it'd be too much hassle. After all, I'd have to get home to Watford, get changed and then get back in to London. She then made me promise to go out with them next Friday and, to avoid any problems about drinking or trains, I could stay at her place if I wanted.

Thinking about it now, although it's great that she asked, I have a feeling that going out with her could end up becoming very complicated. I mean, what if she pulled? How would I feel about trying to sleep in one room and having to listen to her getting a good seeing to in the next? Now that would be strange. Still, at least it'd settle the orgasm bet.

22.45 p.m. – At home

I don't know where this has come from but, all of a sudden, I feel incredibly depressed. Friday night and I'm indoors on my own. Again. I should have made the effort and gone out with Liz after all. But I suppose the fact that I didn't probably says more than enough.

Saturday 19 February

14.20 p.m. – At home

Spent the morning with Lou and the kids but while having Joe and Katie around usually cheers me up no end, now I feel worse than ever. And it's Katie's fault. She sat on my lap and told me that her teacher had said that, because it's a leap year or something, on 29 February women could ask men to marry them. And if no one asks me, she's going to, because she thinks I need a wife to look after me. What could I say to that, except of course that if she did, I'd say yes, because she's so gorgeous.

But to be honest, it was all I could do not to start crying. What is it they say? Out of the mouths of babes . . .

21.10 p.m. – At home

After spending an entire afternoon wallowing in self pity, I've realised that, despite my early-year optimism, I can feel myself sliding even further into my own personal rut and I don't want that. So I've reached a decision. I need a change. I've decided to drop everything and go and see Mum in New York. Tomorrow. I haven't seen her for nearly two years and the change will do me the world of good.

Luckily, Julia has spent most of the week dropping hints to me about her new place so I scribbled a note explaining that I had a family crisis so was taking two weeks off and shot round there to drop it through her letter box. Half lie, half truth.

But as I was pushing it through the door, it opened. And I was amazed to see that, despite the time, and the fact that it was Saturday night, she was decorating her living room. She actually seemed a bit embarrassed that I was seeing her covered in paint and wearing scruffs but I must say, she looked quite sweet. After she'd read the note and told me not to worry about anything, we had a quick coffee and I left her to it.

When I got home, I called Liz on her mobile and told her what I was doing and explained the reasons why. Bless her heart, I don't know where she was but she offered to come over and see me. I put her off though, by telling her that my flight is at five thirty and I have to be up early to get there and book in. That wasn't the real reason of course. I just don't want her to see me this down because, truth is, I still don't know where it's come from.

After making me promise to bring her back something nice, she said a slightly tearful goodbye and was gone. And now I feel even worse.

Chapter 4

March

Sunday 5 March

17.25 p.m. – At home

Well, I'm back. And to be honest, I'm glad. It wasn't that I didn't enjoy myself, because I did. I was just ready to come home. And I feel like a brand new bloke. Because when I was in New York, I finally woke up to what it is that's been causing all these problems: it was me.

The thing that helped me to do that was a book. Not any book, but one of those American self-help manuals I'd always thought of as pure dross and never imagined in a million years I would ever actually read. *The Somebody*, it's called. I saw it in a drugstore one day and bought it purely out of curiosity. The bloke who wrote it is a fucking genius.

It explained that you can only ever change your life if you really *want* to change it. And once you understand that, then you must accept that the only way to effect that change is by modifying the whole you rather than altering just a part. But just as importantly, it highlighted the simple truth that you can't change anything until you get to like yourself. Because if you don't, how can you expect others to?

The more I read, the more I realised that this geezer was talking about me. I thought I'd been trying to change things, especially since New Year, but my efforts were only half-hearted. I hadn't really done anything much except try to get my head straight. But even that could hardly be deemed a success and I certainly hadn't done anything to change the outside. I was still the same scruffy, overweight and very unattractive slob I had spent ten years turning myself into. Something that was driven home to me one night when Mum asked me when I had last seen an advert for a stomach enhancement operation.

And so I've returned from New York with a whole new outlook, not just on life but on Billy Ellis. I've had a new haircut, put myself on a huge diet and have brought back a whole new wardrobe of Tommy Hilfiger, Lacoste and Helley Hansen gear. But, most importantly, I've come back full of optimism. I want to change my life and if it knocks me back a step, then I take two forward to compensate; take something positive from every single negative. From now on, that's the way it has to be.

19.55 p.m. – At home

I've finished unpacking and checked my answerphone. Three messages – in two weeks. As usual, I'm hardly in demand. The first two of those were from the football team. Both left on the day I flew out and both calling me every name under the sun for not turning up again. The last message was from Liz telling me to call as soon as I get home.

22.10 p.m. – At home

Just spent over an hour on the phone with Liz telling her about New York and catching up on the gossip at work. Not that there was much, although my sudden disappearance did not go unnoticed.

I haven't said anything about what happened to me out there. I'll save that for when we go out one night.

Monday 6 March

09.45 a.m. – At work

Day one of my new life. And the sight of Ginger on the train this morning was not a bad way to start it. I'm actually pretty sure that I caught her looking at me a couple of times. Maybe she missed my stunning early morning charm.

My arrival at work was greeted with a pile of paper on my desk together with a note from Julia asking me to go in and see her straight away. I guess she was worried that whatever family crisis had caused me to drop everything and shoot to New York might have left me a bit fucked up.

However, by the time I left, I think she was convinced that I am perfectly sane. She even complimented me on my new suit. Although given the cost, so she bloody should have.

12.20 p.m. – At work

The morning has been spent dealing with work and phone calls from various lads. Of course, there is no way they can or will show any sign of concern about anyone else's welfare, but it is gratifying to know that deep down, beneath that gruff, abusive exterior, some of them do have a few dregs of compassion and actually care about what is going on. Sean also filled me in on results which, sadly, involved yet another away defeat. Still, at least my home attendance record is intact.

14.30 p.m. – At work

Spent lunchtime with Liz. I didn't realise how much I'd missed her until we met and judging by the strength of the hug she gave me, I suspect she missed me a little.

After giving her the bottle of Chanel Number 5 I'd bought, I told her that I'm going to take her out one night so that we can have a proper chat. Because one thing I have decided is that the time has arrived where I have to come clean with her about everything: fears, hopes, dreams, the lot. For although I'm determined to move forward, I know that I can't do it on my own. And if anyone can help me, she can.

22.35 p.m. – At home

Nipped over to see Lou and Ray to fill them in on Mum and how she is. Gave the kids their obligatory presents and, once again, fell into the trap of offering to take them swimming on Sunday. I don't know how they do it but I fall for it every time.

23.10 p.m. – At home

The first day of the rest of my life is over. And, apart from being starving hungry, it hasn't been half bad.

Tuesday 7 March

09.10 a.m. – At work

Bumped into Sue on the way to work and she told me she loves my new haircut. I quickly returned the compliment pointing out that, as usual, she looks stunning. A bit cheeky possibly, but it left her with a smile on her face.

10.05 a.m. – At work

Mike has just rung and asked me if I'd heard the rumour that Kev was still seeing the ugly bird from personnel. I said I hadn't, but good luck to him if he was. Somehow, I don't think that was the reaction he was expecting.

11.40 a.m. – At work

I am obviously on some kind of roll. Liz has just called and told me that she needs someone to go to a party with her on Friday night and I'm it. God knows where it is, but given that I never go to parties, mostly because I'm never asked, I can't see that really matters.

16.10 p.m. – At work

More details have emerged about the impending party. It's actually at Liz's parents' house and, if I want, I can stay overnight.

However, to avoid any chance of me getting the wrong idea, she made it plain that I won't need to bring any condoms with me as under no circumstances will I be needing them. I don't really know if I'm pleased about that or not.

21.45 p.m. – At home

A good day. I cheered up Sue, upset Mike and got invited to a party. God I'm hungry.

Wednesday 8 March

09.50 a.m. – At work

Clearly, something has happened to the lads since I've been away because Kev has just called and asked me if I'd heard that Sean, the bloke who once ate seven Big Macs in one go because I bet him 20p he couldn't, has turned veggie. Like Kev, I am stunned by this. And obviously, as someone who will not eat anything unless it once had a face and could make a noise, I will dedicate a good portion of my spare time towards making sure he sees the error of his ways. Well, old habits die hard. Besides, I still haven't forgotten that I owe that smug veggie twat in Sainsbury's. Winning Sean back can be my revenge.

While I had Kev on the phone, I asked him how he was getting on with the ugly bird from personnel. It's obviously serious because he gave me a mouthful and told me that, in future, I have to call her Sophie.

15.20 p.m. – At work

Missed lunch as I had a long meeting with Julia. I'm still not sure what's going on there, but I do know that I don't want to find out. Mind you, she does have this way of licking her lips that could be considered quite sexy. If I was looking of course. At the moment, all it's done is remind me that I'm thirsty and hungry.

Funnily enough, for the first time, I've actually considered the notion that in my desire to become thinner, I might have to cut back on the Budweiser. Don't know about that so much. Giving up the chicken nuggets is one thing, lager is something else entirely.

22.45 p.m. – At home

Bumped into Mitch at Sainsbury's. She apologised for not calling but has, apparently, lost my number. A likely bloody story. When I told her I'd been in New York anyway, she said she'd been there about six months ago so we went for a coffee to exchange memories.

Aside from that, the place was a bit of a washout. Although I did manage to buy a bag of pork scratchings to send to Sean in the morning. I know they are, or were, his favourite pub snack and are probably the only thing that would survive intact until morning. Even in my current state of perpetual hunger, the very thought of sticking pig scabs in my mouth fills me with horror.

Thursday 9 March

09.30 a.m. – At work

Met Sue again on the way into work and, once again, complimented her on looking fantastic. Despite my previous encounter with her, the more I think about it, the more I fancy the idea. Just to see what it would be like of course.

09.40 a.m. – At work

Have just dispatched a small Jiffy bag containing one bag of pig scabs to Sean and, for good measure, put in a note telling him they were from Mike. I couldn't resist.

14.20 p.m. – At work

An e-mail from Liz has just arrived reminding me not to forget to bring my stuff in the morning as we'll be leaving for her folks' house straight from work. She still refuses to tell me anything about either where we're going or what they're like. Something which would normally fill me with dread but, in this case, I'm actually quite excited. One thing I have absolute faith in is that she, of all people, would never set me up. And if she's keeping something from me, there has to be a perfectly good reason.

19.45 p.m. – At home

Arrived home to find a message from Mitch on the machine only asking if I'd like to meet for a drink one night! After doing a lap of honour around the flat, I rang her back, coolly apologised for not being in earlier and told her that yes, I'd love to. Simple as that.

Fuck me, this is it. On Monday night, I've got a proper date with a proper woman. And a decent looker as well. Things are looking up.

Friday 10 March

09.25 a.m. – At work

Arriving at work with an overnight bag has prompted a great deal of discussion among my workmates. Discussion which inevitably revolves around a dirty weekend with Liz and, as they are happy to think that, I'm happy to let them. To be honest, I'm quite enjoying the attention.

A quick but discreet check with Sean has revealed that his mail has arrived, but he didn't mention the pig scabs. I smell a rat.

11.10 a.m. – At work

Shit. I've been so wrapped up in things this week that I've forgotten the game tomorrow. And because I don't know what time I'll be back from Liz's, I don't know if I'll be able to make it or not. Christ almighty, I remember the grief the lads gave me when I told them I was giving up away games. This would be ten times worse.

11.15 a.m. – At work

Bollocks, Liz is in a meeting. Left a message for her to contact me urgently. And then sent her an e-mail just for good measure.

12.35 p.m. – At work

Still no call from Liz, and Mike has just asked me what's happening tomorrow. Shit, he must be getting suspicious. He hasn't mentioned anything about pork scratchings either. Which can only mean they have arrived at Sean's desk and either he hasn't opened his mail yet (unlikely) or he's eaten them (very likely). If this is true, then he hasn't even survived the first challenge, which will be a nightmare for him and a *coup* for me.

14.20 p.m. – At work

Rumours of my possible absence from the hallowed terrace tomorrow have erupted. To placate them, I have had to tell the lads what I'm doing and, more importantly, who with. This has stopped them in their tracks because, to a man, they would all do the same and they know it. I did, however, neglect to tell them that although I'm going away with a gorgeous woman, sex is not on the agenda. It's taken me long enough to come to terms with that; I don't think Kev could handle it at all.

14.25 p.m. – At work

Just sent Liz another e-mail telling her what happened at lunchtime and asking for more information about tonight. Much as football pisses me off sometimes, I can't imagine what life would be like without it. The very thought of missing my first home game for seven years is already giving me withdrawal symptoms.

15.30 p.m. – At work

Liz has finally returned my call and told me not to be a wanker. However, she still refuses to tell me where we're going but insists if I want to be back for football, I will be. I do not feel comforted.

15.50 p.m. – At work

A very unhappy Mike has just paid me a visit and dumped an unopened bag of pork scratchings on my desk. By all accounts, Sean stormed into his office about five minutes ago and, in front of everyone, went ballistic at him for trying such a childish stunt. Even though I denied any involvement and suggested it was probably Kev, I am quite impressed that Sean managed to resist the temptation. Looks like it'll be meat pies and hot-dogs all round at the game tomorrow then. That's if I make it, of course.

17.30 p.m. – At work

The weekend is upon me. For the first time in ages, I will not be going to the pub straight from work but, instead, will be going off with a gorgeous woman to God knows where for an evening of God knows what. Life might have been shit for a long, long time, but, once in a while, it's fucking magic.

I've made sure my season ticket is in my bag though. Just in case time is tight tomorrow.

Sunday 12 March

19.25 p.m. – At home

If I ever write my autobiography, there are certain days and events which will feature prominently. My first proper kiss (Claire Stiles, aged nine) my first sexual encounter (Claire Stiles, aged thirteen) my first shag (unknown female, aged seventeen) and my first car (Peugeot 306). Hopefully, at some point, meeting my wife and the date of my first born will make an appearance, but one thing guaranteed to be included is this weekend. It was fucking amazing.

When Liz asked me to go to a party, she neglected to mention one very important detail: it was to celebrate something. Not a simple birthday or an anniversary, but her dad's release from prison. And by the time she got round to telling me, it was as we approached the imposing gates of what was a very substantial property in the Berkshire countryside. But, as if that wasn't enough of a bombshell, she followed it up with another one. Her dad had been in prison for the importation and distribution of hard-core pornography. And judging by the size of the house, not to mention the quality of cars in the drive, we weren't talking about the odd dodgy video either.

In any other circumstance, arriving at the front door of a porn baron's house for a Friday night party would be up there on my top ten wish list. But in this instance, I don't know who felt the more embarrassed, Liz or me. Well I do, it was her. I could tell it from the look in her eyes, the tone of her voice and even by the way she turned off the ignition. This was an area of her life that she had kept secret from everyone and now she was opening it up to me. Given that we'd only known each other for a few weeks, it was a massive risk for her to take and so I did the only thing I could do. I reached over, gave her a hug and made a crack about being annoyed at her for not telling me to wear clean pants for the orgy. It did the trick perfectly.

As it happened, there was no orgy. Nor were there piles of porn lying all over the place or page three bimbos throwing themselves at all the male guests. Everything turned out to be surprisingly normal. Well, that's if normal is a huge house with an indoor pool and a tennis court in the back garden. Her mum was great, her two brothers, despite a sad affection for West Ham, were just normal lads and her dad turned out to be a nice bloke who just happened to have made a lot of money from porn. Hardly the stereotypical criminal dynasty and certainly not what I would have imagined had she told me all this in advance.

I didn't ask exactly what he had done to get sent down, but Liz told me he had been away for six months and the party was to welcome him home. It actually turned out to be great and it wasn't until about three that I made it to bed. Alone, as Liz had forecast.

Following a night spent having strange dreams about secret cameras and call girls in my room, I woke up at about seven and went downstairs to find the old man in the kitchen making a cup of tea and smoking a cigar. Frighteningly, he was also stark bollock naked. A situation he was obviously more comfortable with than I was, given the fact he didn't even blush.

After declining his offer of tea and toast, mostly because I couldn't help thinking that if he wasn't bothered about getting dressed, he was hardly likely to have washed his hands, he picked up his breakfast and led me through to the pool. He then began asking me about my relationship with Liz. Not in any nasty way, but I suppose like any dad, he was a bit wary of any bloke his daughter was friendly with. Mind you, given that he'd brought her up on the proceeds of his porn empire and had only just got out of the nick, I can't imagine how he expected me to top that.

As I was busy trying to avoid looking at his wedding tackle, while all the time assuring him that Liz and I were no more than very good mates, things became even more surreal when her mum walked in. After coming over and giving him a kiss and cuddle, she asked me if I'd slept well before slipping off her dressing gown and diving into the pool. For a split second, I thought my worst fears had been realised and she was also naked, but thankfully a cursory glance revealed she was only topless. Still hugely embarrassing, but a whole lot better than the alternative. Especially when I remembered that he'd been inside for six months and so God only knows what they had been up to last night.

After a few minutes trying to avoid looking at either of their respective bodies as I fought back images of them having sex, I made my excuses and headed for the kitchen only to find Liz and her eldest brother eating breakfast. Although a bit disappointed to see that she was fully clothed – but relieved that he was – my mood improved tenfold when he told me that as the Hammers were playing on Monday night, he would take me back to Watford and if I was up for it, bring me back rather than leave me there.

As we were discussing the possibility of getting him a ticket, the old man walks in, still naked of course, and asked what we were up to. Without even mentioning his state of undress, Liz tells him what was going on and next thing I know, he not only offered to come as well, but was on the phone to someone in the printing game sorting out tickets for one of the boxes.

This led to what I can only describe as a top afternoon. Not only did I get to watch an excellent 2–1 win from the comfort of a box – with free booze on tap, I might add – but I also managed to off-load my ticket to a tout and ring the lads on a mobile and give them a wave so they knew I was there. God, how the other half live.

By the time we got back to Liz's parents' place, it was full of people again and we spent another late night getting pissed and having a laugh.

After a late breakfast, thankfully in the company of a fully clothed set of parents, the old man took us all to the pub for lunch, more booze and a lot of laughs. By the time Liz decided it was time to leave, I almost felt like crying. I could have stayed there forever. Her old man may be a porn king, an ex-con and like sitting around in the nude, but in my opinion, he's a top man. And if he can get free football tickets on tap, he's my fucking hero.

On the way back to Watford, Liz opened up a bit more and told me a little about what it was like growing up. From some of the things she said, I got the impression that although she's not ashamed of her old man, she's not exactly proud of what he does. Which kind of explains a bit more about why she is like she is.

After all, she doesn't have much of an opinion of the average male and certainly doesn't take any shit off anyone. But then again, coming from that kind of money, she doesn't really have to.

Still, she seems to be doing all right on her own now. And any bird who can provide a weekend like that once in a while is fine by me. It's just a shame no one else is ever going to know about it.

Monday 13 March

09.10 a.m. – At work

Clearly, since I told the lads I was going away with Liz on Friday, the rumour mill has been working overtime. Something that was not helped by my appearance in an executive box on Saturday, which has got them all worked up into a frenzy. So much so that it has taken less than five minutes for a deputation to turn up at my desk demanding to know about my weekend. I would love to tell them because I know they wouldn't believe it – shit, I can't and I was there! But as a gentleman, and because I know it would devastate Liz, I have declined to comment. Something which has not gone down well with some of them. Especially the lads from marketing who are still desperate to have their bet settled.

09.20 a.m. – At work

Just rung Liz and told her I had the best weekend ever. I also told her that I owe her lunch so will be seeing her later. That should keep the lads on their toes for a bit longer.

10.20 a.m. – At work

Holy fuck. I've just remembered I have a date tonight. A real-life date. I hope to Christ she doesn't ask me what I got up to at the weekend.

14.50 p.m. – At work

Just come back from lunch with Liz where I finally plucked up the courage to ask her why her old man walks around naked. She just laughed and said, 'Why not? It's his house.' Which is a fair point although I should remember it if he ever invites my mum round.

I also told her all about my date tonight and, as she's well aware of my gift for fucking things up, she told me to relax and just be myself. If I do that, she said, somewhat sarcastically I suspect, no woman could help but fall in love with me. As I think about that now, although touched by her support, I can't help but feel a bit miffed. Deep down, I had kind of hoped she'd be ever so slightly jealous.

19.00 p.m. – At home

In thirty minutes I have to meet Mitch at a pub in town. Although this is what I've been after for ages, the honest truth is that I am shitting a brick. 'Be yourself,' Liz said. That'll be right. After New York, I haven't got a bloody clue who I am any more.

23.50 p.m. – At home

I once read somewhere that your ideal person is someone you've never met. You see a person on TV or in a film, think they look nice and friendly but when you get to meet them in the flesh, they turn out to be arseholes. After tonight, I kind of get that. When I first met her, I thought that Mitch was a nice bird, but now I know she isn't. It wasn't that she was an arsehole, well not totally, it's just that she's one of those legions of sad birds who have embraced the whole ladette culture. Not because she believes in what it stands for, but because she thinks that as a thirty-two-year-old single bird who's spent her life being pissed around by blokes, it's what she should do.

As I sat there, listening to her complain about her ex-boyfriends while she drank beer from the bottle and devoured a chicken jalfrezi like it was going out of fashion, I suddenly realised that women like her have really fucked things up. Not just for themselves, but for blokes like me. They gather in groups to moan about being on their own and how every man they meet is a bastard but don't understand that we're all shit scared of them. We don't know where we stand any more because they've moved the goal-posts and not told us where they've put them. That's *why* the only blokes they meet *are* bastards. They're the only kind who are prepared to put up with their crap because they aren't looking for anything other than a leg-over. And once they've had that, they're off.

But all the time they're slagging us off, women like Mitch are busy turning themselves into female versions of us. Complete with every bad habit they've been trying to rid us of for the last fifty years. Is that what equality has finally come down to? Being able to get pissed, swear a lot and eat ring-burning curries just because men do?

In the end, I couldn't wait for it to be over. And after paying my half of the bill – surely one of the few advantages to being a bloke these days – I dumped her in a taxi and walked home. Tonight was not a success. There wasn't even a chance of a leg-over although after watching her eat that jalfrezi, I don't know if I could have done the deed even if I'd wanted to. I know what a chicken biriani does to my arsehole in the mornings. The thought of what that's going to do to hers is not sexually attractive. Not even when you're as desperate as me.

Tuesday 14 March

09.05 a.m. – At work

Although disappointed about last night, I am determined not to let it drag me down. So much so that on the way into work, I did something I've never done before. I told a middle-aged woman standing next to me on the train that her hair looked fantastic. It didn't, not really. But she blushed and smiled and I know that it cheered her up. And it did the trick on me as well.

09.45 a.m. – At work

Just spoke to Liz and told her about last night. She has told me to meet her for a drink after work which sounds like an excellent idea.

22.15 p.m. – At home

As we chatted, I finally bit the bullet and asked Liz for her help. After last night, I know that if I am ever to find someone, I need to know as much as I can about what women actually want from a bloke. Because if Mitch taught me one thing, it was that I haven't got a fucking clue.

Her response was just as I expected. If I need or want to know anything, all I have to do is ask. No subject is taboo and no embarrassment is allowed. But what I didn't expect, was for her to ask that the arrangement be reciprocal. If she wants to know anything about men and what we need, want or are looking for, then I have to tell her and on the same terms. Initially, I was stunned by this, but the reality of the situation soon began to dawn on me. I never realised it before, but looking at her tonight, it was obvious. She's beautiful, sexy, and very independent yet she's also intimidating. And that's why she's alone. In that respect at least, her and Mitch are exactly the same. What a fucking waste.

Wednesday 15 March

16.20 p.m. – At work

I've decided to give Sainsbury's a miss tonight. After Monday, I don't want to bump into Mitch. She might expect a repeat performance and I don't fancy having to turn her down. Christ almighty, that would be a first. Mind you, I am kind of curious to know how she got on with that jalfrezi.

20.25 p.m. – At home

Bollocks. Arrived home to find a message on the machine from Lou reminding me that I was supposed to be taking her kids swimming last Sunday and didn't turn up. After giving me three days to ring and apologise, she got bored of waiting and called to give me shit. I owe them, big time apparently.

23.15 p.m. – At home

In the end, I changed my mind and went to Sainsbury's for my Wednesday night lech fest. Although, to be honest, I'm not quite sure if it was a good idea or not.

Thankfully, Mitch was nowhere to be seen and so I was making the most of a remarkably high nipple count when I was suddenly confronted by what looked like a bowling ball on legs. At first, I didn't recognise who she was and stood there like an idiot listening to this short, round woman excitedly jabbering on and asking me how I was and what I'd been up to until the penny suddenly dropped. It was Tessa Jordan who I used to go to school with.

If I thought time had been unkind to me on the physical front, it's been positively vicious to her. She's enormous! Then again, she was a bit on the lardy side at school, although I seem to remember that she was also quite pretty in a 'mumsy' kind of way. Don't know what happened there then.

After telling me all about how she had just moved back to her parents after splitting from her old man because he's an arsehole, she suggested that we go out on Friday to catch up with old times. And because I couldn't think of a way to turn her down, I now find myself having a second date in one week and both courtesy of Mr Sainsbury's.

Thursday 16 March

09.30 a.m. – At work

Just rang Liz and told her about my meeting with Tessa last night but did not get the response I expected. She took exception to me referring to a fellow female as an egg-on-legs and I am, according to her, 'fatist'. Quite how this can be so when I have spent a lifetime in combat with my own personal flab escapes me but I have no inclination to argue. Christ knows what's rattled her cage.

14.30 p.m. – At work

Apparently, the lads at work are getting a bit miffed by my continued absence. As a result, they told me at lunchtime that, straight after work tonight, we are all off out for a serious session of Budweiser lager and Chinese food.

I am touched by this. After all, it's as near to a show of close friendship as any of my lifelong mates would ever willingly exhibit. The problem is that I hate mid-week sessions. I've done enough of them to know that I will end up shitfaced and will certainly feel like crap in the morning. It's also going to play havoc with my diet which is going remarkably well, all things considered. I've noticed that my trousers feel looser than they have for many years. Then again, it is a while since I've been blitzed; it might do me good.

Friday 17 March

10.45 a.m. – At work

God almighty. As I thought, I do indeed feel like shit. Not because I was blitzed, I hardly drank more than the standard ration last night, but because I fell asleep on the poxy train on the way home. By the time I woke up, I was in Milton Keynes and, inevitably, had to wait for hours until I could get on something going south. It's not the first time this has happened, it's not even the bloody tenth, so I should be used to it by now.

Commuting is one of the very few drawbacks of living outside London and is made worse by the fact that, although all the other lads live in Watford, they travel by different routes. And although I am usually glad about that, on nights like last night, it's a pain in the arse.

Of course, I could have done what some people do and stuck a sign on my lap asking someone to wake me up at Watford Junction. But having seen some of the inhabitants of last night's train, a sign which read 'I'm asleep, my wallet's in my jacket pocket' would probably have been more appropriate.

15.20 p.m. – At work

I have just had the bollocking of my life from Julia who returned from lunch with one of the high-ups from head office and found me fast asleep on my desk. This has obviously amused the rest of the staff in my department who returned from lunch to find me pushing out the zeds and took the unilateral decision to leave me there in the hope that such a situation would arise. Even Sue was in on it, which has disappointed me somewhat. Still, no doubt I'll see the funny side at some point. Probably in about a year or so.

15.55 p.m. – At work

News of my roasting has obviously filtered through the building at an alarming rate. First Kev and then Liz have rung to take the piss. Now, not only do I feel like shit, I feel like an idiot. A winning combination if ever there was one.

Saturday 18 March

01.15 a.m. – At home

At last! It took three attempts but I finally went on a date that could be deemed a success.

It's funny, I've never really thought about going out with a fat bird before. I'd always imagined it would be kind of embarrassing. Even as I was getting ready tonight, I was hoping that she wouldn't turn up. Or if she did, that no one I knew would see us.

But tonight has taught me a lesson. After all, I've complained about women not caring about what's beneath my surface enough. I suppose I've been guilty of that very same thing for years. Because she did turn up and she looked great. And if we had bumped into anyone, so what? I was too busy enjoying myself to care.

How much of that can be put down to the fact that we spent most of the night talking and laughing about the people we went to school with, I don't know. But I've come home feeling absolutely shattered, yet quite pleased with myself.

I even got the impression that if I'd pushed my luck a bit, I could have got her back here. But given my total lack of success in that area, I'm hardly the best person to judge that so maybe it was a good job I played safe and took her home. There's always next time although I guess that's something I really should ask Liz about. She'd know.

Still, think positive. It was a good night and, with any luck, the first of many. All in all, it's been quite a week.

23.15 p.m. – At home

A lazy day and I feel all the better for that. After listening to Watford scrap their way to another bloody draw as I caught up on all my domestic stuff, I rang Liz and filled her in on last night. Although being told that if I'd had the slightest inkling that I was on for a shag – her words not mine – I should have gone for it, was not really what I wanted to hear. Never mind.

Sunday 19 March

13.00 p.m. – At home

Decided to troop down to watch the lads play today and tell them in person that I've given up playing football for good. As usual, they lost and, as expected, it was my fault even though I was fully dressed and standing under an umbrella. However, now it's done, I feel a whole lot better, although I would have appreciated a bit more of an effort to get me to stay on. Clearly, I will not be missed.

21.10 p.m. – At home

Took the kids swimming this afternoon and, for once, I managed to spend an entire afternoon there with no dramas and no embarrassing episodes.

In fact, other than my usual hatred of single dads and all things under eleven, I had quite a good time. Wonders will never cease.

Monday 20 March

09.20 a.m. – At work

Ginger was on the train this morning and, for some strange reason, she reminded me of Tessa. God knows why, physically, they couldn't be more different if they tried. But, as we had a good time on Friday, I've decided to call her later and ask her if she fancies another night out. What have I got to lose?

12.05 p.m. – At work

A boring morning was broken only by the news that the ugly bird from personnel has given Kev the heave-ho. Usually, such news would be a godsend but for some reason, I can't help feel a little sorry for him. I've been there and suffered. It's not nice. I doubt some of the others will be so understanding.

12.30 p.m. – At work

Julia has just summoned everyone in the office for a meeting and informed us that, in three weeks, the company have decided to send twenty-five employees from various departments off for a weekend's sailing to help them 'bond'. Apparently, people from every section of the company will be invited and if we are among the lucky ones attendance will be compulsory unless we have already booked a holiday or can provide a very good excuse.

Inevitably, the chosen weekend includes a home game. And although football is a perfectly rational and reasonable excuse for anything as far as I'm concerned, I know it won't cut any ice with any of the high-ups. Experience has shown me that not only do they all hate football with a passion, dumping on someone lower down the food chain is all that keeps them going.

15.00 p.m. – At work

Lunchtime was dominated by the impending doom of the corporate weekend. Like the majority of blokes, I am a fatalist and so I know that, unless I can do something, I will be one of the sad souls picked to go.

This requires a great deal of thought and not a little cunning. Because I know full well that, while they may appear to be united, the others will all be trying to get out of this individually by shitting on the rest of us. And as usual, unless I act fast, I'll be at the bottom of the pile.

15.50 p.m. – At work

I knew it! That bastard Mike has just rung and told me he will not be included on the list of possibles because he went to his head of department and said that, as he has a season ticket, the company will have to re-imburse him if he misses a game on their business. He then convinced his female boss, who is possibly the most gullible woman on the planet, that getting into Vicarage Road costs almost £65 per game (after all, as he told her, how else do players earn those huge salaries?) and, as that would have to come out of her budget, he is safe. I am tempted to tell her that the true cost is only £27 and that Mike could easily off-load his season ticket, but that would be well out of order.

I wonder if that'll work with Julia?

16.20 p.m. – At work

Just had a call from a very excited Liz who told me that she's put her name forward to go on this trip and asked me if I'm going. When I reminded her of my sad addiction to Watford Football Club, she called me childish and then said that most hated and ridiculous of phrases, 'It's only a game'.

Why is it women have no sense of loyalty or tradition when it comes to sport? Maybe that's what their problem is.

16.50 p.m. – At work

Liz has just rung me back and asked if I fancy a drink tonight because she needs cheering up and she knows I can do it. How sweet.

23.15 p.m. – At home

A strange evening. And one which has left me feeling very confused. For the first time since we met, I've begun to consider the possibility that my friendship with Liz might not be as straightforward as I had thought.

After leaving work, we were walking towards our usual drinking hole when she suddenly burst into tears. No warning, no nothing. Just blubbing. And so instead of sinking a few Budweisers, I ended up sitting on a park bench giving her a cuddle and letting her get on with it. A not entirely unpleasant experience, it has to be said.

Once she'd settled down a bit and I'd taken her back to her flat, I finally found out what the problem was; she told me that being on her own is really starting to get to her.

Although I have every sympathy with that, I am quite possibly the world's least qualified person to help her out with advice on the matter. But one thing even I know is that nothing cheers a woman up like a bit of flattery. And so I sat her down, put my arm around her and told her that it's only a matter of time because she's beautiful, funny and intelligent, and that any bloke with a brain in his head would be mental not to fancy her. And then she did it. She reached up, gave me a kiss on the cheek and said 'Oh Billy, you're so lovely' before snuggling down with her head on my chest. Within about ten minutes, she'd fallen asleep.

Now I'd lay money on the fact that it was no more than a gesture. And that when she said 'lovely' it was in the strictly 'nice' context, but I can't help wondering. And the more I wonder, the more uneasy I am.

23.40 p.m. – At home

Liz has just rung to make sure I got home all right and apologise for the way she behaved. Although I'm glad she called, hearing her dusky voice utter the words 'I'll make it up to you, I promise' has not calmed me at all. In fact, it's made it even worse. I'd just about got used to thinking of her in a non-lustful way but now I've actually begun to imagine what it would be like to have sex with her. Fucking amazing comes pretty close.

The stupid thing is, the more I think about it all, the more it's actually started to make sense. After all, she got the right hump today when I told her I didn't want to go sailing and wasn't exactly pleased to hear about Tessa either. Could it be that she's jealous? Maybe all that 'I just want to be friends' stuff was a test to make sure that I wasn't just another bloke trying to get my grubby hands on her? And now that she's sure I'm not, maybe she doesn't know how to tell me.

What if she's waiting for me to catch on? She could have been dropping hints for weeks and, me being me, I've missed them all. Bloody hell, was that why she took me to meet her folks?

This is all too freaky. God knows what I'm going to be like when I see her tomorrow, but to add insult to injury and mess with my head just that little bit more, when I answered her call, I noticed a message on the machine which turned out to be from Tessa, who wants me to call her.

Of course this raises another problem. Do I go for it with Tessa and possibly blow any chance with Liz, or do I hang on and wait to see what happens there and blow my chance with Tessa? If it was as simple as a choice between egg on legs or sex on legs, there would be no choice. But I don't even know if I have either luxury. Fuck me, why is my life so complicated?

Tuesday 21 March

06.25 a.m. – At home

A rough night last night. This thing with Liz is doing me in. What if I'm right? The more I think about it, the more certain I am that her mood last night wasn't just your average self-pity – Christ, if anyone knows what that sounds like, I do – it was more than that. It was almost a plea. But a plea for what? For me? Why not? Is it so outrageous to think we'd make a good couple? Not as far as I'm concerned. We get on really well and I think we're quite close.

But what if I'm wrong? Not only could I lower myself to new levels of twat-dom, but saying or doing the wrong thing could spoil our friendship. And I don't want to do that. Then again, maybe I already have because I can't get this idea out of my head and, all of a sudden, she's turned back into this gorgeous creature I lusted after until we got to know each other. Now I do want to get my grubby hands on her. And I'm fucking annoyed with myself for thinking like that.

Which returns me to my original problem. What the fuck do I do now?

09.35 a.m. – At work

A bad start to the day. Not only have I been struggling to work out how to deal with the Liz thing, but on the train, I tried to cheer myself up by repeating my morale-boosting exercise of the other day. Sadly, it was not a success. In fact, when I told the young lady concerned how much I liked her suit, she told me to fuck off. Very nice.

Then I arrived at work to find out that someone had pulled that old favourite of a stunt, and diverted every extension in the office to my phone.

And as if all that isn't bad enough, I've just remembered that I've got the small matter of a sailing trip to get out of. And thanks to this bastard diet, I'm bloody starving.

10.15 a.m. – At work

First things first. Liz and Tessa can wait. I have to get this game thing sorted. I can't hang about and hope I don't get chosen, I have to make sure I'm not. In fact, I've decided that rather than piss about, I am going to apply my new-found spirit of going for it to this problem. Sod the rest of them. I don't want to go sailing and so I'm not going to. End of story. I'm going to sit down with Julia and simply tell her I'm not going and why. Hopefully, she'll understand. If she doesn't, tough shit.

10.40 a.m. – At work

Just spoke to Sean who has told me the hot news that Kev and the ugly bird from personnel are back on. This must be love. Either that or there's some sordid and very unpalatable reason that I don't even want to think about.

11.40 a.m. – At work

Liz has just called and asked me if I fancy a quick drink at lunchtime. And now all that unease has resurfaced.

It's pretty obvious, even to me, that something has got to be said. Otherwise this is going to ruin everything. Either that, or my testicles are going to explode. Because all this talk of sex is making me desperate.

14.15 p.m. – At work

A quiet lunch. Liz apologised again and I tried to pluck up the courage to say something. Without success.

15.20 p.m. – At work

Sometimes, once in a while, I amaze myself. Well, that's not strictly true. What I actually mean is that my brain amazes me. Like a lot of people, when I'm pissed my brain takes over and keeps my mouth working just enough for it to spout complete and utter bollocks which more often than not lands me in major trouble. But, for some reason, it also kicks in when I'm sober and in a state of panic. The big difference is that without the numbing effects of Budweiser, it occasionally comes out with a gem. A moment of bullshitting history that demands to be written down and immortalised. I have just experienced one such moment.

Fuck knows where it came from, but rather than explain about wanting to go to a game, I heard myself spouting all kinds of shite about having a morbid fear of the sea and not wanting to embarrass myself in front of everyone. Before I knew it, she was almost eating out of my hand and that was that. I'm off the danger list!

16.10 p.m. – At work

Have just completed the ringing round and now everyone knows I am not going on the trip. I haven't told them why though, just in case anyone grasses me up.

Life is good. Well, at least some parts of it are.

19.30 p.m. – At home

Tessa has just called and, before I knew it, we were arranging to go to the pictures tomorrow night.

Although quite pleased that any woman would want to go out with me, it has added even more confusion to an already stressful situation. After the other night, I'm fairly sure that if I push it a bit, Tessa would come across with the goods. But if we do have sex, what will it lead to? I don't know if there's any kind of future there and in truth, I don't know if I'd want it. But what I'm fairly sure of is that if something is going on with Liz, sleeping with another bird could damage it. And is a simple leg-over worth that? How the bloody hell would I know?

21.10 p.m. – At home

For some reason, I felt a bit guilty about my date with Tessa so rang Liz to make sure she's OK. Which she is. We then talked bollocks for about fifteen minutes and she went off to have a soak in the bath. Sadly, my offer to come down and scrub her back was turned down. I think the term used was 'you wish'. Pretty accurate as it happens.

I didn't tell her about tomorrow night though. Just in case.

Wednesday 22 March

13.20 p.m. – At work

Of all the things I didn't need, a healthy dose of irony would have been high on the list. But that is exactly what I got in the pub at lunchtime as my relationship with Liz was, once again, the topic for debate.

Although I am still slightly flattered that the lads think I actually have any kind of chance with her, the fact that their discussions inevitably revolve around her sexual performance and the quality and nature of her orgasms is really starting to piss me off. I don't know if women talk like this about blokes, but I bloody well hope not. In the end, in an effort to shut them up, I finally came clean and told them that all we are is mates. Nothing else.

Of course, no one believes me and so I lost my rag and had a go at them but all this did was attract more piss-taking and, once again, I was forced to retreat back to the office. Blokes are such wankers.

23.10 p.m. – At home

Just got back from my date with Tessa and, sadly, it was a bit of a disaster. Not because of her and anything she did – she looked great and the film was top drawer – but because, as we came out of the pictures, we bumped into Mike and his latest conquest. Unfortunately, as soon as I saw him, I remembered that Mike had spent much of the fourth form lusting after Tessa so it wasn't really a surprise that he remembered her instantly. After a brief chat, his girlie dragged him off in the direction of the pictures but I could see from the look on his face that by the time I got into work in the morning, everyone would have the full SP: Billy Ellis, sad bastard, spotted at pictures with fat bird from school.

Fucking marvellous. And to cause me even more grief, Liz is going to find out that I went on a date and didn't tell her. God only knows what she'll think about that. And I didn't get my leg over either.

Thursday 23 March

06.20 a.m. – At home

I've suddenly realised what I did last night. And I don't just feel bad, I feel ashamed.

For the first time in as long as I can remember, a woman actually took me out and just because she isn't a size twelve and six foot tall, I got embarrassed when someone saw us and worried that they would take the piss. What kind of wanker am I? More importantly, how would she have felt if she'd known what was going through my head?

It wasn't as if I didn't even have a good time. I did. Actually, I had a great time. She tells a joke better than anyone I know and has one of those giggly laughs that is funny all by itself. And that makes what I did even worse. I'm a prize cunt, pure and simple.

I'll have to call her later and take her out again. I owe her that much at least.

09.10 a.m. – At work

After the realisation of this morning, I've come into work ready to accept whatever piss-taking comes my way as a punishment, and a richly deserved one at that. I can't believe I was such a prick.

09.20 a.m. – At work

Called Liz and told her that Tessa rang me last night and as I was at a loose end, we went to the pictures.

She actually seemed quite pleased, which has thrown me a bit. I was half hoping she'd get a bit of a strop on.

09.45 a.m. – At work

Strangely, no one has said anything about last night yet. That can only mean one of two things, either Mike isn't in, or he's too busy to spread the news.

10.10 a.m. – At work

I am stunned. No, that's an understatement. I'm fucking stunned.

Mike, who is to romance what Dale Winton is to Rugby League, has exhibited a quite remarkable degree of maturity by not telling all and sundry about last night. It seems that not only is he concerned about dropping me in the shit with Liz (who he still thinks I am shagging), but he clearly still has a soft spot for his old fourth-form flame. Indeed, if I wasn't in shock, I'd have sworn that there was a pang of jealousy in his voice when he left me with the words 'fair play to you mate'.

That's as near an exhibition of camaraderie as I have ever heard him utter. I am quite touched.

11.20 a.m. – At work

Called Tessa and, thankfully, it seems that my fears of this morning are groundless. She said she had a great time last night and would love to do it again. She'll call me over the weekend.

I can't believe how relieved I feel. But this has taught me a valuable lesson. One mistake I won't make again in a hurry.

23.55 p.m. – At home

Went out with Liz after work tonight but it was all a little odd. After telling her about last night, although not the bad bit, we talked about what happened on Monday. When she started to get down again, I tried to cheer her up by telling her that if she wasn't married by the time she was thirty, *I'd* marry her. Sadly, the response I got wasn't what I was hoping for. 'Fuck me, if it got to that stage I'd top myself' did not do my self-confidence any good. In fact, it hurt.

So, in the spirit of self-defence, and not a little revenge for such a cutting remark, I bit the bullet and told her why I think she's on her own. At first, being told the anti-bloke barriers she puts up scares blokes off did not go down too well. But once she realised that I was telling her for her own good, she calmed down and we changed the subject.

At least I know where I stand now. Fucking nowhere, that's where. And I can't help but feel more than a little gutted. Although maybe she didn't really mean it.

Friday 24 March

09.15 a.m. – At work

Another crap journey into work. If I could be arsed, I'd complain.

Why does every bastard with a mobile phone have to talk so loud? I don't give a fuck about where they're going or what they're doing at the weekend so why do they all feel that I want to know? The mobile may be a marvel of technology but to me, all it's done is facilitate an epidemic of fantastically boring and trivial conversation.

09.40 a.m. – At work

Liz has just called to apologise for the fact that I had to spend another night listening to her moaning and to tell me that after a restless night, she's realised I am right. She is a bit anti-bloke and she can see how that could be seen as intimidating. But she does base it on the fact that most of the blokes she meets are twats who she would rather die than spend time with. Which is fair enough I guess.

10.30 a.m. – At work

Rumour has reached me that the list of twenty-five names going on the sailing weekend has been circulated to department heads. How many are from this department, lord only knows but I know at least three volunteered to go which should drop the odds somewhat.

All we need now is for Julia to turn up and break the bad news.

11.00 a.m. – At work

Just had a call from Mike: he's not going.

11.05 a.m. – At work

Just had a call from Kev: he is. Excellent.

11.15 a.m. – At work

Just had a call from Mike: the ugly bird from personnel is going. Barry the wanker is not.

11.25 a.m. – At work

Just had a call from Liz, who is also destined for a weekend on the ocean wave and is thrilled to bits. She's never been on a boat before. Fuck me, where is Julia?

11.45 a.m. – At work

After leaving everyone in suspense for over an hour, Julia finally arrived and announced to all and sundry that five people will be going from our department. Thankfully, there has been no change of plan and I am not one of them. Even better than that, Sean is. Which means that two of the Watford supporting stalwarts will miss a game and I will be able to take the piss out of them for ever. Joy of joys.

11.55 a.m. – At work

I've just realised that Julia isn't going on the trip either. Sneaky cow. I wonder how she pulled that?

15.30 p.m. – At work

Most of the afternoon has been spent winding up Kev and Sean, although in truth Kev doesn't seem that bothered. Something I suspect has a lot to do with a certain ugly female.

Sean, on the other hand, is gutted. Even more so now because his pathetic attempt to rile me by claiming that 'at least I'll be able to shag your bird' simply allowed me to point out to him that Liz actually thinks he's quite possibly the saddest male in the company. Something which I know will have hit him hard because he takes stuff like that personally.

16.20 p.m. – At work

I actually feel a bit bad about what I said to Sean. Having a dig at someone is one thing, but that was a bit harsh, especially as it isn't true. She actually thinks he's second saddest. Top honour being held by Barry the wanker.

Not much I can do about it now though even if I wanted to. How do you tell a bloke that the most gorgeous woman in the company doesn't really think he's a complete tosser, but he is almost there? Especially when he's going to be spending a weekend on a boat with her.

22.30 p.m. – At home

Arrived home slightly the worse for wear to find a message from Dad asking me if I was still alive and another from Tessa asking me to call. Ignored Dad and rang Tessa to find that she was out again. For someone who's just split up with her old man, she certainly gets out and about.

Sunday 26 March

12.15 p.m. – At home

A fucking top day yesterday. Not only did the lads get a 1–1 draw with Spurs, but Sean and Kev's impending absence from the hallowed home allowed Mike and me to spend an entire day taking the piss. Although overjoyed at both their discomfort and the fact that, for once, it wasn't me on the receiving end, I can't help but feel a little sorry for them. When you've put in as much time as they have, missing a game for anything other than major illness or a death is a tough pill to swallow. Still, life's a bitch as they say and it could have been worse: it could have been me.

After finally getting bored with taking the rise, the four of us decided to forsake our usual Saturday night session and hit a club to partake in some serious leching. This resulted in a rapid trip around our respective homes for both a change of clothes and more refreshment. The trouble was, by the time we actually got to a club, we were so pissed the doormen wouldn't let us in and so we were forced to adjourn to O'Neill's to decide what to do. Thankfully, inside were not one but two groups of women out on hen nights. And within both parties were a number of birds Kev and I knew from our time at college. Amazing as it seems even now, it quickly became clear that, for once, we had stumbled into females who were actually glad to see us. They had passed 'let's get loud and pissed' and were now at the 'let's snog anything that moves' level. And who were we to let them down? I mean, it's not often that a woman, any woman, wants to stick her tongue down my throat, but plenty did last night and I bloody enjoyed it. Even the ones who smoked were welcome, although I drew the line at the old bird with the grey hair. Sean didn't though, and even in my drunken state, that was not a pretty sight.

Sadly, as with all hen nights, any chance of taking things further was ended at closing time when the mood suddenly changed to 'all blokes are arseholes who let you down', at which point the four of us retreated for our own safety. Still, I have to say, it was nice to do a bit of tonsil wrestling again. It's been bloody ages and badly missed.

15.30 p.m. – At home

Just returned from a quiet hair of the dog to find a long message on the machine from Tessa telling me that her old man turned up on Thursday and they've decided to give things another try. As a result, she's heading back down south this afternoon. Although I'm glad for her, I'm a bit pissed off for me. After the events of the last few days, and especially last night, the thought had been gnawing away at me that she might, possibly, provide me with much more than a good night out once in a while. Bollocks.

17.10 p.m. – At home

I'm depressed and I don't know why. It's not as if I fancied her that much, if at all. Well, maybe I was beginning to. I don't know. I suppose it's because the possibility was there and now it's not. Like another door slammed in my face. I should be used to that after all this time, but I guess I never will be. To be honest, I don't really want to be.

22.00 p.m. – At home

Just had a long chat with Liz and told her what's happened. Having someone on tap to moan at is a bloody godsend. I feel better already.

Monday 27 March

12.50 p.m. – At work

Despite Liz's efforts, I had a shit night's sleep last night and have come into work feeling down again. As if that wasn't bad enough, I keep imagining Tessa staring tearfully out of a car window as she's being driven away. God it's pathetic.

14.50 p.m. – At work

Have just seen Mike who asked me how I was getting on with Tessa. When I told him what had happened, he seemed a bit shocked and bizarrely asked me if I was all right. When I asked him what he meant, he simply said that he thought we looked good together. I was, and am, amazed. And now I feel even worse.

16.20 p.m. – At work

I have been thinking about what happened with Mike earlier because it shook me a bit. In all the years we've been knocking around together, that's the first time we've ever really had what could be called a serious adult conversation.

I suppose this just confirms something else I've been thinking about lately, that since I met Liz, my relationship with the other lads has changed. Up to that point, we spent almost every lunchtime in the pub and had a drink most evenings, but now, it's more unusual. And it's not just me either. Kev has been seeing a lot of the ugly bird which only leaves Mike and Sean. Does this mean our little group is breaking up? There's just as much abuse, granted, but a lot less winding up than there used to be. I wonder if we're making that leap from a bunch of lads to group of friends?

It'd be a shame if we were, but to be honest, it's about bloody time. Even I was starting to realise that, much as I enjoy football and the odd night out, spending all our time together was getting a bit sad. It's certainly true to say that, given the choice between them and Liz, Liz would win every time. Even when she is being a pain in the arse.

Tuesday 28 March

20.00 p.m. – At home

A nightmare of a day. I can't seem to shake this stuff about Tessa. I even turned down the offer of a drink with Liz tonight which, with hindsight, was a stupid thing to do. After all, she's the one person I can really talk to about all this stuff.

Wednesday 29 March

10.25 a.m. – At work

Bumped into Liz on the way into work and had a quick chat about everything that's been going on. She has this ability to boost me up at a stroke which makes her a top bird. What would I do without her?

22.15 p.m. – At home

Sainsbury's was a waste of bloody time tonight as I bumped into Mitch on the way in. After a few minutes of forced conversation, I managed to drag myself away, but knowing she was there made me feel too uncomfortable to even think about doing any serious leching. I wonder what the exact protocol is for telling a bird that you would rather stick pencils in your eyes than go out with her again?

On the way home, I came to a monumental decision. In terms of my relationship with the female sex, I've come a long way in the last few months and I'm not going to let a couple of knockbacks affect that progress. And now, after my tonsil tasting of the other night and my near miss with Tessa, I am more determined than ever to get my leg over something soon. I don't care who or what it is, the only stipulation is that I'm not going to pay for it. The time has come to take things up a gear.

Thursday 30 March

10.25 a.m. – At work

I have come to work today full of vigour and enthusiasm. Not to mention a little vindictiveness.

The reason is that Saturday is April Fools' day. And, as with normal tradition, if it falls on a weekend, we celebrate it, if that's the right phrase, on the preceding Friday. That's tomorrow. And if, as I am increasingly suspecting, our days as lads are rapidly drawing to a close, I plan to get revenge for all the times the bastards have done me over the years. After all, you can't beat a bit of ritual humiliation and although more often than not, it's me who is the victim, this year I intend things to be different and for the first time in ages have gone on the offensive.

I am ready. They won't know what hit them.

Friday 31 March

08.55 a.m. – At work

An early start this morning. In fact, I was in work at seven o'clock. And, armed with a tin of WD40 and some clingfilm, have rigged the male toilets. Every seat has been sprayed and every pan, both standing and sitting, has been covered with a very tight and almost invisible plastic film. Either way, unless they are observant, whoever goes to the bogs first will get an oily arse or a splashback. In a perfect world, they'll get both.

To avoid falling for any similar stunt, my plan is to treat any mail, phone calls or requests to be somewhere or do something as suspect and, if possible, delay them until either later on today or possibly even Monday. Furthermore, I have no intention of going to the toilet or drinking anything that does not come out of a sealed bottle. No bastard is going to get me this year.

As I await the impending screams, I can't help but feel a little nervous apprehension. I wonder if they felt like this in the trenches?

09.10 a.m. – At work

Success! Sarah has just come in almost pissing herself. By all accounts one of the accounts managers has just suffered a particularly nasty episode while having his daily nine o'clock dump. I can't imagine how it must feel to have your turtles' heads bounce back up and actually try to squeeze their way back through your arsehole, but I doubt it's very nice. Still, at least it'll be waterproof now. And it should start in the morning.

09.20 a.m. – At work

Excellent. One of the security guards has been reported coming out of the toilets covered in urine after experiencing a particularly nasty backfire.

11.35 a.m. – At work

My early start to the day has proven to be an astonishing success. So much so that the total number of victims stands at seven. One of whom, thankfully, was Kev who is now sitting at his desk in a pair of shorts while his trousers are in the boiler-room drying off.

Inevitably, while half the women are moaning about us being childish idiots and the rest are pissing themselves laughing, a manhunt of unprecedented proportions has begun. Thankfully, it is focusing on Barry the wanker. Mainly because I planted the empty WD40 can in his bin.

12.00 p.m. – At work

Well, that's that. I have survived the morning without a single prank being played on me and, as we always end our japes at midday, I am safe. What's more, I have staged what is possibly the most spectacular joke ever played in this building and sit here safe in the knowledge that no one knows it was me. The only problem I have now is keeping it to myself until the time is right to own up.

Then again, judging by some of the threats being made to Barry the wanker, that might not be for a good few months yet.

12.15 p.m. – At work

After the success of this morning, more good news. Liz has just mailed me and offered to take me out for a curry tonight. Although I'll have to hang around for a while in the pub as she has to work late. Bummer.

14.25 p.m. – At work

Fallout from the toilet prank has begun. Julia has been called to a meeting of all the high-ups, who are determined to stamp out this kind of childish practice once and for all.

What's the bloody world coming to? Don't they realise that such things are all that keep us sane?

15.00 p.m. – At work

Oh my God. Sue has just been over and sheepishly asked me if I fancy going for a drink after work tonight. As she has been looking especially attractive of late, and I have been feeling increasingly frustrated, I immediately accepted despite what happened last time. Now I feel both terrified and excited at the prospect. I just hope to fuck no one else finds out. I don't know if I could go through all that *Forty & Fab* stuff again.

15.15 p.m. – At work

Just rung Liz to cancel tonight. She's not thrilled to be stood up for an older bird, but will settle for a full and detailed report in the morning.

Chapter 5

April

Saturday 1 April

00.45 a.m. – At home

I should have guessed really. In fact, I don't know why I didn't. It would have been a first, not to mention a bloody miracle, if the day had gone by without me being a victim of at least one wind-up. Although walking into a pub with Sue to be greeted by a roar of laughter and about fifteen assorted workmates waving porno mags above their heads was quite possibly the single most humiliating moment of my life and certainly not what I needed after this week.

The only thing that kept my spirits up was an apology from Sue ('they made me do it, honest') and listening to the others grudgingly admitting that whoever set up the toilet prank is a genius. Even Kev, still slightly damp, had to agree and I look forward to the day when I own up. Although I decided not to do it tonight. Barry the wanker was still issuing threats and looked extremely irate.

The other small crumb of comfort was that I did manage to piss everyone off. When I realised that my date with Sue was a sham, I rang Liz and re-arranged our meal. And when I told the lads I was doing the off, they got the right hump as they were expecting a full-on session. Probably at my expense. Tough shit.

As it happened, I doubt a night on the piss would have been more enjoyable anyway. Liz was back to her old self and so we spent the whole night discussing the rights and wrongs of girl power and the notion of women asking men out. Obviously, as a bird, she thinks it's all a good thing but as her sole argument revolves around the 'if it's good enough for you blokes . . .' stance, and her definition of a gentleman is someone who takes his weight on his elbows, I think I'll stick to my own opinion.

When I got home, there was a message on the machine from the old man asking me to ring him. As I know he always stays up late on Friday and Saturday, I gave him a call to hear the bad news that he isn't going to Telford after all but is instead getting married again. Rich frumpy widow and life of leisure in the South versus new job, move and life up North; no contest really. Even in my bloated and Budweiser-corrupted state, I can see the logic in that.

Sunday 2 April

20.10. p.m. – At home

Thanks to a dodgy curry on Friday night, most of this weekend has been spent either puking or shitting. However, my initial fears that a bad batch of Budweiser had hit the UK were soon allayed by a call to the Foster's-drinking Liz who confirmed that she was also suffering. In typical female fashion, it is of course, my fault that we are both ill. After all, it was *my* idea to go out, *my* idea to have an Indian and *my* idea to have a prawn curry. Although I seem to recollect the events of Friday entirely differently to that, I let her get on with it as even I know that nothing makes a bird feel better than blaming a bloke for everything. At least I was spared the nightmare scenario of going to a game with the shits as the lads lost at Everton yesterday. The memory of Kev getting hit by a dose of the Saturday skitters about three seasons ago is still fresh in the memory. In the end we had to make him move away from us. It wasn't nice.

Sadly, as my suffering was at its height, my old man and potential mum invaded, unannounced, for an evening of sparkling conversation and good food. Well, I suppose that's what they were hoping for, although I doubt the noise of her future stepson shouting for Arthur down the porcelain telephone was quite what she was expecting.

To be honest, there's something about her I just can't warm to at all. I don't know what it is but I do know one thing, beauty may be skin deep, ugly goes right the way through.

This morning, feeling much better, I rang Liz to see how she was only to hear that she was still in bed suffering. She certainly sounded rough, but turned down my offer to nip down to Camden to look after her by telling me to fuck off and die. Nice girl. As a result, aside from a walk to the newsagent's to get the papers, today has been spent lying on the sofa watching Sky Sports and eating biscuits and crisps. Hardly good for the diet, but at least it's settled my stomach a bit.

Monday 3 April

10.20 a.m. – At home

I still feel like shit so called a sickee today. Rang Liz as well and she's also at home suffering. Poor cow.

13.50 p.m. – At home

Just had a call from Mike who told me that Barry the wanker is fighting a rearguard action following April Fools' day. He has now sworn revenge on the guilty party and is telling everyone he knows who it is. Some hope.

Mike also told me that they had a shit night on Friday and it was all my fault. Kev was especially annoyed as he had turned down a date with ugly just to be there. To be honest, although pleased that they miss my sparkling wit, bank balance and ability to get them home safely, I can't really see what their problem is. They humiliated me in front of almost everyone I work with (again) and then expect me to go out on the piss with them as if nothing matters. In the past, I guess I would have done just that but now, I have an alternative. And Liz is just more interesting.

And there's always the chance, however remote, that if I get her pissed enough, she'll sleep with me.

Tuesday 4 April

09.20 a.m. – At home

Called another sickee and also spoke to Liz who has done the same even though we both feel a lot better. There's a lot to be said for lazing around all day. It's good for the soul.

11.45 a.m. – At home

I'm bored out of my skull. I've called just about everyone I know in an effort to hear a human voice but only Liz is at home and she's sorting out her underwear drawer or something so doesn't want to come out to play.

I'm sick of playing FIFA 2000 and Gran Turismo 2 and daytime TV is killing me with its mix of crap, bullshit and anti-male propaganda. If my sole ambition in life was to appear on *Trisha*, I'd hang myself. Where do they find these people? And why are so many of them from up North?

17.30 p.m. – At home

I don't care how I feel in the morning, I am going back to work. I can't stand this boredom and solitude any more.

20.15 p.m. – At home

Bloody hell! Julia has just rung and offered to pop round and see if I'm all right. When I told her I'd be back at work in the morning, she sounded almost disappointed and said she'd see me then.

Christ, I couldn't have her round here. Not only does the place look like a shit-hole at the moment, but if anyone found out, I'd die.

Wednesday 5 April

11.15 a.m. – At work

Ah! How I've missed work. Within five minutes of sitting at my desk, I have been told that the latest rumour sweeping the company is that Liz and I have not been sick at all but have, instead, been away on a long and very dirty weekend. There have even been suggestions that calls to my house have been diverted to a mobile phone to give the illusion that I was at home. The fact I don't even own a mobile phone has clearly escaped everybody but, nevertheless, I have spent most of the morning telling everyone that there's nothing going on. Something which, to most people I work with, is as good an admission of guilt as they will ever hear.

I don't know if Julia has heard all this, but she is acting very strangely. When I went in to see her this morning, rather than go through her usual interrogation, she came round and sat on the desk in front of me displaying what I can only describe as long, and quite shapely, legs. If I didn't know better, I'd even swear that the little lumps in her skirt were evidence of suspenders.

What the bloody hell is happening in this office?

12.50 p.m. – At work

Liz has just rung and told me that she has decided that, at some point today, I am going to pay for poisoning her over the weekend. What the fuck is that all about?

15.10 p.m. – At work

Well, I have to hand it to her, she's clever. For weeks I've been denying that Liz and I are anything but mates and what does she do? In front of a packed office, she walks in looking more stunning than ever and plants a full-bore smacker right on my lips. Before I could say anything, she'd given me a sly wink and pissed off leaving me to deal with the explosion of shit which immediately blew up in my face.

16.30 p.m. – At work

A deputation has just arrived from marketing, not only demanding that I resolve the orgasm bet but offering me money for the information. Despite my desperate desire to get even, I am much too fond of Liz to do anything like that and once again, denied everything.

16.45 p.m. – At work

Just rung Liz and congratulated her on making my afternoon a misery before telling her how close she came to becoming known as a gasper. Her response was to tell me that she is. And I should have taken the money because we could have split it.

19.40 p.m. – At home

Liz has just called to apologise for this afternoon. She said she had overstepped the mark by using sex as a weapon for revenge and hoped I wasn't offended or think any less of her. I told her I wasn't and congratulated her on her cheek. Although if I'd have had the nerve, I'd have said that in the morning, I'll be throwing her across her desk and rogering her senseless in front of *her* workmates. But I haven't, so I didn't.

It hasn't stopped me thinking about it though. Especially now that I know she's a gasper.

23.15 p.m. – At home

An amazing but ultimately disappointing evening at Sainsbury's. As I was flicking through the new edition of *Total Football*, I was astonished and delighted to notice Geri Halliwell, the world's greatest example of womankind, on the front of the new *Maxim*. Obviously, this required further examination and, after sneakily removing the inevitable shrink wrap – surely the most sadistic marketing trick ever employed by the media – was soon staring longingly at the semi-naked form of the goddess that is the former Ginger Spice. As I was busily trying not to look too desperate, I was accosted by a rabid dyke who began harassing me about the exploitation of women and why scum like me were encouraging what amounted to prostitution.

I thought this was a bit rich and so casually pointed out that if having millions of pounds in the bank and being recognised the world over is regarded as exploitation, I would willingly change places and have some of that. What's more, judging by the cheeky smile on Geri's face, it clearly hadn't taken much pressure to get her posing. At this, she started shouting abuse at me, which not only drew a sizeable and highly amused crowd – among which, I noted, was the smug veggie bastard – but in the end, got her thrown out by a security guard.

Suitably embarrassed for the second week on the trot, any chance of a decent lech was ruined and so I sped round, got what I needed and headed home. I bought *Maxim* though. Well, you have to don't you.

Thursday 6 April

15.20 p.m. – At work

Over a lunchtime pint, I told the lads what happened to me at Sainsbury's last night. Once they had finally finished laughing, we discussed the issue at length and Kev decided that the only women who have a problem with this kind of thing are ugly ones. Primarily because no one in their right mind ever looks at them. He has a point, but I suspect that things go a bit deeper than that. This is one for Liz. Speaking of which, the repercussions of her assault on me still continue. The latest is that the rumour has reached the ears of Julia.

It took ages to convince her that Liz and I really are no more than friends and it was all a wind-up. I think she got it in the end and certainly seemed happy enough when I left her office, but you never know with her. I still haven't worked her out.

21.45 p.m. – At home

Went for a post-work drink and a pizza with Liz and, among numerous other things, discussed the issue of porn. Something we are both highly qualified to discuss but for different reasons. Not surprisingly, she made some very interesting points about why men get off on looking at naked birds but women don't really get off on looking at pictures of nude blokes. According to her, it's because most blokes' bodies are bloody ugly.

The female form on the other hand, with all its curves and variations, is extremely attractive to us blokes. The other difference, also according to her, is that women like to be looked *at*. They like to feel the centre of attention and, as far as she is concerned, if someone wanted to bring out a proper porno magazine for women, what they should do is fill it with good-looking blokes peering lustfully out from the pages. It's all about eye contact apparently.

When I pointed out that when I look at women, most of them get the arsehole, she added without a trace of sympathy that it depends on who is doing the looking and, more importantly, what she imagines is going through his head at the time. For example, if she caught her beloved George Clooney giving her the eye, she'd be made up because no matter what *he* was actually thinking, *she* would imagine it was lust which would *make her* feel horny. But if she caught sight of Barry the wanker giving her the once over, because *she* thinks he's a prick, she'd do her best to discourage him. Probably by smacking him in the mouth.

Although good and interesting stuff, I can't help but wonder how anyone who thinks about stuff like this can possibly be surprised that blokes like me are confused.

Friday 7 April

09.30 a.m. – At work

Travelled in with Ginger on the train this morning and, with Liz's words of wisdom still ringing in my ears, gave her a knowing smile while consciously thinking of our precarious position in the league in an attempt to confuse her. I don't know if it worked or not because, once I thought about that, I was too depressed to care.

10.10 a.m. – At work

Kev has just rung to plead with me to swap places with him on the sailing trip. As if.

14.25 p.m. – At work

A joyous lunchtime spent taking the piss out of Kev and Sean who, at seven thirty on Saturday morning, will be arriving at Southampton for two days of sea, sea and more sea punctuated only by an overnight stay in the Isle of Wight. For two people going on an all-expenses weekend away, they are remarkably miserable. But I suppose that's what happens when you are about to miss your first home game for almost eight years. Never mind, Mike and I will tell them all about it.

16.25 p.m. – At work

Just been up to see Liz and tell her to bring me back a stick of rock. Bless her heart, she's all excited. She's never been on a sailing boat before. Mind you, neither have I, but given the choice between that and Watford at home, well, there is no choice.

18.10 p.m. – At home

As Sean and Kev will be away for the weekend, the rest of us have decided to hit a club and go on the pull. What this phrase actually means is 'get pissed, have a laugh and then eat something we really shouldn't'. We never pull; or, at least, I don't.

Saturday 8 April

10.20 a.m. – At home

Shit, what a night. God knows how the two of them are feeling, but if it's as rough as me, then I doubt if bobbing up and down on the ocean will be doing them much good.

I can't even begin to imagine what they're telling Liz about what I got up to, but then again, it is all her fault. After all, she told me all about the eye contact thing and it was only natural for me to try it in actual combat.

There was I, giving my very best soft-eyed and kindly look to this fantastic blonde piece with cleavage about a foot long, when she suddenly comes storming over, thrusts her tits in my face and says 'Have a fucking good look, 'cause this is as close as you're ever going to get to them you pervy bastard!' Clearly, proof, if any were needed, that she was not reading my signals correctly. A point brought home even more forcibly when her boyfriend suddenly appears and tries to lump me one.

After this, the night took its usual dive when the bouncers appeared and threw us out. Leaving us with no choice but to adjourn to Mike's house for a Chinese take-away after which we ended up sitting around until about three in the morning talking bollocks.

At least I had a lie in. The two reluctant deck-hands had to be up at five to get into London to pick up the coach.

18.55 p.m. – At home

Just got in to find a message on my machine made on an obviously dodgy mobile from somewhere in the Solent reminding me to do Sean's lottery for him. Much easier than it sounds given that I have no idea what numbers he wants me to put on. Oh well, what you've never had, you never miss.

Today was actually a bit of a washout. It wasn't that the game was crap (another draw though, not good enough. We're down), it was that, without the others there, it was kind of flat. There wasn't the banter in the pub either and with Mike having to shoot off to take his bird to the pictures, I was left with a choice of a pub crawl with Tom the psycho or an evening indoors on my own. Not much of a choice really, which is why I'm at home. I don't want to end up in a cell again.

20.00 p.m. – At home

Just watched *Blind Date* in the hope of seeing something decent in a skirt but instead was treated to the usual conveyer belt of Scouse/Northern slappers and Scouse/Northern prats. Is that what passes as entertainment these days? Watching a series of wankers make twats of themselves on national TV?

And why are there so many tampon ads on these days? They're bloody gross.

20.20 p.m. – At home

Just had a call from Sean asking me about the result and the lottery numbers in that order. I told him that, despite the result, we'd actually been brilliant, which I know will make him feel even worse, and that I didn't know what the lottery numbers were because I haven't checked. After hurling abuse at me and making me put them up on Teletext, he was delighted to find that he'd won £10. He was then less than thrilled to hear that I hadn't put his numbers on, although the inevitable 'yeah, right' leads me to believe that he thinks I'm trying to wind him up. I was going to ask him how Liz was getting on but his money ran out.

20.30 p.m. – At home

Just had another call from Sean asking me about his lottery numbers again. He is clearly at that worried stage, but doesn't want to have a go at me just in case I'm setting him up. I don't know why he's so bothered, it's only a poxy tenner.

20.40 p.m. – At home

Just had another call from Sean, this time freaking out at me. He is now saying that because I didn't put them on, I will have to settle the debt personally and give him the £10 out of my own pocket. Something which is highly unlikely to happen this side of my death.

I can imagine exactly what he's doing now. He'll be red with rage and calling me all the names under the sun. But all the time, he'll be clinging on to the hope that I'm winding him up and when he gets back, I will hand him a nice, crispy ten pound note. Fucking idiot.

Sunday 9 April

13.00 p.m. – At home

Just been down to see the lads play and have a beer.

Tragically, they won for the second week on the trot, which merely confirms the general opinion that I was holding them back all the time.

Monday 10 April

09.20 a.m. – At work

Sean has just been down and, without even mentioning his trip, angrily demanded I hand him ten pounds. Told him to piss off.

10.25 a.m. – At work

According to Mike and Kev, I am being bang out of order for not settling my debt. What fucking debt is that exactly? While drunk, someone tells me six numbers and not only expects me to remember them, but also to hand a pound of my own money to the nearest newsagent in the hope that they will be selected. I'd like to see that come to court.

15.15 p.m. – At work

I have been sent to Coventry for not paying my debt. Good. At least I won't have to listen to them moaning.

15.55 p.m. – At work

Just had a chat with Liz and got all the gossip about the trip. No sexual contact has been reported but lots of (free) alcohol was consumed and a good time was had by most. That is until nine on Saturday night, when an unnamed individual began cursing the name of yours truly.

16.30 p.m. – At work

I'm still *persona non grata*, which suits me fine. At least I can get some work done in peace.

Tuesday 11 April

09.20 a.m. – At work

A nightmare on the way in today and, once again, it came courtesy of British Rail or whatever they call themselves these days. Having drunk far too much last night while watching the Monday night game on Sky (just for a change), the desire to empty my bladder became overwhelming by the time we got to

Harrow and so I was forced to use the toilet on the train.

I hate train toilets. You never know when they were last cleaned, nor do you know who or what has been in there before you. Years of going to football has given me enough of an insight to realise that they are used for far more unsavoury activities than the one for which they were designed and I still cannot even pass one without thinking of Kev and Mike and their experience with the woman from Grimsby in 1994.

This alone is a good enough reason for me to try to avoid touching anything other than myself whenever I am inside one. I cannot even begin to imagine what they are like for women because the mere thought of sitting down on a toilet in a train sends shivers down my spine. I don't even wash my hands afterwards. Mostly because using one makes me feel like taking a shower anyway.

But this morning, I had no choice. And after battling my way through the obnoxious scum that are other commuters, I forced my way into the cubicle to find that, not only was I not the first to use it that morning, I was probably not even the fiftieth. It was a hell beyond description.

Inevitably, as I escaped from the stench emanating from the numerous bodily fluids swilling about in the sink and on the floor, waiting outside to follow me in was a woman. Not just any woman of course, but a gorgeous young woman. I warned her, I really did. But she looked down her nose at me in that condescending way that women do when they think that a male is making some kind of childish joke about something he has just done and pushed past me. Slamming the door behind her.

A few minutes later, she came storming out, slightly ashen-faced it has to be said, and upon seeing me, proclaimed in an extremely loud voice that I was disgusting filth. She then launched into a tirade of abuse, first about me and then about men in general. A subject that seemed to generate a great deal of sympathy among the other women on the train. Never has the sight of Euston station seemed so welcoming.

12.45 p.m. – At work

Mike has just arrived at my desk and casually asked if I intend to settle my debt. Clearly, we have passed the sulking stage and are now at the 'point of principle' stage. I needed that this morning, so to make myself feel better, told him to tell Sean to sod off.

15.20 p.m. – At work

To avoid the traitors that are my 'mates', I stayed at work over lunch and spent an hour with Sue discussing, among other things, the subject of affairs. Something which she is perfectly placed to discuss having divorced her old man for just such an indiscretion. The funny thing is, even though she threw him out over two years ago, I could see from the look on her face that she isn't really over him yet. Although whether that's because she misses him or is just plain lonely, I don't know.

Mind you, having spent an hour sitting not two feet away from her, it seems to me that her old man must have been off his trolley to go looking elsewhere because she's amazingly attractive. Then again, to quote another of the old man's sayings, you don't know what goes on behind the bedroom curtains do you?

19.50 p.m. – At home

Thankfully, no one I knew was on the train tonight, so my encounter with the manic power dresser didn't come back to haunt me. I don't imagine I'll be so lucky in the morning.

I'm starting to get a bit pissed off with the lads now. I didn't expect anything better of Kev but Mike was a bit quick to jump on my case. It's not as if I've done anything major either. Well bollocks to them. If they want to sulk, fine.

Wednesday 12 April

09.10 a.m. – At work

Weighed myself this morning and found out that I've lost half a stone since I got back from New York. Excellent! And thankfully, aside from a few odd glances, my train journey of yesterday did not come back to haunt me and so my day has started very well. In the past, the pessimist in me would have taken that as a bad omen, but now I feel distinctly positive about today.

11.30 a.m. – At work

More good news. Julia has announced that she needs to feel the sun on her back and, as a result, will be heading abroad for a week next Friday. The other bonus is that as the number two in this department, it will be placed directly under my control.

What that is supposed to mean is that I have to mind the shop for her while doing all my own work and for no extra money. What it means in real terms is that I delegate all my work to everyone else and sit in her office doing fuck all.

14.55 p.m. – At work

As the lads are still not speaking to me, I spent lunchtime in Liz's office talking to her and the other girlies. A good thing as it happens, as the more time I can spend alone with women, the more relaxed I feel. Not only that, but being as all they do is gossip, I learnt a few things that could come in very handy. Not least of which is that Julia has a new bloke. No wonder she's been more cheerful lately.

22.50 p.m. – At home

Another success at Sainsbury's tonight. While looking through the sirloin steak, I struck up an innuendo-laden conversation with a thirty-something brunette called Jill about the merits of red meat.

138 • *Dougie Brimson*

After adjourning for a coffee, we discovered a mutual dislike of all things French and arranged to go out for a drink tomorrow night.

Hating the French, now there's a chat-up line if ever I heard one. Clearly, my early morning optimism was well placed. Today really has turned out to be a blinder.

Thursday 13 April

09.35 a.m. – At work

Rang Liz and told her about my date tonight. She laughed and then called me an old slag. Not very friendly really.

11.15 a.m. – At work

Just had a visit from Mike, who has repeated his assertion that I should pay Sean ten pounds and settle this feud. Repeated *my* assertion that they can kiss my arse.

23.30 p.m. – At home

Sadly, my date with Jill was not a success. Clearly, I need to rethink this whole Wednesday night at Sainsbury's tactic because, aside from Tessa, who I knew already, it just isn't working.

Don't women understand that when they go out with a bloke for the first time, he doesn't want to hear about what wankers their predecessors were or how they're desperate to have kids because their biological clock isn't just ticking, the alarm's gone off? It seems pretty fucking obvious to me. But as I sat there tonight, listening to her drone on and becoming more convinced by the second that this was a shag on a plate if I wanted it, I suddenly realised that she wasn't interested in me at all. All she wanted was a sperm donor and I was probably just the latest in a long line of blokes she had tried to pull. And with any normal bloke that would be fine, but not with me. If I get a leg over, great, but I want it to be because a woman wants to have sex with me as a person, not as an ingredient.

Sadly, Sainsbury's seems to be full of women who are increasingly desperate. Either for sex, babies or just company and, if nothing else, that's incredibly sad. But it's not my fault. Women backed themselves into this corner and now a lot of them are suffering the consequences. And while I don't feel much sympathy for them, I don't intend to take advantage either.

Friday 14 April

15.20 p.m. – At work

Just spent an age with Julia going through all the detail of next week. You would have thought she was going away for a bloody year the way she went on. I think she forgets I have done this before. Then again, maybe she's been told about what happened two years ago which is why she's so concerned.

Mind you, it was my first time in charge and I was keen to make an impression. Although that doesn't excuse my level of stupidity. I mean, fancy telling everyone that the high-ups had reviewed their non-smoking policy and decided to relax the smoking ban in our office. All on the strength of a memo signed by B. Hedges. What a dickhead. When the (non-smoking) caretaker came in with the cleaners that night and found a haze of nicotine and piles of dog-ends, he almost had a coronary. Thank Christ I managed to keep quiet although I never did find out who set me up.

16.15 p.m. – At work

The blokes are still not speaking to me, so that's almost a week. I don't know what they're trying to achieve, but no way am I handing over a tenner just to get in their good books.

Saturday 15 April

16.00 p.m. – At home

Went out with Liz last night but after the two of us spent the evening moaning about our respective lack of partners, we ended up getting so depressed we decided to adjourn to her flat to get totally bombed. Something we finally achieved at about four o'clock this morning. It's taken me all day just to get to the stage where I felt fit enough to travel home on the train, and even that was touch and go.

Nice place she's got, but very girlie. She hasn't even got Sky! Strangely, given her family background, she didn't seem to have any porn either.

20.00 p.m. – At home

Just rang Liz, who is out. I don't know how she does it. I feel like death. Roll on *Match of the Day*. Although as Watford lost again, I don't know if I can be arsed to watch.

Sunday 16 April

19.30 p.m. – At home

As I hadn't seen them for a while, I went to Lou's to spoil the kids for the day. After lunch in Pizza Hut, where they ate way too much, we went to see *Toy Story 2* for the fourth time. They loved it, so did I.

Sadly, I am in pain now after a frantic game of football in the back garden ended with Ray joining in and almost crippling me with an Eric Cantona style attack on my groin.

Now I need a bath and an early night. I'm the main man tomorrow and want to be on top form. Although someone to rub my groin would be handy.

21.00 p.m. – At home

Holy fuck! I always knew that, one day, the goddess that is the former Ginger Spice would change my life, and finally, she has.

If she hadn't been on the front cover, I'd never have bought *Maxim*, and then would never have sat in the bath reading an article about flirting. An article which has not only shaken me, it's turned a fucking great lightbulb on right over my head.

I can't believe I've been so bloody stupid. How did I miss it? All those cheeky little smiles and quick glances. The way she licks her lips and keeps touching me when we're talking. And that thing she does with her hair, it's all here like a bloody script. If this is right, Julia's been giving me the come-on for months.

The more I think about it, the more obvious it all is. All that asking me about stuff to do and places to go in Watford. She was waiting for me to ask her out! Bloody hell, she even wanted to come round here last week and I turned her down. What the fuck is up with me? Much as she gets on my tits, and still scares me a bit, she is quite fit. I don't know how the lads would react though. Shagging the boss is a bit extreme. Then again, being as they aren't speaking to me, it hardly matters.

And of course now it's too late. She's off on holiday with her new geezer. Bollocks.

Monday 17 April

12.45 p.m. – At work

A mental morning. Julia might well have been giving me the eye, but that hasn't stopped her leaving me a bloody great list of things she wants doing including my ideas for staff appraisals. Still, at least having access to her office means I can go through all her drawers, although nothing interesting has turned up yet.

The lads still aren't talking to me. Hopefully, they had a shit weekend.

21.10 p.m. – At home

Christ, it's tough at the top. I'm bloody shattered. It's bloody lonely as well. I've hardly spoken to a soul all day and haven't even had the bottle to give anyone a bollocking.

Tuesday 18 April

22.35 p.m. – At home

I'm knackered. My plan to delegate all my work has backfired badly, mostly because everyone else is so bloody lazy, I can't risk my annual bonus by leaving stuff up to any of them. Shit, I wonder if Julia sits there thinking that about me?

I'm also becoming increasingly confused about this flirting thing. If it's true, then what do I do when she comes back? It's one thing being ignorant and not knowing, but knowing and being aware is something else. Especially when the idea is becoming increasingly attractive.

I haven't mentioned this to Liz yet. Much as I think of her, I don't know if even she could keep something like this to herself. I was there the other day when they were talking about Julia's new bloke and it wasn't nice or supportive. God knows what they'd be like if it were me!

As far as the lads are concerned, I'm still on the shit-list, although to be honest I haven't missed them that much. I haven't had the bloody time.

Wednesday 19 April

12.45 p.m. – At work

Weighed myself again this morning and found that I'm even lighter! God knows why women make all this fuss about dieting, it's bloody easy. I've even started to think about joining a gym, which aside from getting me fit, might provide a replacement for Sainsbury's as my hang-out joint. I have always had a thing about sweaty, panting women. Maybe that's why I like porn so much. Or maybe I like sweaty, panting women *because* I like porn.

14.10 p.m. – At work

Just spoke to Liz and told her I won't be going on the hunt at Sainsbury's tonight as I'm going to be working very late. To compensate, she has asked me if I fancy going to a party at her friends' house in Camden on Friday night. Although delighted by the invitation, I'm a bit disturbed to think that she has other friends. I don't. Well, only the ones who aren't speaking to me. Is she as close to any of them as she is to me I wonder? Bloody hell, how selfish a question is that?

14.50 p.m. – At work

Bollocks. Just checked my diary and realised that the MOT is due on the car next month. This means that my annual encounter with smug bastard garage mechanics is almost upon me.

22.35 p.m. – At home

My late night at the office was made all the easier by Liz turning up with a bottle of wine and a pizza. She really is a top bird so why the fuck doesn't she fancy me? I still don't get that. I've certainly never met anyone like her. Not only is she gorgeous, but she's funny, we seem to get on, her old man's loaded and she has ready access to porn. She's the perfect bird, we'd be great together!

Shit, I can't get into all this again. It'll start to get me down.

Thursday 20 April

11.30 a.m. – At work

A bad morning. All this stuff with Julia and Liz is really playing on my mind but for different reasons. Bloody women, they're like a curse.

I'm going to have to sort out this thing with Liz soon. If I don't, it's bound to cause problems at some point and I don't want that. The thing is, how do I make what is potentially the most important question I will ever ask sound perfectly innocent?

I could do with some advice about how to handle Julia as well. She's back after the bank holiday.

13.55 p.m. – At work

An interesting visit to my office from Mike just now asking about the game on Sunday. I was torn between telling him to fuck off or just forgetting the whole thing and carrying on as normal. In the end, after weighing up the pros and cons and considering that not one of my three so-called mates have spoken to me for almost two weeks, I told him to fuck off.

15.20 p.m. – At work

Amazingly, having finally realised that I've got the arsehole with them and not the other way round, Kev has just called and, without so much as an apology, asked if I fancy a night out with the lads tonight. Cheeky bastard. I told him to fuck off as well. Childish I know, but it made me feel better.

17.00 p.m. – At work

Just called Liz and asked if she fancies a drink after work. I've decided to ask her about Julia and then, if the situation presents itself, drop in a few hints about the two of us and our 'future'. I know what she said before but I'm still not convinced she was thinking straight. After all, she was a bit depressed.

23.10 p.m. – At home

Just got in after a few drinks with Liz, although I am not really any the wiser. Her response to my suspicions about Julia were a bit vague although she did point out that, if such an obviously aggressive bird as Julia wanted to ask anyone out, she wouldn't piss about, she'd just do it. She does have a point there.

As for the subject of the two of us, that also remains a mystery. Because I bottled it.

Friday 21 April

09.25 a.m. – At work

My last day as boss and thank God for that. The last time I stood in, it was a piece of piss but this week has been madness.

Although I'm sure that ninety per cent of Julia's work is self-inflicted, I will look at her in a whole new light in future. In more ways than one as it happens.

09.40 a.m. – At work

Clearly, the lads are worried about the fact that I almost certainly won't be getting any rounds in on Sunday because Kev has just been down and asked what's happening. As I haven't seen anything of Sean, never mind had any sniff of an apology, I lied and told him I had been asked to go in one of the boxes. Predictably, he was a bit shocked, then annoyed and then left with his tail between his legs.

I feel bad now, but then again, I haven't done anything wrong so why should I? The problem now is that, as I can't sit with them, I have to work out how to off-load my season ticket stub and get a replacement ticket. As it's Arsenal, that's not going to be easy.

16.45 p.m. – At work

As expected, the only thing I've heard from the lads since this morning has been the gnashing of teeth. Bollocks to them all, that's what I say.

17.25 p.m. – At work

That's that then, back to normal next week and, thanks to the bank holiday, it'll be Tuesday before Julia returns. In the meantime, it's party-on tonight which means straight from here to Camden. After the week I've had, I can't wait. Although I'm still worried about the game on Sunday.

Saturday 22 April

17.45 p.m. – At home

Well not exactly the evening I had imagined, but a blast nevertheless. It turned out that Liz's friend was a bloke called Darren. Well, to be more specific, a gay bloke called Darren. And although camp as a busload of Butlins redcoats, he was a bloody good laugh and clearly regards Liz as a diamond bird. Thankfully, that's the only thing we have in common. As a hetero and proud of it, I just can't get my head around some of the more unsavoury aspects of male homosexuality.

As for Liz, she was in her element and it seemed to me that she had the time of her life. So much so that, for a while, I was worried she'd get pulled by someone. But it became pretty clear that she wasn't interested in anything other than laughing. Nothing wrong with that. Nothing at all. The only downside was that Fiona was there but, seemingly, she had forgotten all about our disastrous blind date as she never mentioned it. She never mentioned the bloody money she owes me either.

God knows what time we got back to Liz's. It must have been late as I didn't wake up till about eleven thirty and she was still asleep. Although sorely tempted to look in and see if anything was peeking out from beneath the duvet, I made a coffee but despite making as much noise as possible, she didn't wake up and so I drank it, scribbled a note and came home.

Not a bad move as it happens. By the time I got to my front door, I had turtle's head syndrome. And there's something about having a dump in a bird's flat which fills me with terror.

I was actually sitting on the bog when she rang me up, called me a dickhead for not waking her and then told me to get back down there as soon as possible. Another party beckons.

Sunday 23 April

19.30 p.m. – At home

My seven-year, unbroken home attendance record has been broken. Not because I couldn't get there, but because I got arrested. And it was all bloody Liz's fault.

If she hadn't invited me to a poxy party, I'd never have got wrecked last night. Then I wouldn't have slept in and been late getting to Vicarage Road. And if I'd been there early, I'd have sorted out my ticket situation in plenty of time instead of having to argue about the price with a bastard scum-of-the-earth tout right outside the away end. And if I hadn't done that, the police wouldn't have thrown the two of us in a van and carted us off. And because the bastard tout, who was obviously a seasoned veteran of such occupational hazards, immediately blamed me for everything and told the police he was buying not selling, he ended up getting released and I ended up sitting in a cell for almost three hours. Which was the length of time it took to find the copper using the station's brain-cell. Once he turned up, he realised that if a twenty-nine-year-old bloke could stand in front of him and explain with a straight face that the reason he hadn't used the season ticket he had in his pocket was because he wasn't speaking to his mates, chances are he was telling the truth. And so he gave me a bollocking and kicked me out.

Of course, Watford knew I wasn't there and so broke their season-long habit of playing shite by turning in one of their best home performances for months. At least according to Teletext. They still lost though. No change there then.

To make matters worse, I now feel like shit because I've only just had something to eat and I can't for the life of me remember much about last night. Which usually means I did something stupid. Great.

Monday 24 April

10.15 a.m. – At home

Rang Liz last night to blame her for all my troubles but instead received the devastating news that my Budweiser-numbed brain did indeed let me down last night. With a vengeance.

Apparently, when we got back to her flat, I started drinking brandy. Something which is fatal for me as it always makes me broody. Proof of this came when she told me that I was so pissed, I tried to get her to agree to the idea that, as we are both single, and therefore have no sex life, we should get rid of all our frustrations by having sex with each other. All the time. Something which would also help us to practise our sexual technique so that when either of us did eventually meet someone, we would know we were doing it right.

After more brandy, and to make matters even worse, I then told her that I think she's gorgeous and that we should get married. Not just because we get on, but because I want lots of kids. And then I went into one of those drunken low-spirited moaning sessions before falling asleep on her settee.

Hearing her recount all this, especially as she made it sound like she was giving evidence in court, was not a pleasant experience. Although thankfully, she doesn't seem to realise that the only time most twenty-nine-year-old single blokes will ever say what they truly feel is when they're pissed out of their minds. Instead, she thinks it's all one big joke which is a bloody relief. But coming on top of missing a game and spending time in a cell, hearing her say 'you fucking wish', for about the fifth time was one kick in the knackers too many. And as far as our relationship is concerned, quite possibly the best contraceptive I have ever encountered.

19.35 p.m. – At home

Needed cheering up so spent the day with Lou and the kids. It worked perfectly. There's nothing like listening to an eight-year-old excitedly trying to explain why Pokémon is so brilliant to make you realise that nothing else is really that important.

Tuesday 25 April

09.25 a.m. – At work

Shit. Julia's back. On top of everything else, now I have to work out if my theories about her flirting with me are correct or, more likely, another product of my increasingly warped imagination.

I must say though, she does look fit. Maybe this new geezer she's got is doing her good. Or good at doing her, I haven't worked out which yet.

10.30 a.m. – At work

Have just briefed Julia on everything that's gone on and what's been done while she's been away.

Didn't catch any obvious flirting although I did get a nice flash of cleavage as I was looking over her shoulder. Why is that suddenly so sexy?

10.50 a.m. – At work

Liz, or, as she now calls herself, Mrs Ellis, has just called to take the piss. Although relieved in a way that she thinks it's funny, I can't help but feel a little gutted about the way it's all turned out.

Is the idea really that ridiculous? I still don't think so, although she obviously does. So I guess maybe now I'll never know.

12.00 p.m. – At work

About ten minutes ago, Julia dropped a package on my desk. Foolishly, I though it was a present and got quite excited. But when I opened it, I found two rolls of film and a note asking me to get them developed. That's me put back firmly in my place then.

14.20 p.m. – At work

Just put Julia's films in Boots and had a quiet beer on my own. Something which is becoming increasingly boring. This thing with the lads is getting on my tits but the problem is, because we're blokes, this will never get sorted because none of us will ever admit we were wrong.

Mind you, if I'd have handed over the tenner in the first place, I'd have got to see the game Sunday and my record would be intact. The one bonus is that at least none of them will ever know.

Of course, if we were birds, this would already have been forgotten. They're much more sensible than us.

15.15 p.m. – At work

Bumped into Kev about half an hour ago and casually asked him what he thought of the game on Saturday. A bit of a gamble seeing as I'd only seen the highlights on Sky News.

Thankfully, he talked as if nothing was wrong and told me that they'd missed me in the pub because it was my turn to get the first round in. Typical. Still, at least a bit of ice has been broken.

Wednesday 26 April

13.00 p.m. – At work

On the odd occasion, life is indeed, sweet.

Over an early lunch, I collected Julia's photographs from Boots and, while scanning through them on the way back to work, discovered nine of her sunbathing topless. I immediately returned to Boots and ordered a second set. This time, jumbo sized. She might be my boss, but judging by these pictures, she has top tits. Besides, you never know when such things might possibly come in handy.

14.15 p.m. – At work

Have just caught sight of Julia staring at me from her office. She has a sly and extremely dirty looking grin on her face which, according to *Maxim*, is classic flirting.

God knows what she's thinking about. But, judging by her expression, latex is almost certainly involved somewhere.

16.30 p.m. – At work

The more I think about it, the more I'm beginning to suspect that darker forces are at play here. Julia could have walked into any chemist's and got those pictures developed herself but she didn't. I think she gave them to me because she actually *wants* me to see her with her tits out.

It makes perfect sense. For fuck's sake: she must know I'll have a look through them. But she also knows that I'm not stupid enough to put them on general release, or even tell the lads because it'd be instant dismissal.

So is this just the latest instalment of her pulling technique? Or is it simply the fact that she gets her rocks off knowing that I'll be looking at her in a state of semi-undress and this build-up is all a part of the game? Come to think of it, this could well be a part of the old domination thing. After all, if she thinks I'm lusting after her, she has power over me. Maybe my idea about her in a latex cat-suit wasn't so wide of the mark after all.

What she doesn't know, of course, is that I've already seen them. So at least I can work out what I'm going to say when I hand them over.

20.00 p.m. – At home

Thanks to Boots excellent service, I collected my photos on the way home. It was expensive, but worth it. They really are magnificent jugs. I'm actually starting to think of my boss in a whole new light.

23.10 p.m. – At home

Just returned from Sainsbury's. For once, I didn't go for a lech, just some shopping, but nevertheless, the nipple count was fantastic. On top of that and these pictures, I am almost, but not quite, titted out.

Thursday 27 April

10.20 a.m. – At work

I've just handed Julia her pictures. The cheeky cow only had the nerve to ask me if I'd had a look. When I said of course not, she went bright red, gave me another of her grins and told me that she was relieved because she'd only just remembered that there were some of her sunbathing and they might be embarrassing. Mind you, she went even redder when I told her that I doubted that.

God, I love *Maxim*. Why have I been wasting my time reading the bloody *Daily Mail*?

11.50 a.m. – At work

As I've been busily working out what to do about Julia, Kev has just called and asked if I'm going for a beer at lunchtime. I'm amazed. Is this an olive branch I wonder?

13.30 p.m. – At work

All is sorted and forgotten. I apologised for not putting his numbers on (even though I didn't do anything wrong) and Sean apologised for being a wanker. A heated debate then began about whose turn it was to buy the first round at the next home game, and in the end I relented and offered. It's good to be back. Although not good enough to tell them about my photos!

Mike also told me about our traditional trip to the last away game of the season. Thankfully, in typical bloke fashion, they had always assumed I would be going and have both tickets and travel sorted. More importantly, as the tradition also involves going in fancy dress of some kind, he's also sorted the costumes. This year, a minibus full of monks will be heading north to Middlesbrough stopping at God knows how many places on the way.

Christ knows how long it'll take, but it's the end of season and we're going down. It has to be done.

22.30 p.m. – At home

Went for a beer with the lads after work to mend some more fences and had the annual 'do we/don't we' season ticket debate. As usual, it's 'we do'.

Sadly, the session was brought to a premature halt by Kev, who turned up with the ugly bird from personnel in tow. She's obviously memorised my records for some reason, and reminded everyone that my birthday is in two weeks. I knew I didn't like her.

Friday 28 April

09.50 a.m. – At work

Julia has just turned in late again and, as she passed my desk, gave me a knowing and quite sexy smile. This is becoming more interesting by the minute.

I don't know if I'm ever going to have the bottle to take it any further, just in case I'm completely wrong. But it's fun thinking about it.

11.50 a.m. – At work

Just had a call from Liz asking if I fancy a drink after work. She has something to tell me, which sounds a bit ominous.

22.00 p.m. – At home

Liz dropped a bombshell on me tonight. She told me that she went out on Wednesday night and met someone. According to her, they kind of clicked and she already thinks there might be something in it.

I know it's selfish and terrible, and I know I should be pleased as punch for her. But the second she told me, I felt like someone had kicked me in the bollocks. And suddenly, I feel very lonely.

Saturday 29 April

06.35 a.m. – At home

Thanks to the bastards at Sky Sports, at eleven thirty today, Watford play Manchester United at Vicarage Road. Normally, a fixture of orgasmic, if ever so slightly terrifying proportions. But today I can't get excited about it at all. In fact, I'm not even sure I fancy going.

After Liz's news, I've spent the night trying to come to terms with the one thing I've been trying to avoid having to face up to for weeks if not months. I guess deep down I've probably known it ever since we first met. But after last week, and now this, it's clear that Liz doesn't fancy me and, no matter what I think and hope, she never will. Because the plain truth is that she's out of my league. And there's nothing I can do to change that. Which is actually a bit of a cunt.

08.15 a.m. – At home

Great. Just what I didn't need. The fucking postman has not only brought me my bastard Council Tax bill, but he's also delivered a stack of mail from single men who have answered what is apparently *my* lonely hearts advert in the 'Boy seeks Boy' section of the *Watford Observer*.

If I wasn't so pissed off, I'd almost laugh at the irony of it. I need lager. Lots of it.

19.30 p.m. – At home

What a poxy day. Dicked by Man Utd, dumped by my dream woman and pursued by a pile of sad losers from the local rag. I couldn't even get pissed, although it wasn't for want of trying. It just wouldn't happen.

To make things even more complicated, the only thing I could think of in the pub after the game was that I didn't really want to be there at all. It was as if by being in the Red Lion, even after a short time away, I was slipping back into the rut I'd just about climbed out of.

But without Liz to talk to and spend time with, there's no one to stop me doing just that except me. And at the moment, I just can't be arsed.

23.55 p.m. – At home

I have to admit, reading through these lonely hearts adverts as I was waiting for *Match of the Day* has actually cheered me up a bit. Because in a perverse kind of way, they've shown me that I'm not the only bloke out here looking for someone to take care of.

The funny thing is, some of them actually sound like quite nice blokes. Although I could have done without the photos. I'm sure I recognise a few of them from somewhere.

At least none of them are competition. Maybe I should introduce them to each other?

Sunday 30 April

20.45 p.m. – At home

After recent events, I've spent the day on my own doing some serious soul-searching. And coming on the back of what happened last weekend, I've finally accepted the inevitable: that Liz and I will never be anything more than mates and I have to forget any chance of anything else.

However, rather than feel sorry for myself, I've decided not to be so bloody selfish and feel pleased for her. I know how important this could be and what a step forward it is and I have no right to either resent it or be jealous. If this bloke can make her happy, then good for her, and for him.

But one thing I have decided is that, if a geezer has come on the scene, I need to take a step back. I don't think I could handle seeing her with anyone else, not yet. So I'll steer clear for a while. At least when they're together. It's only fair.

Mind you, if he messes her about, I'll kick the shit out of him.

Chapter 6

May

Monday 1 May

22.15 p.m. – At home

Rather than face today on my own, last night I rang Lou and told her that if she and Ray hadn't planned anything for the kids, they could spend the bank holiday with their favourite uncle.

Not surprisingly, she almost bit my bloody hand off and so I've spent today being dragged around London Zoo. How can two under tens eat, cost, run around and go the toilet so much in such a short space of time?

Tuesday 2 May

09.25 a.m. – At work

Back to work and Liz has just called to ask how my weekend was. Not that she listened to a word I said, because in a voice which sounded more happy than I've ever heard it, she was too busy telling me that her new geezer is top and that I have to meet him.

Although I would rather die, I suppose at some point I'm going to have to. But please God don't let her tell me when they start having sex. That's stretching friendship too far.

10.55 a.m. – At work

Just returned from Julia's office after being summoned. Although she said she wanted to talk about my appraisals, she spent most of the time telling me how she gave her new bloke the elbow over the weekend because he turned out to be a wanker. Then she started going on about wishing she was back on holiday and spending time on the beach. A hint even I picked up on. I'm bloody convinced she's giving me the come-on. Either that or she's on heat.

Now there's one for an agony aunt. Dear Marge, my boss suspects that I've seen pictures of her topless and now I think she's trying to pull me. What should I do? PS, She's got great jugs as well.

Dear Billy, fill your boots mate. PS, But if you're reading it wrong, don't forget to collect your P45 on the way out.

14.30 p.m. – At work

Didn't fancy the pub at lunchtime so stayed at work to be treated to the delights of a bloke-slagging fest by the women in the office. Apparently, their latest attack revolves around the assertion that we are all scum because we aren't romantic any more. Coming from a group of females who are known to hunt as a pack, that's a bit rich. Not that I said anything of course. I'm not that bloody stupid.

What really pisses me off is that, if they're so bloody equal, why don't they try a bit of romance themselves? I wouldn't mind someone sending me flowers and shit like that. I could certainly do with a bit of flattery and a cuddle once in a while.

15.30. p.m. – At work

A sneaky late-lunch visit to McDonald's has just resulted in more than the quarter pounder and fries I had been after. I was just about to walk out with my brown bag in my hand when I caught sight of Sean hiding in the corner desperately trying to conceal the half-eaten Big Mac he had in his hands. Hardly the diet of the average veggie.

16.25 p.m. – At work

Despite telling everyone in the entire company about Sean's desperate failure on the veggie front, I still don't feel as cheerful as I'd like and so have accepted Kev's invitation to watch the reserves in action tonight.

22.30 p.m. – At home

Another pile of lonely hearts replies greeted me when I got home but the joke has already started to wear thin. Not just because I've got no chance of ever finding out who was responsible, which kind of defeats the whole object of a wind-up as far as I'm concerned, but because I feel a bit guilty about being involved in what is basically a piss-take at the expense of a few lonely blokes. The fact they're gay is irrelevant. I know what it's like to be on your own and it isn't funny. Replying to something like this must have taken a lot of bottle and not a little desperation. I couldn't do it, that's for sure.

Mind you, it could be worse, I could be cursed with a love of reserve team football. That was quite the saddest evening out I've ever spent. And I have a lot to compare it to.

Wednesday 3 May

09.15 a.m. – At work

After a bizarre dream about aliens with blue heads chasing me around the desert, I have somewhat bizarrely arrived at work in a positive frame of mind.

Having jumped on the scales this morning, I've found out that I've lost more weight and am now at the stage where my trousers are definitely in the too big category. My face also seems a bit less round as well, which is cool. Although no other bastard's noticed.

10.10 a.m. – At work

I've finally decided to sort myself out a gym. The only problem is that, working in London and living in Watford, I'll only be able to get there late at night or early in the morning. Hardly the best in terms of leching but at least I'll get fit.

10.20 a.m. – At work

Just called some gyms in Watford and found out how much they cost. It's a fucking scandal. Still, with nothing better to do tonight, I'll take up their polite invites and check out a couple on the way home.

14.10 p.m. – At work

Gave the pub a miss at lunchtime and went hunting for suitable gym attire. Much as I'd happily wear my 1993 Watford away shirt and a pair of plimsolls, I have a sneaky feeling that I'd be immediately marked out as a yob and so best toe the fashion victim line.

In the end, I came away with a white Fila shirt, Adidas shorts and some new trainers. I also brought a rather tasty dark blue Ellesse tracksuit. I'm a label junkie.

15.10 p.m. – At work

Thankfully, my busy morning has kept the saga of Julia out of mind but now it's returned to haunt me.

I've just caught sight of her leaning over her desk and I could see so far down her cleavage, I know what colour underwear she's wearing. She might be my boss, but the thought of feasting my hands and not just my eyes on those jugs is becoming increasingly appealing.

In fact, it's only really the fear of humiliation that's holding me back. That and the fact that the lads would have a field day and make my life a misery.

16.00 p.m. – At work

Liz has just called to see how I am and find out what's been going on.

I think she might be a bit worried that I've got the hump with her which is why I haven't called. That couldn't be further from the truth really.

22.00 p.m. – At home

Have arrived home from my local gym with my bank balance severely depleted but a smile on my face and a stirring in my loins.

I knew it was a good idea as soon as I clapped eyes on the blonde bird on reception. Everything after that was a bonus. It was like walking into Sweaty, Panting Babes R Us. The place was packed out with fanny, most of which was extremely fit – and I don't mean in the sense that they can run a long way. More importantly, the gym also has a sauna, a jacuzzi and a small pool. All incredibly useful facilities from a leching viewpoint. The only downsides were that there were also loads of blokes there but, that said, it still beats Sainsbury's hands down. Then again, it bloody should do for that money.

Thursday 4 May

09.30 a.m. – At work

Despite another crap night's sleep and another weird dream, this time about Dracula of all people, I feel remarkably cheerful. I've decided to take the plunge and pay my first visit to the gym tonight. Just to get a feel for the place. And the women of course.

11.25 a.m. – At work

At last! Someone has noticed I'm losing weight. And a bird as well. According to Sally from the office, I am apparently, looking 'chipper' whatever that means. Although I suspect if I watch *Neighbours* I'll find out. I hope it's something good.

23.00 p.m. – At home

I ache in every fibre of my body, but I wouldn't have missed tonight for the world.

Is there anything more erotic than the sight of a slim blonde bird in a tight white vest sitting on a multi-gym and gasping for breath? I don't think so.

Friday 5 May

09.10 a.m. – At work

I'm as stiff as a board. Even places I didn't know I had are painful and the train was a bloody nightmare. Every jolt found some new muscle to pull or tweak. I knew all this keep fit was bad for you.

10.00 a.m. – At work

Just had a call from Liz and she's invited me to a party on Saturday night so that I can meet her new geezer. Thankfully, the end-of-season trip to Middlesbrough dictates that I will be too far away and then too pissed to attend.

Much as I miss her company, I'm still not ready for that particular confrontation.

10.25 a.m. – At work

Liz has just called again and asked me to meet her for a drink at lunchtime. She thinks we need to talk.

That's not good. When women say that, it inevitably means that some poor bloke is in the shit. Lately, it's usually been me.

11.45 a.m. – At work

Bollocks. I've just had one of those moments where you know you shouldn't say something but, by the time your brain registers, it's too late.

Having bumped, literally and painfully, into Julia, she suddenly, and totally out of the blue, commended me on my new slimline frame. When she asked me how I'd lost all the weight, I told her that I'd been on a diet since New York but had also just joined a gym.

Even as I was speaking, I knew what was coming, and sure enough, she told me that she's been looking for a good one since she moved up here and could I recommend mine. Jesus, I don't know why she doesn't just lay down on the floor and tell me to get in there.

Then again, I wish she would. At least then I'd know one way or the other.

12.30 p.m. – At work

My encounter with Julia has got me thinking again. Mostly about what a twat I am.

I spend all my time moaning about being single and here's a woman, dropping world record-sized hints about wanting to meet up somewhere but as usual all I can do is worry about what other people will think. Well fuck that. She might be my boss and she might be a bit intimidating, but she's single, fit and available. I'm gonna go for it. Next chance I get.

14.20 p.m. – At work

Lunch with Liz was a giggle. I've missed our chats and it was good to have a laugh, even though I still feel like I've been ten rounds with Prince Naseem.

Over an astonishingly good bottle of Budweiser, I came clean and told her my theory about giving her and her new geezer a bit of space. In her usual understanding manner, she told me not to be a prick because, as far as we're concerned, nothing has changed at all. Something which came as a huge relief to me.

Much as I hate to admit it, he's clearly doing her good. She looks fantastic.

I also told her about my situation with Julia. She told me to take a deep breath and go for it this afternoon. So I'm going to.

15.45 p.m. – At work

Bloody typical. Just as I'd wound myself up to go and see her, Julia has had to shoot out for the rest of the afternoon. I guess it'll keep till Monday.

16.25 p.m. – At work

Thank God today is almost over. I'm in so much pain, it hurts even to think about how much pain I'm in.

As tomorrow will be both a long day and a seriously major piss-up, I have decided to go home early and catch up with some sleep. Much as I'd love to go to the gym, if I did I think I would die.

Saturday 6 May

07.00 a.m. – At home

My body still aches, but luckily, thanks to the beers I had watching telly last night, the pain in my head is somehow managing to subdue it. Why do I do this to myself?

Sunday 7 May

10.55 a.m. – At home

A bloody nightmare yesterday. Why do hire vans always seem to break down on the way *to* games and never on the way back? No one would really give a shit then. But no, that would be too easy.

Of course, because we couldn't get it fixed or find a replacement, and the rescue service wouldn't pay for seven lads to go on by train from Doncaster to 'Boro and then come home again, we had to miss the game and return to Watford. Just what you need when you're sober and dressed as a monk.

We got some right odd looks on the train as well. Especially when two nuns got on at Nottingham and we're all sat there with cans of Carlsberg.

By seven o'clock we were back in Watford and so went on the piss and the inevitable dip in the rancid pond. Sadly, thick woollen cloth tends to absorb rather a lot of water and we all ended up weighing about twice what we did when we went in. More annoyingly, because we were soaking wet and caked in shit, no doormen would let us in anywhere and so we ended up sitting outside Burger King getting wrecked on cans and freezing our bollocks off. We then started to receive abuse, first from groups of birds on their way to various clubs and then from groups of lads who, to a man, thought we were sad wankers. An opinion I had a great deal of sympathy with.

In the end, I'd had enough and headed for home. But as no taxi driver would let me in their car, I was forced to use a bus which proved highly embarrassing as, by now, my damp habit was starting to smell. Never was the sight of my own front door so welcoming.

I feel like shit now though. It must be that bloody pond water. God knows what's been in there over the years but I must have swallowed about a gallon of it last night. That's too disgusting to think about.

16.20 p.m. – At home

Just been to the pub for a few beers and something to eat to counter the effects of the contaminated pond water. I feel much better for it as well. I always knew lager had medicinal properties.

22.45 p.m. – At home

The old man and his frump have just left following another surprise visit. This time to announce their official engagement. God knows what she thinks of me because, like last time, I spent a good portion of the evening throwing up.

Bastard council. I wonder if I can sue them for poisoning me?

Monday 8 May

09.30 a.m. – At work

After the vomit-a-thon of Sunday night, I slept like a log for the first time in ages and have made it to work feeling a lot better but still not a hundred per cent. Don't know what I dreamt about last night, but I have a vague recollection of Fred Astaire. Best keep that one to myself.

10.25 a.m. – At work

Shit, shit, shit, shit. God knows why, but the thought has suddenly struck me that I'm thirty tomorrow. Aside from the obvious dismay I'll feel as I leave my twenties behind, I have something more important to worry about. I do not intend to suffer a repeat of the flab-o-gram episode of last year. It took fucking ages to get all that baby oil off me. And I had to throw away a new pair of Calvin Klein pants. I have to take the day off.

10.35 a.m. – At work

Yeesssssss! Julia has grudgingly given me tomorrow off. I was going to appeal to her better nature and tell her the real reason but, instead, lied through my teeth and told her I have to attend to a personal matter. In a way, I suppose that's true. I have to preserve what little dignity I have left.

11.50 a.m. – At work

Liz has just called and asked me if I'm doing anything for my birthday. How did she know about that? I'm sure I've never mentioned it to her. Told her I had nothing planned but kept quiet about taking the day off. I have a sneaky feeling she's up to something.

14.30 p.m. – At work

Everyone I work with is a wanker. Especially my so-called mates. Having guessed that I would pull a stunt to avoid the normal birthday humiliation, they hit me a day early. As a result, I am sitting here wearing nothing but a pair of overalls borrowed from the caretaker after a lunchtime encounter with a stripping granny, a tin of treacle and a bag of flour.

As if that isn't bad enough, I now have to sit here pretending to have enjoyed being made to look a total prat in front of a pub full of regulars, most of whom I have known for years and all of whom have now seen my meat and two veg for the second year on the trot. I wouldn't have minded so much if she'd had decent tits. But having a pair of hairy icing bags thrust in your face is not the stuff wet dreams are made of.

Still, it's almost certainly cured me of any lingering older woman fixation. I'll never be able to look Sue in the eye again.

16.55 p.m. – At home

Having discovered that the one and only shower in our office block was broken, I was forced to ask Julia if I could shoot off early to avoid the shame rush hour would have heaped upon me. Even she had to agree to that although I don't think she was best pleased. Maybe she's got no sense of humour. Not the kind of thing you want to discover when you're on the verge of asking a bird out. In fact, if she hadn't looked so pissed off, I'd probably have gone for it then and there.

Never mind. Now that I'm cleaned up, I think I'll hit the gym early.

21.40 p.m. – At home

Having learnt from the other day and carried out only a mild workout tonight, I spent the evening indulging in some serious leching. Top notch stuff but different from Sainsbury's in that it's impossible to tell who is single. On the plus side, there's no tubby birds and no old biddies.

Tuesday 9 May

09.30 a.m. – At home

> *Happy birthday to me,*
> *Happy birthday to me,*
> *Happy birthday dear Billy,*
> *Happy birthday to me.*

Jesus Christ, I'm thirty. Almost halfway to my pension and still single. I suppose I should try and look on the plus side, but to be honest, I can't find it. I mean, life begins at forty not thirty. So if you take that theory a step further, the next ten years are going to be crap and then I die.

I didn't even get any cards. Dad never sends them and Mum's could turn up any time between now and Christmas. I would have thought Lou and the kids would have sent one though. And Liz.

The only mail I did get were a couple more lonely hearts which has got me wondering about placing a proper one in the 'boy seeks bird' section? It could be quite a giggle to see what kind of response I get. Just out of curiosity, mind. I'd never take it any further than that.

10.15 a.m. – At home

I'm bored. I hate days off. I even thought about going into work but that would have meant admitting to Julia that I had tried to work a flanker. Not a good idea as, at some point in the future, I'll almost certainly have to do just that.

11.55 a.m. – At home

Liz has just rung to wish me a happy birthday and tell me that a card will be on my desk in the morning. She still sounds annoyingly happy but I can't begrudge her that any more. If I'm honest, I'm only jealous.

15.25 p.m. – At home

After sitting around for a while, I decided that if no one else was going to buy me a birthday present, I'd buy myself one. As a result, I finally gave in to the inevitable and went out and bought myself a mobile phone. And just for good measure, I lashed out and got a palmtop computer as well. One which I can use to keep my diary up to date as I'm on the move.

I feel quite excited, even though I have no idea how any of this electronic wizardry works.

20.10 p.m. – At home

In the end, I gave up trying to work out how to change the tune on my phone and went to the gym. I feel knackered now but bumped into Mary Jones who used to live two doors up from us. She looks bloody gorgeous but, sadly, is happily married and therefore, unavailable. Disappointingly, when I told her I had never married, she didn't seem in the slightest bit surprised.

20.40 p.m. – At home

Just had a stream of calls. One from Lou wishing me happy birthday and telling me I can pick my present up at the weekend after I've taken the kids swimming, again, and three from various lads telling me to get down the pub pronto. The drinks are, apparently, on me.

Wednesday 10 May

05.30 a.m. – At home

Even after huge amounts of lager, mostly at my expense, I haven't been able to sleep as a result of another weird dream. This seems to have been going on for ages now and it's doing me in. I wouldn't mind so much if I could work out what the bloody hell they were about but they are all so, well, weird.

In this one, I was standing on a platform with David Mellor addressing an audience made up almost entirely of ex-politicians and famous journalists. For a while, I was going on about sport in general, but then I began campaigning for the European Parliament. Mellor was getting the right hump with me and, in the end, decided that, to shut me up, he'd put it to a vote. But when they counted up the votes from the audience, I'd been beaten by this bloke who was dressed up to go fishing! He had the rod, the waders, the bloody lot. When he said 'I don't know that much about deep sea angling . . .' I woke up. I've got to sort this out.

Maybe it's all the Budweiser I've been drinking lately? God, I hope not.

10.15 a.m. – At work

Thanks to David Mellor, I missed my train and had to wait twenty minutes for the next one. As usual, this meant that I spent the entire journey contemplating which ruse I should employ to disguise my late arrival. Should I adopt my usual trick of grabbing hold of various files from off of the front desk and walking into the office in a manner that suggests I've been there for ages or, should I simply sneak in the back door and hope no one sees me?

As I was pondering this potentially job-threatening decision, I was totally unaware that standing right next to me on the train was, nightmare of all nightmares, Julia. God knows what she was doing there but 'Morning Billy, late again?' was all she said, cleverly avoiding the fact that if she was with me, she was late as well.

After overcoming the initial shock of her being there, I replied with a simple 'Yes.' And then, thanks to my brain kicking into panic mode, and in a voice that was not only calm and controlled, it was almost arrogant, added; 'I'm sorry and all that, but I was having sex and well, you know how it is.'

Clearly, judging by the look on her face, she did. 'Billy!' she exclaimed. 'But I always thought . . .'

'That I was a sad git?' I interjected, surprising myself with my quick thinking.

'Well . . . yes actually,' she responded. Then, clearly racked by curiosity, she asked: 'Who was the lucky girl?' and then ruined the moment by adding, 'It was a girl?'

'Of course it was a bloody girl,' I exclaimed in a voice that would have made Mickey Mouse sound effeminate. 'You don't think I'm . . .'

'No-no, not at all,' she replied, in a voice which clearly showed that, like Liz before her, she'd had her doubts. Doubts which I suppose had been reinforced by my failure to respond to the numerous sexual signals she's been sending me lately.

I actually learnt a lot this morning. Not only did Julia confirm my suspicion that, unlike the lads, most of the women at work know my relationship with Liz is nothing sexual and still have me down as a bit of a loser with homosexual leanings, but I also discovered that she wasn't quite as scary as I had thought. She is actually quite friendly outside the office environment and, at close quarters, quite attractive.

11.35 a.m. – At work

Having seen another side to Julia this morning, I finally got up the courage to go for it and, about ten minutes ago, went and asked her if she fancied a meal one night this week.

Judging by the look on her face and the fact that after weeks of flirting with me she turned me down, I suspect my 'admission' that I'd slept with someone only hours before meeting her on a train has not done me any favours in the pulling department. Now I feel like a total twat and, what's worse, she keeps giving me disapproving looks.

I wonder if sometime in my future there will ever be a situation with a woman where I actually come out on top?

14.00 p.m. – At work

After an hour spent trying to avoid eye contact with Julia, I've spent lunchtime in the local library because I need to get the problem of my sleep sorted out. This is especially important if, as I am beginning to fear, it is lager that is causing these bad dreams.

Of course, if it does turn out to be Budweiser, that in itself would surely constitute a bad dream. Imagine, a life without those little brown bottles. Christ that's not a bad dream, that's a living bloody nightmare.

Thankfully, the local library had a number of books on dreams but, the more I read, the more certain I am that such examinations of the subconscious are rubbish. Not one of them mentioned David Mellor even once.

16.25 p.m. – At work

Julia was obviously busy at lunchtime as news of my phantom sex life was clearly the main topic of conversation in the pub although, thankfully, she seems to have missed out the part about me asking her out. Maybe she's embarrassed.

But as a result of her handiwork, everyone in the office is looking at me in a new light. Even Kev came down from accounts and stuck his head round the door, but 'top man' was all he said before disappearing back to his ledgers, calculators and twenty-seven thousand a year.

This afternoon is passing by in a warm glow of smugness. I'm going to enjoy milking this for a while.

Thursday 11 May

06.45 a.m. – At home

The mystery of the bad dreams has been solved! Thank God, it isn't Budweiser after all.

Last night, after an evening spent avoiding phone calls from all and sundry, desperate for information about my phantom sexual conquest, I made the staggering decision to go to bed early and pass on my daily dose of Playboy TV. After crashing out at about ten thirty I soon found myself on an American battleship during World War Two. The Japanese were attacking and all hell was breaking loose when I suddenly woke up. Or at least I thought I had because even though I was apparently in my own bed, I could still hear guns firing and American sailors shouting. Then, I realised that all this noise wasn't coming from a battleship in the Pacific at all, it was coming from the flat next door. I banged on the wall and hey presto! The Japs packed it in.

As I lay there, the truth finally dawned on me. Dave, who lives next door, is a cabbie. When he comes in from work late at night, he sticks on the telly in his bedroom and, due to the fact that I am a fairly light sleeper, my subconscious by-passes the audition stage and I become an extra in whatever late night show or rubbish movie he watches. Of course, when he turns the telly over, it screws up whatever it is I'm doing. That would certainly account for some of the stranger nights I've had recently.

All I've got to do is to ask him to turn the telly down, it's that simple. Mind you, I hope he watches porn sometimes. Otherwise some of the things I've been dreaming about lately are sick.

11.50 a.m. – At work

The entire morning has been spent fending off more questions about my apparent sex life. The sad thing is, the more I talk about it, the more I'm starting to actually believe it myself. Thankfully, I haven't dug myself in too deep and, to be honest, it is proving very effective with the females in the office. Even Sally gave me a knowing smile when she came in this morning. Liz just wants to know who it is. 'Someone I met' is not going to hold her at bay for long.

13.50 p.m. – At work

Avoided the pub to keep the lads gossiping and, instead, spent the time trying to work out the finer details of my phone with little or no success. Funny, my palmtop cost me ten times more and is a piece of piss.

15.25 p.m. – At work

Liz has just called with more questions about my phantom conquest and an offer to make up a foursome with her and her geezer. That'd be fun: her, him, me and the invisible woman.

16.10 p.m. – At work

Questions about my sex life continue. I'm getting bored with this now. Lying is bloody hard work.

Still, at least I've finally worked out how to change the ringing tone on my phone. I know it's childish, but is there a better tune than the theme song to *The Simpsons*? I don't think so.

22.00 p.m. – At home

Went to the gym tonight and spent most of the evening leching at a stunning brunette in a lycra top that was so tight a blind bloke could have read what the bumps around her nipples said. 'Suck here,' probably.

Friday 12 May

11.55 a.m. – At work

Julia has just visited my desk to give me the devastating news that, like it or not, I am going to Mitcham on Monday to spend the week helping them sort out their sales strategy for the next twelve months. This is a very, very bad thing. Five days on my own in arsehole town. What a fucking nightmare.

What makes it worse is that I get the sneaky feeling that this really is meant as a punishment. She could have sent any one of a dozen people so why pick on me? I guess my stunt the other day pissed her off even more than I thought.

14.30 p.m. – At work

Spent lunchtime in the pub with the lads. Something which made a nice change given recent events although, sadly, the discussion revolved around Sunday and our last game of the current season. Traditionally, this will mean that we will be on an end-of-season blitz and end up splashing around in the town centre pond again.

If I do go in, something which is highly likely as I've done just that for the last five years, I really must remember to keep my bloody mouth shut this time. I can't afford to be ill Monday. Julia really would get suspicious.

15.15 p.m. – At work

Sadly, not even the sight of a grown man with tears in his eyes has made any difference to Julia's stance and I am going, like it or not. It was nice of Sean to try though.

22.45 p.m. – At home

Had a quick drink with Liz after work and told her that my conquest was actually just a one-nighter from the gym rather than anything serious. She seemed happy with that and, although I don't like lying to her, it'll be good to get back to normal. I also finally relented and asked her how she's getting on with her geezer and what his name is. Fine and Paul, in that order.

Feeling slightly depressed by this, I headed homeward, stopping off in The Red Lion where the lads were in full swing. Clearly, the post-season party has begun early but, still feeling knackered, I left them to it and came home for something to eat. Maybe I'm getting too old for this lark. I am over thirty after all.

Saturday 13 May

17.45 p.m. – At home

Just got back from a day with Joe and Katie. As it was Saturday, there was nothing much worth leching at down at the pool, although at least it wasn't rammed out with single dads. I must say, having caught sight of myself in the pool windows a few times, all this dieting and gym stuff is working wonders with my shape. My beer gut has all but gone and my shoulders look positively hunky. Shit, if it were physically possible, I'd fancy me myself.

After swimming, I took them up to the ground to show them around a bit and indoctrinate them into the beast that is Watford FC. I also ended up spending a small fortune buying each of them a Watford shirt. A long overdue purchase as, with Ray not being a football fan, I daren't take the chance that they'll end up following anyone else. Bloody hell, imagine my niece and nephew supporting Spurs. Or even worse, poxy Chelsea. I couldn't let that happen, that's not far off child abuse in my book.

Sunday 14 May

10.50 a.m. – At home

Oh God. Once again, I excelled myself last night and reached new lows in the 'how to make a twat of yourself' stakes.

I'd just sat down to have something to eat and take the piss out of the northerners on *Blind Date* before heading down to the Red Lion, when Mike rang and told me to get down there right away. Never one to turn down such an invite, I stuffed my pie and chips into my face and shot down there only to find the place packed out with happy Hornets singing and shouting with all their might. Something I dutifully joined in with as normal.

However, at some point, I suddenly realised that I badly needed a shit but, as the toilets in the pub are even worse than those in the ground, my choices were limited to nipping home or heading into town and using McDonald's. It was at this point that someone suggested moving the party to O'Neill's, and as that's not far from my favourite burger bar, I not only seconded this idea, I quickly downed my beer and was off.

The problem was, I was about halfway there when it became crystal clear that I wasn't going to make it. And as the others were miles behind, I nipped down an alley, dropped my trousers and just let it go. It was only when I pulled them back up again that I realised that, in my drunken state, I hadn't actually lowered them enough and a large pile of fresh logs were now sitting inside my strides rather than on the floor.

Torn between scooping them out with my hands and tipping them out, I had just kicked off a trainer and removed one leg when a gate next to me flies open and this old boy comes out and starts hitting me with a golf club. It fucking hurt as well so I had to run away from him with my trousers half on and full of shit plus I was missing a trainer. And to make matters worse, walking past as I burst out of the alley were a group of women who upon seeing me in that state, burst out laughing. Mostly because I think they were waiting for a woman to come out after me. It was only when I fell over and then began to scoop out crap with my bare hands that they started screaming and then throwing stones.

Of course the sensible thing to do then would have been to run home and get in the shower. But me being me, and being pissed, I started to run into town only to find that, for the first time in living memory, the bastard pond had been cordoned off and was surrounded by Old Bill so I couldn't even dive in that. When I'd finally worked out that my only option was to go home and sort myself out, the others had turned up and after trying to explain what had happened for about ten minutes, I gave up and left them to it. But thanks to my overpowering odour, not even the bus drivers would let me on and so I had to walk. Which meant that by the time I got to my front door, my foot was red raw, my leg hurt where I fell over and I stank so bad I had to take my trousers off and dump them in a skip outside.

God knows what today's going to be like. Suddenly, a week in Mitcham seems like an attractive idea.

23.30 p.m. – At home

Well, that's that then, the season is no more. It'll be months before we can venture into the fortress that isn't Vicarage Road again. That means no more matchday piss-ups, no more singing and joking with the lads and no more Rookery. I hate the close season.

I could have done without all the piss-taking though. That's one thing I won't miss. Don't they ever get tired of it?

Monday 15 May

09.30 a.m. – At work

Sadly, Julia has not relented and, in ten minutes, I will be climbing into my car and heading for the living toilet that is Mitcham for a whole week. Great.

Thursday 18 May

16.50 p.m. – At work

Thank fuck that's over. And, as a result of working late every night, I finished a day and a half early as well. Never in my entire life have I worked with a group of people who weren't just unwelcoming, they were positively hostile. And that was just the women; the blokes were just arrogant pricks. Still, given that every one of them was a closet Chelsea fan, what else can you expect? I wouldn't mind if any of them actually went once in a while, but if I heard 'I can't get tickets' once, I heard it a hundred times. I may not be the best Watford supporter in the world, but at least I actually make the effort to go, which makes me tons better than those tossers.

The thing that pisses me off the most is that I was there helping *them* out, not the other way round. Thanks to me, they'll get through this year OK, but did I get anything resembling a thank you? Did I fuck.

Still, it's all over now, and having just informed Julia in no uncertain terms that if I am ever forced to set foot in their office again, I will kill myself, it will hopefully never be repeated. And I left my palmtop in my desk drawer as well so couldn't even seek refuge in my diary. Not that there was much to tell: 'went there, hated it, came back' just about sums it up.

17.10 p.m. – At work

Just called Liz and the lads to let them know I'm back and have received the astonishing news that Barry the wanker is putting on the beers tonight to celebrate his engagement. Amazed as I am that any female with any degree of imagination would want to spend as much as a second in his company, of greater concern is the fact that I will miss out on drinking Budweiser at his expense. My car's outside with all my gear in and I'm sure as shit not leaving it around here. That means it's a night on the Coke for me.

20.05 p.m. – Casualty

Fate is a funny old thing. At lunchtime, all I wanted was to get back to Watford and shower the last remnants of arsehole town off of me and now, here I am, waiting in a casualty department with someone I don't really know wondering if I'm ever going to get home again. Thank Christ I put my palmtop in my briefcase. At least I can write in it while I'm bored. And I'm bored, big time.

Inevitably, this is Kev's fault. The pub was rammed out with people from work and he's standing there, larging himself up telling a joke about fishing at the Grand National and how you get reduced odds for a place. As he reached the punch-line (which actually is 'you get reduced odds for a *plaice*') he swung his arm out and caught a tubby blonde bird called Emma from admin. She staggered backwards, tripped over my briefcase and fell, the short journey earthward leaving her arm sticking out at a very odd angle from the rest of her body.

The funny thing was, she didn't cry, she just swore, a lot. However, she was clearly in shock, and Sean shouting, 'Christ almighty, look at that!' was almost certainly the last thing anyone in such obvious pain would want to hear.

Of course, having a handy car parked just across the road, and being sober into the bargain, I was immediately commandeered to take her to casualty rather than wait for an ambulance. But did any of her mates volunteer to leave the free beer and come with us? Did they bollocks. Clearly when it comes to a choice between alcohol and amigos, women have the same priorities as men.

20.40 p.m. – Casualty

Is it me or are the waiting rooms in casualty departments really the closest thing to hell on earth? Why are they all so dirty and why do they all seem to be populated by smelly, grubby, foul-mouthed dregs? And that's just the staff.

Judging by the lack of activity among the nurses and the queue of in-breds staring at the soundless telly, I can only imagine that I'm going to be stuck here for hours and this bird Emma has turned out to be a bloody nightmare. She might be pretty in a

'Sharon from *EastEnders*' kind of way, but she's spent the whole time bleating on and on about how her shoulder hurts and how she is going to sue the arse off Kev for assault. Although sympathetic to her plight, and very supportive of the fact that she plans to drag Kev through the courts, I have decided that the fact that it was actually my briefcase she fell over is best kept to myself. At least for the time being. I don't need tonight to get any worse, and the last thing I want is her turning on me.

It isn't even as if I can escape. Her flat-mate is out, her mum and dad are on holiday and, unsurprisingly if her current mood is anything to go by, she has no boyfriend to call on. As a result, I am stuck here. You can't leave someone in casualty on their own, can you? Especially when, like me, they commute in. And as she comes from Bushey, which is on my way home, it probably means I'll have to take her home as well. Jesus wept.

21.10 p.m. – Casualty

Hurrah! Someone has actually decided to take a look at Emma's arm. However, the sight of a real-life doctor has turned her from a hard-nosed stroppy cow into a gibbering mess. She even pleaded with me to go into the cubicle with her and hold her hand. A request I grudgingly agreed to, even though it was exactly what I was hoping for.

After all, not only am I desperate to get out of this hell-hole of a waiting room, but the sight of a bird's arm being wrenched back into its socket is not something you see every day. And I am kind of hoping that they'll take her top off, which will certainly make the whole evening worthwhile. I've noticed that while she might be a bit on the plump side, beneath that blouse lurks a chest of fairly respectable proportions.

21.35 p.m. – Casualty

Clearly, the move to a cubicle has been designed to disguise the fact that we will have to wait for ages yet. The doctors have obviously been called to an emergency tea-break or something, but at least Emma has fallen asleep.

22.45 p.m. – At home

I'm back at home and thank fuck for that. I couldn't stand it any more.

It was OK for a while. Emma was asleep and I was trying to work out a way to undo her blouse without waking her up, and then they brought someone else into the next cubicle. 'Quick nurse, I need a bucket' was the first warning sign, although the all-too-familiar splash of vomit hitting floor was the clincher. If her flat-mate hadn't turned up to save me, I'd have probably done a runner anyway. The stench was foul.

I've obviously not been missed, judging by the fact that there are no messages on the machine and only assorted bills and lonely hearts replies on the mat. That's almost thirty I've had now, so it obviously works. It has to be worth sticking in a legit one, if only for the crack. I'm going to get on to that tomorrow. And I'm also going to have another crack at Julia. I'll tell her what I told Liz, that my sexual conquest was a one-night stand. Well, if it worked once, no reason why it shouldn't work again.

I'd better check up on Emma as well. I actually feel a bit guilty for leaving her there like that. I don't even know how her flat-mate got to the hospital, but I hope it was by car and not by train. My Peugeot may be knocking on a bit, but it's a damn sight more comfortable, not to mention quicker, than the average Silverlink cattle-wagon.

I bet two minutes after I left, someone came to see her. And a pound to a pinch of shit they made her take her blouse off as well. That'd be just my luck to miss that.

Friday 19 May

09.25 a.m. – At work

Despite being in my own bed for the first time in a week, I had a restless night last night, although this time it wasn't caused by aliens, Japanese soldiers or even David Mellor, it was caused by pangs of guilt. Something that was made even worse by the fact that the moment I walked into the office, everyone was asking me how Emma was and I feel like shit because I don't know.

09.45 a.m. – At work

Liz has just called down to welcome me home. She looks fantastic as usual but, like a lot of other people, seemed a bit surprised I didn't know anything about Emma. Not what I needed.

Of course, the second she left, all the usual childish bollocks started. No wonder she thinks most blokes are low-lifes. How would some of these wankers feel if I started talking about the size of their sisters' tits? Not as annoyed as me that's for bloody sure.

11.30 a.m. – At work

Just spent an hour with Julia moaning about Mitcham but she didn't seem to give a shit so I didn't bother trying to set her right about my 'date'.

Like Liz, she also looks fantastic today. It must be something in the water. Or maybe they're all flushed with joy at having me back.

14.15 p.m. – At work

I couldn't face the pub. I'm too depressed. The whole thing with this Emma bird affected me although it's not really guilt about leaving her there, it's more to do with me. I mean, there I was, supposedly looking after a young woman who was alone and clearly in a great deal of pain, and all I wanted to do was get a good look at her tits and then get the hell out. What does that say about me? Am I really as sad and desperate as everyone seems to think I am?

14.45 p.m. – At work

Despite my guilt, I finally managed to pluck up the courage to call Emma at home and she told me that she's fine and will be back at work on Monday. She also thanked me for looking after her and offered to take me out for a meal tomorrow night to show her gratitude. An offer which I immediately accepted. Well, a free meal is a free meal.

17.00 p.m. – At work

This afternoon has gone by in a bit of a blur. I'm quite stunned at the thought that I've been asked out, albeit by a little tubby bird, but that's not the point.

I wonder if women feel like this when I ask them out? Mind you, most of them simply say no which solves a lot of problems.

22.30 p.m. – At home

Had a quick chat with Liz on the way home and told her all about my impending date. For some reason, she felt it necessary to inform me that Emma is really lovely. I'm not sure about that. I guess she's sort of pretty. But the only thing I really know about her is that she could moan for England.

I haven't told the lads, though. At least not yet, because they're going to have the right hump when I do. I've realised that tomorrow is FA Cup final day which traditionally means that we watch it in the pub together and get slaughtered because we're not good enough to be there. I don't suppose that they're going to be thrilled when I tell them that I've got a date with a fat bird and not only have to stay sober but have to sneak off early.

Saturday 20 May

09.25 a.m. – At home

Another very restless night. Christ knows why I'm getting wound up over what's basically nothing more than a meal with someone I hardly know. And given that it's Cup final day, any right-thinking bloke would have simply blown her out in the first place. After all, it's a special football day and one which should be celebrated in big style.

18.45 p.m. – At home

Amazingly, for me at least, rather than tell the lads some complete bollocks, I bit the bullet and told them the truth about my meal with Emma. Equally amazingly, they were quite cool about it, although when psycho Tom asked what she looked like, Kev's description of her as 'short, blonde, plain face, top tits, fat arse' did slightly piss me off a bit. Sometimes I wish that, for once, one of them could just say something nice about someone. Me preferably.

Of course, they didn't let the fact that I was on Coke affect my status in the drinking pool. Perish the thought. After all, what's six bottles of Budweiser between mates. And at least I got a slice of lemon with my drink.

It's so good to have mates who are supportive.

Sunday 21 May

08.30 a.m. – At home

I suppose I should be flattered. But I'm not; I feel like a mug. And I'm bloody angry. Not just at Emma, but at Liz as well. As she was busily extolling the virtues of her tubby mate, the one thing that she neglected to mention was the very same detail which almost got me battered the last time she set me up on a date. Like Fiona before her, Emma is on the rebound. Big time.

I should really have guessed when she told me on Friday that she would book a table. Because, like last time, the restaurant she chose turned out to be 'theirs'. And as we sat there making polite conversation, I also failed to spot that she had one eye on me and the other on the door waiting and hoping that he would come in. Which of course, he did.

Not that I took any notice. In fact I thought everything was going OK until I went to the toilet. Next thing I know, I'm standing there with my dick in my hands as this twat is standing behind me giving it the large one and offering me out. Funnily enough, that was when I realised who and what he was. Although considering that he was with another bird, albeit a fucking ugly one, I still can't see what his problem was.

However, given that he was about nine stone in his clothes and I was suddenly seriously pissed off, I told him that if he didn't fuck off, I would batter him senseless. Something I have never done before but probably will do again as it made me feel a whole lot better. He obviously got the message anyway. By the time I had come out, he had gone.

Judging by the grin on her face as I sat down, she was clearly buoyed up by this moral victory, but she soon came down to earth when I pointed out that I wasn't best pleased at being set up like that and was doing the off. I hope she felt as embarrassed sitting there on her own as I did walking out on her.

That's twice this has happened to me now. What the bloody hell is going on? Have restaurants become the new weapon in the battle between exes? And if so, shouldn't someone warn the poor bastards caught in the middle? Me, for instance.

Bloody hell, I hate first dates. Next time I'm going to choose the restaurant or it's no deal.

13.00 p.m. – At home

To get rid of some of my resentment, I've just spent a few hours down the gym and have returned to find three messages on my machine. One from Liz asking me how last night went and two from Emma apologising for the stunt she pulled. Given that I could have ended up getting a kicking and I feel seriously let down, especially by Liz, they can both fuck off.

15.45 p.m. – At home

Been to the pub but no one was there and so in my pissed-off state have come home to pig out and sulk a bit more on my own.

What pisses me off the most is that *she* was supposed to be taking *me* out to thank *me* for taking *her* to hospital because *she* had dislocated her arm. It wasn't as if I was even on the pull. Christ almighty, they say blokes treat women like shit but, if my experiences are anything to go by, bloody women can be unbelievable.

18.10 p.m. – At home

Liz has just called to find out what happened last night. She actually thought that because I hadn't been at home earlier, I'd ended up staying at Emma's last night. Fat bloody chance. In her defence, once I told her what happened, she did apologise for not telling me and offered to fill me in on the detail. An offer I declined because I don't give a shit.

19.45 p.m. – At home

Emma has just rung and told me she was bang out of order last night. At least that's one thing we agree on. But if she was waiting for me to offer her a second chance, she was disappointed. I hope.

21.40 p.m. – At home

After what has been a shite day, to cheer myself up, I've written out an ad for the 'boy seeks bird' section of the *Watford Observer*.
'Single thirty-year-old male, GSOH, own home, car and good job seeks single woman with no children who won't try and get him a good kicking whenever they go out for a meal. No ugly or fat birds need apply.' That should do nicely!

Monday 22 May

10.10 a.m. – At work

Liz has just been down and apologised again for not telling me about Emma. She sounds genuinely sorry and so she should be.

But I can't stay angry at her even if I wanted to and so have told her to forget it. At least her visit cheered the lads up. She looks even sexier than normal today which leads me to draw only one conclusion. Paul got the treatment at the weekend. Lucky bastard.

10.50 a.m. – At work

I've just screwed up and lobbed in the bin the revised advert I was going to send off.

I just couldn't do it because, despite all this *Sleepless in Seattle* bollocks, I can't imagine that anyone other than a serious loser would ever stick something in a lonely hearts column let alone answer one. And if I'd have sent that in, I'd have admitted that I was indeed a sad loser. And I'm not ready for that. Not just yet anyway. Although if things don't pick up soon, I'll be getting pretty bloody close.

Even Julia has stopped giving me the eye now.

16.20 p.m. – At work

Have just had a call from Liz telling me, not asking me, to meet her for a drink after work. A bit forceful perhaps, but it sounds like a bloody good idea to me. I could do with getting shit-faced although I hope to Christ she doesn't start telling me about Paul and what he's like in the sack. That's information I just don't want.

22.45 p.m. – At home

It seems that setting me up has become something of a habit among the females at work because I turned up at the pub to find, not Liz waiting for me, but a very embarrassed and apologetic Emma. Although not initially thrilled, I gave up having the arse in the end because she kept giving me the kind of look Lou's kids give me when they want something.

Anyway, from what she told me, I can kind of understand why she felt the need to have a pop at this geezer as he sounds a top-notch wanker. Fancy dumping your bird of over three years on Christmas day. And not just dumping her, but telling her that she's already been replaced. Not even Sean would do that and he's an arsehole of the first order. Yet despite this twat's obvious lack of Christmas spirit, it had taken her all this time to get over him and Saturday was the first date she'd been on since. She'd chosen the restaurant because it was her favourite not his and had certainly never even contemplated the idea that if he did show up it might turn nasty.

Oh well, all's well that ends well. I actually quite liked her in a matey kind of way but I don't know if I could do the deed. She's slimmer than Tessa, and a bit prettier, but not as sexy. I don't know why, she just isn't.

Tuesday 23 May

09.25 a.m. – At work

Rang Liz with the intention of winding her up by giving her shit for setting me up last night but instead, have been given the shock of my life.

Bizarrely, she said that Emma had already rung and told her I hadn't flipped my lid but had stayed and we'd got on OK. She then went on to tell me that she's been trying to get me together with Emma for ages, as she always knew we were perfect for each other. The problem, apparently, was that Emma wasn't having any of it which is why she never told me before.

I'm really fucked off by this. It's not just that she's already got us down as a potential couple, it's the fact that she's got my level down as a short, plain tubby bird. Bloody hell, no wonder she wasn't having any of it when I tried it on with her. Obviously I'm not up to scratch.

11.50 a.m. – At work

After a morning reflecting on both last night and Liz's revelations, I have decided to consume a lot of alcohol when I get home this evening.

21.20 p.m. – At home

Rather than get pissed, I stopped off at the gym on the way home to try and clear my brain through exercise as opposed to excess.

It didn't work. Mostly because being in a large building full of gorgeous women only reminded me what a failure I am.

With this in mind, I have decided that, if Emma is available, and willing, I should at least try and take advantage even if I don't fancy her. I need to have sex. Badly. And if she's all that's on offer, she'll do. For now anyway.

Wednesday 24 May

09.15 a.m. – At work

Got off the train at Euston and almost tripped over Emma on her way to work. Considering that we both use the same route every day, it's amazing that we've never met up before. She looked quite nice actually. And after a brief chat she chased off up the platform to catch up with her mate.

As she went. I did notice that she took a quick glance back over her shoulder. Even someone as thick-skinned and stupid as me understands a look like that. It means she's interested. And very shortly, I will be in there. Lucky girl.

10.35 a.m. – At work

There, after all this pissing about, it's done. A slightly modified ad from the one I wrote the other day has been put in the post. I feel a bit of a fraud for doing it. After all, I'm not going to go through with anything, I just want to see how many replies I get. If only to boost my confidence a bit. It should be a laugh as well, and if anyone needs that, I do. The replies to the 'boy seeks boy' ad seem to have dried up.

14.25 p.m. – At work

Not surprisingly, word is out about me and my supposed relationship with Emma and, once again, I was the subject of discussion in the pub. I should charge rent on my life. I'd make a bloody fortune.

After the inevitable 'Have you shagged it yet?' from Kev, we somehow became embroiled in a debate about when a woman can actually be classed as a girlfriend. Mike reckons it's when you class her above your mates; Sean thinks it's once you've slept with her more than three times; and Kev will only apply this term to a woman once he has heard her fart. Something which has made all of us see the ugly bird from personnel in a new light.

I don't know what these ideas say about my respective mates, although I have a good idea. But for myself, I think Emma is miles away from anything like that.

16.45 p.m. – At work

Much as I dislike Barry the wanker, I have to admit that, once in a while, he pulls off a cracking wind-up.

Through the simple act of dumping a tin of vegetable soup in the drinking fountain on the first floor, he has turned Suzie from accounts into a sobbing wreck. For some reason, she found the sight of him picking out bits of carrot with his bare hands and then eating them, quite upsetting.

Of course now he's in the shit, although I can at least claim credit for that. As a result of my April Fools' clingfilm prank, stuff like this is still very much *verboten*. Not that I'm going to lose any sleep over what happens to him.

Thursday 25 May

09.20 a.m. – At work

I bumped into Emma on the platform at Euston this morning. As she was on her own, we walked to work together which made quite a nice change as rather than spend fifteen minutes dodging *Big Issue* sellers, I actually had a laugh.

And she does look quite pretty today. I have to admit.

10.30 a.m. – At work

Liz has just called and asked me how I'm getting on with Emma. When I told her I'm not, she gave me a mouthful and told me that she's not going to speak to me again until I've called her. Then she slammed the phone down.

It's good to know that she isn't going to let a little thing like me thinking she's totally wrong affect her judgement. After all, it's only my life. What do I know?

10.50 a.m. – At work

In the interests of keeping her happy, as well as my desperation for carnal experience, I've just called Emma and we're off out on Friday night. She sounded quite pleased I'd rung and, coming on the back of this morning, I am quite optimistic, if not a little excited, that I might finally get my leg over soon. Now that would be nice.

I'm not going to tell Liz though. Not yet anyway. I know she'll be sitting by the phone waiting for me to call and so I'll leave her to sweat for a while. It'll do her good.

12.10 p.m. – At work

As Julia is wearing an extremely tight white blouse this morning, I've spent the last two hours trying to catch her eye to see if I can work out how the land lies. Sadly, I have had no success whatsoever.

Bloody woman. For weeks she was giving me the eye, and now I want to return the favour she doesn't want to know.

15.10 p.m. – At work

Liz has called to tell me that she's just spoken to Emma, and then proceeded to spend five minutes congratulating herself about being right about the two of us. Clearly, she thinks there is more to this 'relationship' than me needing to get my rocks off. Mind you, if Emma called Liz, I suppose she does as well.

I hope they aren't going to get too pissed off when they both find out that's all I'm really after. Nice though Emma is, she's no long-term thing. I'm pretty sure of that.

19.55 p.m. – At home

Thanks to Julia delegating, or should that be dumping, more of her work on to me, I had to work late.

As I'm not pleased by this one bit, a visit to the gym is in order tonight to work off my anger.

Friday 26 May

09.40 a.m. – At work

Emma has just rung to confirm tonight. God knows why. I'd taken it as read.

14.30 p.m. – At work

Sean has just called and told me that he has arranged a 'play-off-a-thon' at his place over the weekend. This means that the four of us, plus assorted others, will spend three days eating, drinking, playing Subbuteo and FIFA 2000 on the Playstation and, most importantly of all, watching the play-off finals. Does life get any better than that?

Saturday 27 May

10.00 a.m. – At home

It might only have been a quiet meal, but I really enjoyed myself with Emma last night. We had a laugh, talked bollocks for a while and then went back to hers for coffee and more chat.

Sadly, although I got a nice cuddle and a kiss on the cheek, there was no leg over. Although to be honest, I didn't push my luck that far. I got the feeling from talking to her that she's the type who responds to a bit of time. And after two years, a few days isn't going to make that much difference to me. Let's just hope I don't have to wait too long and that, when she does come across, it's worth waiting for.

I did meet her flat-mate again though. Helena her name is and, I have to say, she's fit as fuck. Although I can't see me having much of a chance there. Liz would go mental for a start.

Tuesday 30 May

09.30 a.m. – At work

Like most people who like a drink, I have often thought about investing some of my hard-earned in my favourite brewery. After all, by getting bombed on their product as frequently as I do, I would actually be helping to support the company and therefore, my own money. And given that this weekend the four of us must have poured a small fortune down our throats, the share price of Budweiser can only have risen which means that I would actually have made a profit. I can't really see how I could lose out.

But although attractive from a purely financial perspective, it isn't the main reason why this seems like a good idea. Because if I did have a stake in the company's monetary growth, I would at least be able to see a light at the end of what appears to be a very long and vomit-laden tunnel. As it is, I just feel like death.

10.10 a.m. – At work

Liz has just called to ask what I got up to at the weekend. When I told her, she called me and the other lads a group of sad losers and told me that I need to grow up. Very sympathetic. And there's me thinking she's my friend.

    At least I'm finally starting to feel better, although I'm glad it's not my job to clean out the men's toilets on this floor. How can people make themselves be sick on purpose? I'd rather be fat.

11.45 a.m. – At work

Emma has just called and asked how my weekend went but, rather than give her the sordid details, I told her that I'd prefer to know where it went rather than how. She told me that hers had been a bit boring and then asked me if I fancied a walk at lunchtime as she has to nip down Charing Cross Road for something. Not a bad idea as it happens. I could do with some fresh air. Although I doubt I'll get much more than dust and diesel fumes there.

12.25 p.m. – At work

Astonishingly, Kev has just called and told me that all the lads are going for a pint at lunchtime, did I fancy it? How do they do it?

14.50 p.m. – At work

A very worrying development at lunchtime. As we were walking down the Charing Cross Road, Emma put her arm through mine. Not even Liz has ever done that and it's fair to say that it was a bit of a shock. Because as far as I'm concerned, walking along arm in arm with a bird means that you're a couple. And although she's nice and all that, I don't think of us in those terms at all.

Of course, I couldn't exactly shove her away or pull my arm out as that would have been rude. So I had to carry on as if it were all quite normal and I were quite happy. Which I wasn't. Not really. I just hope no one saw us.

15.10 p.m. – At work

I have been thinking about lunchtime. Maybe I overreacted a bit.

So what if she wanted to walk along with her arm through mine. It doesn't really mean anything. Go down any high street on a Saturday and you'll see hundreds of women walking along together arm in arm. Despite what we always believed when we were younger, they can't all be lesbians, so obviously, as far as women are concerned, it's just a gesture of friendship. That's all that this was. I'm sure of it. It's certainly how I'm going to think of it anyway.

15.25 p.m. – At work

Mike has just rung and asked me if I fancy going round to his place after work to help him clean it up. God knows what it must look like but I can remember throwing up in his bathroom on at least four separate occasions. That's something of a record even for me although, to be fair, my bouts of projectile vomiting weren't all down to Budweiser. I seem to remember drinking Bacardi at one point, and I know a few cans of the very cheapest supermarket bitter went down my throat as well. That's never good.

Still, he is my mate and much as I would like to decline his tempting offer, I don't really think I can. Told him to count me in.

16.10 p.m. – At work

Emma has just rung and sarcastically asked me if I was ever planning on asking her out again. After fighting back my initial reaction to answer 'only if you're going to drop 'em this time,' I told her that, in these days of equality, it was her turn to ask me. Which, amazingly enough, she did.

I must say, as much as I don't really fancy her, knowing that someone actually wants to go out with me is extremely satisfying. I wonder if I'll need to take any condoms?

22.25 p.m. – At home

As I should have guessed, the only people who turned up to clean Mike's place were Mike and me. Well, I say clean, it was more of an exercise in stain and odour removal. One for which we really should have been wearing those white paper suits that coppers wear at crime scenes. I wonder if women cause that much smell when they have a blow out? Jesus, I hope not.

Wednesday 31 May

16.35 p.m. – At work

No Julia today, so without her to feast my eyes on, today has been a bit boring. Although after my cleaning exertions of last night, that hasn't been such a bad thing.

Off out to the pictures with Emma tonight. God knows what we're seeing. I just hope telling her to choose the film wasn't a mistake. Maybe I should have mentioned my morbid fear of horror flicks. Now that would be embarrassing, her having to deal with me freaking out at *Scream 3* or something.

23.45 p.m. – At home

Well, if I was in any doubt before, now I'm certain. It's game on with Emma. After the pictures – not *Scream 3* thankfully, but the Harry Enfield film which was shite – we ended up back at her flat and it just happened. The full bore, tongue-down-the-throat snog. Fucking sensational it was as well. I reckon she'd have gone all the way but just as I was about to slide my hand under her jumper, her bloody flat-mate turned up and she got all embarrassed. So that was that.

Still, at least we got to first base and I'm sure it's only a matter of time. After so long without, sex is definitely on the horizon. And I can't fucking wait!

Chapter 7

June

Thursday 1 June

10.15 a.m. – At work

Made a point of bumping into Emma on the way into work to check that she was all right after last night.

After such a long time without any form of sexual contact involving anyone other than myself, I had begun to worry that even my tongue-wrestling technique was of the crap to poor variety. And there was a sneaky feeling that maybe I had gone too far too soon even though she was more than willing. But, as it happened, the cheeky smile on her face spoke volumes and dispelled any doubts I may have had. Clearly, she, like me, has realised that we are moving toward the inevitable close-quarter combat. And why the bloody hell not?

14.20 p.m. – At work

Met Emma for lunch and, not for the first time in the last twenty-four hours, felt a stirring in my loins. Indeed, at one point, as she bent forward and I caught sight of her bra through the gaps in the front of her blouse, I almost felt myself slavering. Clearly, having got past the first stage, lust is beginning to make its presence felt.

The anticipation is killing me. I really must go to the gym tonight.

18.25 p.m. – At home

Met Emma after work and travelled home on the train with her. Ginger was on the train with us, but if she was shocked to see me in the company of another woman, she hid it well.

23.55 p.m. – At home

I knew there was a good reason for having a mobile. I was on the way back from the gym when Emma called and asked me if I fancied popping round. Within ten minutes I was in her flat once again, copping an eyeful of the lovely Helena. Sadly, she was with a bloke, but at least he was a Watford fan which is something.

We all went out for a quick drink which was actually a giggle and then Emma and I indulged in a bit more tongue tasting. I have to admit, she does actually taste quite nice. She's also extremely cuddly in a 'hands-on' kind of way, although there was no sign of an invite to take anything much further tonight.

Thank God it's almost the weekend. It gives me two whole days with a clear run.

Friday 2 June

09.20 a.m. – At work

A late night last night. As I was lying in bed wondering whether or not Helena and Emma ever indulge in a bit of minor-league lesbianism, I suddenly realised that if I do manage to get Emma back to my flat over the weekend, I'd rather not have any evidence of my long-term relationship with porn on show. Not that I'm ashamed of it, but because I don't know how she'd react. For all I know, she might have a stack of wank mags at her flat, but it's more likely that she hasn't. And I daren't take the risk that she'll see something and get the hump. That could have a major effect on my chances of indulging in some live action stuff. Which, after all this time and effort, would be a bastard.

As a result, I spent almost two hours tidying up and making sure that any incriminating evidence is hidden away in the spare room. Something which I should really have done ages ago anyway. After all, Dad's brought two different women back here since Christmas, one of whom he's planning to marry. God knows what impression even a brief glance at my video collection would have given.

10.20 a.m. – At work

Just had a call from Sean asking if I will be joining them for a beer at lunchtime. Coming on the back of a message from Emma telling me that she's going shopping with some of the other girls over her dinner break, this is a welcome diversion.

14.40 p.m. – At work

Although pleased to be in the company of the lads, I have to say that my mind was elsewhere at lunchtime. For some reason, I've suddenly began to worry that because I haven't had sex for so long, I've forgotten how to do it properly. This is bad. I'm certain a close encounter of the inserting kind is imminent and I don't want to mess it up by fumbling around or, God forbid, proving to be a failure, of the premature kind.

The problem is that I've got no one I can ask for advice. Lads don't talk about things like this unless they want the world to know, and if I ask Liz, who seems the best option, I know she'll gloat about her matchmaking skills and then want to tell me about her experiences with Paul. I'm still not quite ready for that.

15.10 p.m. – At work

Concern about my lack of sexual prowess is increasing. I have to put this to one side and worry about it if, and when, the time comes.

15.25 p.m. – At work

Emma has just called to find out if I fancy doing anything at the weekend. Leaving aside the obvious response, I asked her if she fancied a night on the town tonight but, incredibly, she said that she'd prefer it if the two of us had a night in. Holy fuck. Now I'm not just concerned, I'm bloody terrified. And I have to cook.

16.15 p.m. – At work

I bit the bullet and have just spent a quick ten minutes outside with Liz where I told her all about my carnal worries. She laughed and told me to relax, take my time and, above all, think of Emma before myself. This sounds like good advice although, judging by the fact that I can almost hear the sperm bubbling around in my scrotum, it might be difficult to follow.

19.50 p.m. – At home

This is it. In ten minutes, she'll be here. I'm shitting myself. After all these months and all the anxiety, it could be that it's about to happen. I just hope that, if push comes to shove, I can control myself.

I was tempted to follow the example of the guy in *There's Something About Mary* and empty my loins in an effort to relax. But I have a morbid fear that if I do that and all my stock is exhausted, I won't be able to perform at all. And that would be a nightmare.

At least my cooking's up to scratch. Until I started going to Sainsbury's on the hunt, I was strictly a fry-up specialist. But thanks to all the good advice I got from various single women and the odd gay bloke, I'm a dab hand with the old pasta. Not that I'm in the slightest bit hungry.

Sunday 4 June

17.45 p.m. – At home

I don't know how it happened, and to be honest, I don't care. But within twenty minutes of Emma turning up here on Friday night, we were in bed. The sex was fantastic, she was fantastic and, yes, I was fantastic. In fact, we were so fantastic, that we stayed in bed until Saturday morning and then, after watching *Ant and Dec*, we had a quick shower, went back to bed and were fantastic all over again. Something which set the pattern for the weekend as a bin full of condom wrappers and empty Pizza Hut boxes will testify.

Christ knows why I was worried. It's not as if I haven't done it before. And I've watched enough porn over the years to know that the mechanics haven't changed. Some of the finer points need polishing up I suppose. But that will come with practice. And I do intend to practise. Oh yes indeed. With any luck this weekend will be the first of many. In fact I'm even hoping to get a bit more in when I go round there later on.

Life is definitely good. And I was right all along; she does have fantastic jugs. I'm going to have to get my photos of Julia out tonight. Comparisons have to be made.

Although I suspect that a breast in the hand is better than two in a photo.

Monday 5 June

09.40 a.m. – At work

Travelled into work with Emma and we spent the whole time laughing like two guilty schoolkids.

I have to say, she does look especially pretty today. Must be all the exercise she's been getting.

09.50 a.m. – At work

Liz has just called and asked me how Friday night went. As the office is packed out, I didn't really want to say too much other than 'mission accomplished', which drew a yell of delight from the other end of the phone. I guess she's pleased. I just hope Emma gives her a glowing report.

10.05 a.m. – At work

I'm fairly sure that Julia is giving me the eye again. Typical, you wait ages for the first one to come along and there's another right behind it.

14.25 p.m. – At work

Having been forced to work through my lunchtime thanks to the demands of my horny boss, I missed the chance to spend some time alone with Emma. She did nip in to see me though and brought me something to eat, which was a nice thought. She wasn't to know that the smell of egg sandwiches make me heave.

16.15 p.m. – At work

Emma has just called and said that, as we haven't had much time together today, did I fancy stopping off at her flat on the way home. Nice one!

23.10 p.m. – At home

Thankfully, when we arrived at Emma's place, her flat-mate was out and so we were able to indulge in a brief and very welcome post-work tumble.

Interesting how her bedroom was exactly how I imagined it though. All candles and purple walls. The only thing that concerns me was the poster of Ricky Martin on her wall. That'll have to go. I can't have that wanker looking over my shoulder as I'm doing the deed. He'll put me off.

Tuesday 6 June

09.15 a.m. – At work

Met Emma on the way to work again this morning. This is becoming almost a routine but it's one I'm quite happy with. It's a damn sight better than getting the arsehole with Walkman wearers and mobile phone shouters. Besides, she does cheer me up.

10.50 a.m. – At work

Rather than do any work, I have spent a good portion of the last hour in quiet reflection. Not about contracts or sales figures, but about me, Billy Ellis. Because it's suddenly struck me that *The Somebody* was right. Having taken on board what that most brilliant of books told me, I now feel fitter, slimmer and smarter than I have for years and for the first time in as long as I can remember, I actually feel quite happy. Not in the way I am when Watford win and the scum lose, but in the sense that I feel what I can only call content. Getting my leg over Emma has helped, that's for sure. It's certainly given me a massive confidence boost. Something which was much needed after Liz's knock-back.

Of course, usually, as soon as I start to feel like this, the pessimist in me comes out and I spend so much time worrying about it all falling apart that it all falls apart. But for once, I don't feel like that at all. The optimist in me is shouting loud and clear and telling me to sit back and enjoy it.

And why not? Emma seems quite happy with things so I don't see why I shouldn't enjoy it while it lasts. A shag is a shag after all.

Shit, to think that only a few months ago, I was all over the place. Now look at me. Life is good.

14.10 p.m. – At work

Bollocks, I think I upset Emma at lunchtime. We were discussing the merits of Ricky Martin as opposed to Geri Halliwell and when she said she thought it was a bit sad that a thirty-year-old bloke had a picture of a Spice Girl on his living-room wall, I told her that as far as I'm concerned, the ginger one is the perfect woman so why not?

Given that the only things the two of them have in common are height and fairly large breasts, it might have appeared ever so slightly insensitive.

Oh well, I'm supposed to be meeting her after work so, hopefully, she'll have cheered up by then.

16.00 p.m. – At work

Just bumped into Liz who asked me how Emma and I were getting on. She seemed a bit pissed off when I said 'not bad'. What the fuck did she expect? An invite to be maid of honour?

21.40 p.m. – At home

Thankfully, Emma was back to her usual self after my lunchtime indiscretion, so I didn't have to say anything. I'm quite glad really. Thinking about it this afternoon, I realised that whatever I said by way of an apology might have sounded like an admission that I was well aware she was short, fat and dumpy rather than short, slim and gorgeous. I don't suppose that would have been quite what she would have wanted to hear.

Sadly, she did tell me that she has to stay in tonight because Helena requires sympathy and chocolate after being dumped by her geezer who has apparently gone from being a treasure to an arsehole in the space of a week. And so, although a bit pissed off at this lack of leg over, but intrigued that Helena is now available, I've spent the evening in the gym making the most of the time and money I have invested.

Funnily enough, although the place was full of women, leching seems to have lost its attraction. Amazing what a weekend of sexual frenzy can do.

Wednesday 7 June

09.20 a.m. – At work

Julia has summoned me. She is apparently, unhappy about something and when this happens, I'm the one who gets the flak because I'm below her in the shit chain. And guess what? I don't care.

10.00 a.m. – At work

Even though my ears are still actually ringing, I'm none the wiser about what is actually wrong. I hope to Christ freaking out at me has made her feel better. Maybe then things can get back to normal.

14.30 p.m. – At work

I might have missed lunch with Emma, thanks to the demands of her mates and a vitally important shopping expedition, but at least one mystery has been solved. As soon as I related the tale of my morning with Julia to the lads, Barry the wanker came out with the immortal line 'You dickhead Ellis, it's the second week of the month . . . PMS week!'

He then casually informed us that, over the years, he has put together a record of all the women in the company and has worked out most of their monthly cycles. Something which, by all accounts, gives him the edge when it comes to negotiations, be they involving work or sex. He reckons it never fails and is amazed that no one else does the same. Even Sean was aghast at this revelation and immediately began questioning him about the women he works with. A conversation which I not only didn't want to be involved in, but which I didn't even want to hear.

Frankly, I am somewhat disturbed, and not a little embarrassed, that any of my so-called mates would want to know anything so intimate about their colleagues. Especially as one of those colleagues is, for want of a better expression, my girlfriend.

15.50 p.m. – At work

The issue of PMS has been the main topic of conversation this afternoon and has spread to almost every lad in the company. General opinion is that it's a bit out of order for women to expect us to put up with their mood swings every four weeks when they moan about us for being depressed on a Monday morning if Watford lose. The argument that 'they can't help it' put forward by Des the security man was easily dismissed. After all, does anyone really believe we actually choose to support Watford? All blokes know such things are predestined. They're a part of our DNA. And in any case, if Watford win then we're all elated, which does tend to balance things out in my book.

With women, it's all grief. I mean, has there ever been a bird who's cheerful because she's ovulating?

16.55 p.m. – At work

Julia seems to have calmed down a bit and, although I don't know if there's a biological reason for that or not, what I do know is that it's a bloody relief for the rest of us. Jesus, what must it be like living with that? No wonder her geezer did the off.

23.45 p.m. – At home

It seems that our lunchtime discussion about PMS did not remain a strictly male affair. Word of the now infamous PMS calendar has spread through the female ranks and they are not happy. Tragically, they haven't found out who is responsible yet, but have sworn that the guilty party will be discovered and suitable revenge taken. As a result, every woman in the company who has any degree of influence over a male colleague has been charged with putting pressure on them. This includes Liz, who has left a message on my answerphone threatening to tell everyone a fictional account of my evening with her gay mate Darren, and Emma, who shocked me rigid on the way home when she told me that she was quite prepared to do whatever it took to get the information out of me. A task she has worked hard on this evening with not a little relish but, ultimately, no success.

Fair play to her though. Her workmates would be proud of her if they knew how hard she'd tried. And how often.

But much as I dislike Barry the wanker, I cannot grass him up. It not only goes against every unwritten law in the book of lads, but if he hadn't told Liz I was gay, she'd never have gone out with me and we'd never have got to be mates. And of course, he was the one who put on the beers the night I met Emma. So, much as it pains me to admit it, I owe the guy. But it won't bother me when they do find out, because he's a prick of the first order. It just can't come from me.

Thursday 8 June

09.10 a.m. – At work

Arrived at work with Emma to be told the not unsurprising news that, unlike me, Kev was unable to resist the sexual sorcery of his other half and grassed Barry the wanker.

Thankfully, Julia is out today, but nevertheless, this is going to be a most interesting morning.

11.50 a.m. – At work

Terror has spread through the male population at work. Not only has Barry the wanker been suspended for gross misconduct, but a list of all those involved in the initial PMS debate has been circulating among the women.

As it all started as a result of me moaning about Julia's bad mood, something which also seems to have become common knowledge, I have spent the morning trying to avoid glares that would kill a lesser mortal at twenty yards. Even Liz rang me up and gave me an earful although, on reflection, it might not have been a good idea to remind her that I already knew when she had the painters in because she had told me months ago.

Thankfully, Emma is treating my role in this sordid episode with not a little humour. So much so that she even rang me and asked me if I wanted to know when the red mist would descend on her. Although obviously interested in something which will undoubtedly effect my fledgling sex life at some point soon, I sensed that there was more to this than a simple offer of information and so turned her down. Something which clearly met with approval judging by the laughter on the other end of the phone.

16.50 p.m. – At work

After this morning, I've spent the rest of the day keeping my head down and trying to avoid being alone with any women apart from Emma at lunchtime. Thankfully, the mood has calmed down a bit but none of the women seems to have seen the funny side of this at all.

Bloody females, they might be able to talk, bond and share their feelings, but they have no sense of humour at all. Something I think we'll see by the shovelload in the morning when Julia comes back.

22.30 p.m. – At home

Tonight was just what I needed. My flat, Emma and the telly. We didn't even have sex, we just sat there on the sofa having a cuddle, talking and watching the box. The only interruptions were a call from Lou pleading for a babysitter on Saturday night and one from the old man wondering if I was ever going to meet my future mother without vomiting.

Interestingly, when I'd driven Emma home and we were sitting in the car outside her flat, she began going on about setting ground rules and stopping over. The kind of thing which clearly shows that she's been considering our long-term possibilities. I don't really know what to make of that. After so long without sex, it's nice to have finally got some again, but I'm not really sure that Emma is 'girlfriend' material. She's nice and all that, but she's no Liz. And she's certainly no Geri.

Still, if she's happy, I guess I'll just go with the flow and let her get on with it. For a while anyway.

Friday 9 June

10.35 a.m. – At work

The bombshell that is Julia in full flow has hit. Thank God Barry the wanker had already been suspended, because if he'd been here I think she'd have murdered him. As it was, I got the full force instead, which means I now have something else to dislike him for. Words like invasion, privacy and disgusting peppered her tirade and all I could do was sit there and take it. Safe in the knowledge that at least five dictaphones were sitting on desks in the outer office recording it for posterity.

To be fair, she does have a point, of sorts. I was out of order discussing her with people lower down the company shit chain and I know it. But the rest is all down to Barry the wanker and I don't see why I should take the flak for that. Especially since I agree with her. It was a shitty thing to do. Still, if it proves one thing, it's that those tampon adverts on telly are bollocks. All the women on them look delirious; Julia looks like she could kill with her bare hands.

I suppose she'll get over it. Although I doubt if this has done my chances with her any good.

16.55 p.m. – At work

Fallout from Julia has continued all day but I've managed to avoid it as best I can. Thankfully, Emma was free at lunchtime and so we went for a bite to eat rather than the pub. God only knows what the mood must have been like in there.

19.25 p.m. – At home

I am in the shit, big time. And not just at work, but also with Emma. Well that's not strictly true, what I mean is that I will be in the shit after tonight. Because at some point later on, I'm going to humiliate her in public. I don't want to, of course, but it's unavoidable. Because on the way home from work, she told me that she fancies going to a club tonight. That means only one thing: dancing. And I can't dance to save my life. Simple as that. It's not as if I don't like music or anything, I just can't do it. I have zero sense of rhythm.

I'm actually surprised that no one has mentioned this to her already. Whenever a potential girlfriend has come on the scene in the past, Kev has usually taken it upon himself to impart this knowledge to them quite quickly. In fact, his favourite Billy-related story revolves around the time when we were fifteen and he came with me to my cousin's wedding and actually heard my own mum refuse to dance with me.

Largely as a result of that childhood trauma, unless huge quantities of Budweiser are involved, I confine any such activities to my bedroom. Which has kept everyone happy. Not least of all me.

In the interests of my future sex life, I suppose the kindest thing to do would be to break it to her myself. I'm actually hoping she'll be staying here tonight and the last thing I want to do is give her the hump.

19.35 p.m. – At home

Shit, just as I was about to get in the shower, Lou rang and reminded me about babysitting tomorrow night. Funny, I don't actually remember offering. I wonder if Emma fancies it? That's if she's still speaking to me after tonight.

Sunday 11 June

22.15 p.m. – At home

Emma has just gone home after what eventually turned out to be a great weekend. Although, as I feared, it didn't start out too well.

When I picked her up, and told her about my hatred of dancing, she genuinely believed I was taking the piss. It was only later on, when she physically dragged me on to the floor and witnessed it at first hand, that the full horror of the situation hit home. Poor cow, it can't be much fun having people laugh at your geezer. Mind you, she's no great shakes either. She does that Essex girl, foot shuffling dance you see on old replays of *Top of the Pops*.

After a night of passion and a lie-in to watch *Ant and Dec*, Saturday afternoon was spent wandering round various clothes shops. Something which would normally fill me with horror but which actually turned out to be quite interesting. Mostly because, on three occasions, I managed to get myself in a position where I could actually see into the women's changing rooms. A joy which I have never experienced before, although some of the sights I saw were not for the fainthearted.

By seven o'clock, we were at Lou's. Something which, as an only child, Emma was quite happy with, although the sight of me walking up the path with a woman was obviously a bit of a shock judging by the look on Lou's face when she opened the door. Emma was actually pretty cool with the kids and they obviously liked her, if for no other reason than that she took them round a bag of sweets and then let them stay up late while they told her stories about me. Judging by the constant references to 'sad' and 'loser' they've obviously been listening to their mum way too much.

On Sunday, after another lie-in, we went down to Covent Garden and just hung around there all day which was great. And now, because it's work in the morning, she's gone. And I must admit, I actually kind of miss her a bit. Maybe she's starting to grow on me.

Monday 12 June

10.30 a.m. – At work

I've just spent an hour with Julia and, although she apologised for her behaviour on Friday, the result of our meeting is that she isn't speaking to me at all now.

The reason, inevitably, is down to my unfailing gift for saying the wrong thing at the wrong time. But to be honest, this time it is mostly her fault. I mean we don't really have much in common other than that we live in Watford. And despite the fact that I've got photos of her semi-naked and she's been giving me the come-on since she arrived, I don't actually know her that well.

So why ask me of all people why men don't find her attractive? Me, the bloke who can count on the fingers of one hand the sexual conquests he's enjoyed over the years. Could there be anyone less qualified to give such advice? And did she really expect me to come out with anything worthwhile?

Why do women do that anyway? Is it some kind of test? Surely they must realise that every time they ask stuff like 'does this suit me?' they're lining themselves up for upset. The worst one of all is 'how do I look?' – I mean, what are you supposed to say to that? Who in their right mind is going to say to their other half 'you look like a right old slapper in that love, and the old thighs are getting a bit bulky aren't they'?

Still, on reflection, maybe telling her to lose the Myra Hindley hairstyle wasn't the most supportive thing I could have said.

21.55 p.m. – At home

What a bloody day. Amazingly, I'm even a bit thankful that Emma and her ground rules mean I am at home alone because I was able to go to the gym and have a think while I worked out.

Julia is doing my bloody head in. How am I supposed to keep track of what's going on when her mood swings take her from flirt to psycho to manic depressive within the hour?

Tuesday 13 June

09.15 a.m. – At work

As usual, met Emma on the way into work and discussed the issue of Julia. Although tempted, and deeply touched, I declined her offer to come down and give her a slap for me.

10.45 a.m. – At work

Julia has turned up (late as usual) sporting a new hairstyle. It's much shorter and very sexy. In fact, she looks fantastic. Although still slightly wary of her after the last few days, I caught her eye and gave her a wink. Judging by the embarrassed smile, I think she's forgiven me. So is it game on again, I wonder?

21.30 p.m. – At home

Both Emma and I had to do some shopping tonight and so, after an hour in the gym, I went round, picked her up and took her to Sainsbury's. It was strange walking around there with someone else but was actually much more fun in a kind of gloating 'I've got a partner with me' kind of way. Didn't see the veggie loser though, which was a shame.

One thing I did notice was that Emma buys a lot of ready meals which does make me think that, possibly, she isn't the greatest cook. And I wasn't convinced that all those pot noodles were for Helena either.

Maybe I should get her to invite me round for a meal. It is after all, her turn.

Wednesday 14 June

22.15 p.m. – At home

An interesting day. Julia has been giving me the eye again. Something which became increasingly interesting when Emma rang to tell me that she was going to the pictures with some of the girls after work. I was seriously thinking about going in and asking her if she fancied a meal or something when Liz rang and told me to meet her for a drink after work. It's so nice to be in demand after all these years.

She looks great, and life with her geezer is bombing along. I did get another bollocking about Emma though. She seems to think

I'm not taking her seriously enough, which isn't really fair. She's the one doing all the planning and dreaming, not me. I'm just along for the sex.

Thursday 15 June

11.25 a.m. – At work

Emma has got a right strop on. Someone has just told her that I went for a drink with Liz after work and, because I never told her this morning, she thinks I'm hiding something. Given that Liz was the one who got us together, and Emma's known her much longer than I have, plus the fact that she knows that Liz doesn't fancy me at all and is more than happy with her bloke, I don't really know what the fuck she's on about. Bloody women. Are they all mad?

14.10 p.m. – At work

My lunchtime was spent walking around various shops listening to Emma moan about me, Liz and everyone else. Of course, if she'd have gone into Boots the Chemist first, I would have known why she's got the hump. From now on, I guess the seventeenth is going to be a red letter day. Every month.

21.35 p.m. – At home

In an effort to show my sensitive, caring and thoughtful side, I got off the train at Bushey and walked Emma back to her flat. My thinking being that with most of the women still seriously unhappy, I need all the female friends I can get. And if I could exhibit a bit of PMS-related sympathy, so much the better.

Sadly, it was not a success. I made the classic mistake of telling Emma that I understood what she was going through. Something I obviously don't because, as she pointed out in no uncertain terms, as a bloke, and I quote: 'I have no fucking idea at all.' Indeed, it seems that, because I don't face a lifetime of spots, mood swings and water retention, and I have no idea just how painful stomach cramps can be, I have it easy.

Although tempted to point out that at least she doesn't have to shave every morning nor does she have to put up with stroppy menstruating females, I did point out that it was hardly my fault. Something which only served to piss her off even more.

After ten minutes of listening to her moaning on and on about what bastards men are, I finally realised that I was in a no-win situation and I decided to leave her to it. But as luck would have it, on the way home I nipped into the newsagent's to get something to read in the bath. And on the cover of one of the women's mags was mention of an article about PMS. Being in the front line so to speak, and despite the obvious embarrassment that accompanies buying anything remotely girlie, I bought a copy and headed for the flat with it in my briefcase. And bloody good stuff it is as well. Not only do I now know what the signs and symptoms are, I also know how to turn it to my advantage. A process that will begin in the morning on the way to work.

22.00 p.m. – At home

Bit the bullet and rang Emma to make sure she's OK, which she is. And then I followed the advice of *Woman* and told her that I think she's gorgeous, which made her laugh and put me straight back in the good books. These birds' magazines are brilliant.

Friday 16 June

09.30 a.m. – At work

Judging by the huge kiss she gave me on the train, my late-night phone call to Emma seems to have done the trick. On to the next phase then.

11.35 a.m. – At work

News has just come from Des the security man that the flowers I ordered for Emma about half an hour ago have just turned up at reception and are on their way to her office. That means it's time to vanish for a while. After all, if she can't find me, it gives her more time to think about what a top bloke I am.

15.00 p.m. – At work

I finally allowed Emma to catch up with me just before lunch and, as I hoped, she was all over me. By all accounts, the arrival of my bouquet had all the girls in her office swooning and they now think I'm the dog's bollocks. Something which has had the knock-on effect of making her feel both lucky and special.

Quite possibly, that was the best thirty-five quid I've ever spent.

15.30 p.m. – At work

Kev has just rung and asked me what I'd done that was so bad, I had to send flowers to my own bird at work. When I told him I did it because I wanted to, he called me a ponce. He also told me that Barry the wanker will be back at work on Monday. Suitably chastened no doubt.

Saturday 17 June

18.45 p.m. – At home

As expected, horizontal refreshment of the lurid kind was not an option last night. However, thanks to my new-found knowledge, a quiet evening of cuddling, chocolate and *You've Got Mail* on video was all that was needed to keep me in the good books and, I suspect, secure me a seeing-to of the most X-rated kind in a few days.

Interestingly, as we wandered around the shops today, Emma

purchased a new toothbrush which has now taken residence in my bathroom for use at weekends. Although pleased that she intends staying over on a regular basis, it does seem a bit forward. She never even asked me first.

Sunday 18 June

18.15 p.m. – At home

Another quiet day today. After lunch in the pub, we nipped round to see Lou and Ray who tried to get us to take the kids swimming without success.

Much as I enjoy having sex and sleeping with Emma, I can't really picture her in a bikini.

23.20 p.m. – At home

A fucking nightmare time tonight. With Emma wanting to go home and sort stuff out for the coming week, I went down the gym and, after putting myself through a major workout in the gym, I decided to try a sauna.

As soon as I opened the door, I knew it was a mistake. I've never felt anything so hot in my bloody life. But typically, because there were two other geezers in there and I didn't want them to think I was some kind of wimp, I went and sat down.

I'd stuck it out for about ten minutes – just long enough to prove I was up to it – and was about to leave, when the door opens and not one, but two extremely blonde and extremely fit women walk in wearing nothing but white towels and sit down opposite me.

Given my affection for hot, sweaty women, even I realised that being with two of them in a sauna was not a good idea and was about to get out when, tragically, the other two blokes stood up. For some bizarre reason, when they did that, I suddenly thought that if I left as well, these two birds might think something iffy had been going on. So I stayed put.

It was at this point that things really took a downward turn. Because within seconds of the door closing, one of the blondes, who by now weren't just hot and sweaty, they were panting, stood up and dumped yet more water on the hot bricks. And it was something about her doing that which made me think of Swedish porn. My dick whipped to attention so fast, I swear I heard a crack.

What could I do? I couldn't leave. Not with a flagpole sticking out of my shorts. And despite concentrating as hard as I could on the quality of Watford's midfield last season, it just wouldn't go down. So I had to sit there like a fucking idiot praying that they wouldn't start talking to me – that would have made it ten times worse – and pretending I was OK. But I wasn't OK at all, I was melting. Forty-five bastard minutes I was in there. The longest hard-on in history. By the time they left, I was almost passing out.

Never again will I put myself through that. That can't be healthy.

Monday 19 June

09.10 a.m. – At work

After my enforced and extended sauna last night, I can't describe how ill I feel. My head is spinning, I've got no energy and I'm constantly thirsty despite drinking about a gallon of orange juice already this morning. If I didn't know better, I'd swear I'd lost about a stone in weight as well.

11.25 a.m. – At work

At last I'm starting to feel better. Trouble is, I've taken in so much fluid that I can't stop going to the toilet.

11.45 a.m. – At work

Julia has just dropped a bombshell on me. Apparently, she has taken my advice and joined a gym. And not any old gym, but my gym.

Although pleased to be handed another avenue for possible future access, this could turn out to be a very, very bad thing. If the lads find out, this will be regarded as socialising with my boss, which is the worst kind of cardinal sin.

16.35 p.m. – At work

I keep imagining Julia dressed in sports gear and with sweat dripping down her cleavage. Much as she gets on my tits sometimes, I have to admit it is an increasingly arousing image.

Is there some kind of subconscious force at work here? Warning me that I shouldn't play with fire because I might get burnt? Or am I just a pervert?

22.55 p.m. – At home

On the way home from work, Emma suggested we stop off for a drink and then have something to eat back to her place. Despite still feeling a bit off colour after last night, we went and, as I suspected, she is not exactly a dab hand with the pots and pans. She certainly knows her way around a microwave though. And, judging by the number of take-away menus pinned to her noticeboard, a telephone.

Tuesday 20 June

09.30 a.m. – At work

On the way into work this morning, Emma stunned me with an idea which only someone who has no real knowledge of my mates and their personal habits could ever come up with. She thinks that

I should fix up the recently dumped and extremely sexy Helena on a date with Mike. As if. She's way too good for the likes of him. I was even thinking about trying to slide in there myself. Only once I've split from Emma mind.

11.15 a.m. – At work

Just told Mike about Emma's plan. His answer, 'Does she fuck or what?', says more about why this is not a good idea than anything I could possibly say.

14.20 p.m. – At work

Emma has somehow lost all sense of logic and reason. When I told her what Mike had said, she replied, 'He's just shy.' This, the bloke who once stood on a table in the Red Lion, dropped his trousers and, in front of a pub full of Watford fans, invited someone to try and light his fart. Shy is not a word that springs to mind.

16.10 p.m. – At work

Emma has just rung me again and after three whole minutes of 'Please Billy . . . do it for me'-type grovelling, I've given in and have agreed to sort something out with Mike. I know I am going to regret this.

23.15 p.m. – At home

Emma is obviously back to normal. On the train home she began acting like a rabbit on heat and, having dragged me back to my flat, delivered my X-rated seeing-to. With interest.

Wednesday 21 June

10.20 a.m. – At work

My desperate hope that the date idea was just some crazed fantasy appears to have paid off. She hasn't mentioned it once since last night. And I have no intention of ever doing so again.

11.10 a.m. – At work

Bollocks. My hopes have been dashed and my stalling tactics have failed. Emma has cut out the middle man and arranged things with Mike herself. Foursome, Saturday night.

12.35 p.m. – At work

Mike has been on at me all morning trying to find out anything he can about Helena. Given that I've only met her about three times, what can I say? That she's fat, drinks pints, smokes like a chimney and has herpes. The sad thing is, I doubt that would put him off. In fact, it would probably make her his perfect bird. So I suppose I'll have to tell him the truth – that she's slim, very pretty, has small tits, dark hair and is far too good to fall into his grubby hands. And I'm ever so slightly jealous.

14.50 p.m. – At work

There's obviously a competition to see who can give me the most stress today because, after Emma and Mike, Julia has just mentioned that she hasn't seen me in the gym yet.

15.30 p.m. – At work

The 'who can cause me the most stress competition' is over. Liz has just called to suggest that Emma and I go out with her and Paul one night. Coming on top of the Mike and Helena thing, all I can say is, great.

23.45 p.m. – At home

Having just arrived back from Emma's place after another extremely enjoyable bout of sexual shenanigans, something has begun to nag at me.

Judging by recent performances, she clearly knows her way around a bloke. So much so that I'm frankly amazed that I was able to walk up the stairs when I got home tonight. I'm not complaining, not by a long stretch. But I suspect such intimate knowledge can only come from one source: practice.

Of course, as the person who stands to gain the most from this, I should be appreciative of my good fortune and indeed, I am. But I can't help but wonder about how many people I might have to thank.

Thursday 22 June

11.10 a.m. – At work

A strange morning. Julia keeps mentioning gyms, Mike keeps asking me about a woman I hardly know and Emma keeps ringing me and saying disgusting things down the phone. And to think that, a few short weeks ago, I was moaning about my life being dull.

15.30 p.m. – At work

Emma told me at lunchtime that, although she would love to do unspeakable things to me after work, she has no clean underwear left and so has to go home and do some washing. Although naturally disappointed, the domestic in me is breathing a sigh of relief. My flat looks like a shit hole. And if I don't clean it tonight, I know it won't get done over the weekend.

22.45 p.m. – At home

After spending two hours on the flat, I nipped down to the gym for an hour. Although the basic idea was to get the blood pumping, lurking in the back of my mind was the hope that Julia would be there. I might not be her greatest fan on the work front, but I am still quite interested in seeing what she looks like all sweated up. And I haven't given up hope of an encounter either.

Sadly, there was no sign of her but this exercise I'm getting with, if not on, Emma is helping my fitness regime no end. I've even lost a bit more weight.

It's funny, for years I was a tub of lard and lusted after skinny birds with no success. And now, after a few weeks working out in a gym, I feel fitter and better than I have for years and have ended up getting plenty from a short, tubby woman.

Maybe it's true what they say. Life really is a funny old game.

Friday 23 June

14.25 p.m. – At work

After Emma called and told me that she was having lunch with the girls, I reverted to the pub with the lads, where all talk was of Mike's impending date. Like me, at least until recently, he has also been devoid of female company for some time. But, unlike me, he is one of those blokes who has no problem relating every single sordid detail of his infrequent sexual exploits to an eager male audience.

I sense an embarrassing episode of massive, if not monumental, proportions.

Saturday 24 June

18.10 p.m. – At home

A quiet night at the pictures last night followed by yet another day shopping. Something which is rapidly losing its novelty value. Especially since, rather than drag me around Watford, Emma decided that we had to go to Oxford Street because she has nothing to wear tonight.

Having seen her flat, I can confirm that this is bollocks. I've been in shops today that have had fewer clothes in them than her bedroom. Although from what I can gather, most of those seem to have been purchased with the sole intention of wearing only to go shopping for more clothes.

Of course, like any bloke in the same situation – and I saw plenty of fellow refugees from the close season today – I tried to at least pretend I was enjoying myself. But when it's boiling hot, you've been in the same shop three times and have been told at length and at least five times that there are no decent shops which sell clothes for five foot four, size sixteen women, who wouldn't get bored shitless?

I wouldn't have minded so much if I'd actually had the opportunity to buy anything myself. But if I so much as turned my head towards a sports shop, I swear could actually hear her thinking 'keep walking!'

And now, after spending a day in the nightmare that is the West End in June, I'm faced with the foursome from hell. If Mike is on his usual form, it's certainly not going to be pretty which means that, when it all goes wrong, it will be my fault. It's always my fault.

Monday 26 June

10.45 a.m. – At work

To be honest, I don't know where to start because, quite frankly, I'm still in shock. I simply cannot believe that the bloke with us on Saturday night was Mike. He was relaxed, funny and a total gentleman. Everything the Mike I have known for years is not. More incredibly, he and Helena hit it off. So much so, that they actually went out again last night and even, I have since learnt, did the deed. As a consequence, Mike is like a dog with two arseholes, Emma has a huge 'I told you so'-type grin on her face and I'm a bit gutted. Bloody amazing.

22.50 p.m. – At home

I have spent the entire day discussing Mike. If not with Mike himself, with Emma. And if they weren't on about it, either Sean or Kev were. And then, when I popped over to Bushey tonight, Helena started. Is there no escape?

Of course, Emma is now on a mission. Because while I have her, Mike now has Helena and Kev has the ugly bird from accounts, poor Sean has no one. I sense trouble ahead.

Tuesday 27 June

15.20 p.m. – At work

Discussion in the pub at lunchtime initially revolved around Mike and his new-found woman. As I feared, he has reverted to type and I am now more than familiar with the anatomy of Emma's flat-mate. Somehow, she just doesn't seem as attractive any more. I'll certainly never be able to look her in the eye again.

However, once he had finished describing her expertise in the oral area, Kev suggested that, to know such intimate techniques, she must have been about a bit. This led on to a debate about promiscuous women, a subject which I am ashamed to say is still nagging at me.

Although popular opinion in the media seems to be that it's OK for women to sleep around these days, general opinion among the lads in the pub is that it certainly bloody isn't. Indeed, given that most of them would shag anything that walks given half a chance, I was quite surprised at the level of malice involved when talking about the promiscuity of potential girlfriends. Kev went so far as to say that, if he found out that his bird had been with anything more than seven other geezers, he would dump her on the spot. Although, given that I can think of at least eight lads who went through his last one before he met her, including Mike and Sean, I doubt the sincerity of that statement.

It's all bollocks of course. But I suspect it has more to do with our inbred sense of insecurity than any sense of morals. After all, if a bird has been with loads of other blokes, she's got more to compare us to. Then again, after four pints and only a bag of crisps for lunch, what the fuck do I know?

Wednesday 28 June

10.00 a.m. – At work

After a quiet evening in with Emma, I've come to work this morning in a foul mood. Not with anyone else, but with myself. I know it's pathetic and I'm ashamed of myself for even thinking about it let alone caring, but I just can't escape the idea that Emma has been about a bit.

The stupid thing is, I know it's none of my business. She's twenty-six years old and single. What she did before we met has absolutely nothing to do with me, so why am I so bothered?

11.30 a.m. – At work

I'm still worrying about Emma's past, and it's getting so bad I've now begun to wonder if she spent her formative years doing porno movies for Liz's old man. What the fuck is wrong with me?

15.10 p.m. – At work

Emma has just called. She obviously picked up on my mood at lunchtime because she asked me if anything's wrong. Knowing that she's worried about me has made me feel even worse. Now I feel guilty for being a prick, guilty for thinking the worst and guilty for causing her unnecessary grief.

22.45 p.m. – At home

As we walked to Euston tonight, Emma stopped me and asked if she'd upset me. As soon as she said it, I looked at her and for the first time in as long as I can remember, felt a lump come into my throat. Because I suddenly realised that I was being a total prick.

After two years on my own, I find a woman who, for some strange reason, actually likes me, and I'm doing my head in over something which almost certainly isn't true and which, even if it were, I have no control over. What's more, in the great scheme of things, it doesn't even matter. And to make it even worse, she's upset because she thinks she's upset me! I need my fucking bumps felt.

Thursday 29 June

09.25 a.m. – At work

Although I think she believed me when I told her nothing was wrong last night, I've come to work determined to make things up to Emma. I've been bang out of order the last few days and, in truth, feel seriously guilty for the way I've been acting. So a bunch of flowers are on order and a table booked for tonight.

Sadly, she isn't so chirpy. The sounds of Mike and Helena going at it hammer and tongs kept her up half the night. However, as it's her own fault, something I was more than happy to point out, she can't really moan about it.

11.30 a.m. – At work

I have made another decision, this time, one that's a lot more personal. And it's about this diary. The fact is, I'm spending too much time on it. Not at work, that's not really a problem at all, but at home. Over the years, I've got into this habit of writing stuff on floppy and then taking it home every night to download on to my PC. And as I sit there, I write more stuff.

I enjoy it and all that, but it's a habit I have to break because now that Emma is spending more and more time at the flat, I'm getting slightly concerned that she might sneak a look at it one day which could be a disaster. I've even put in a password now and have started to cut and paste the floppy stuff on to my hard drive rather than copy it. That way, I know it's not left lying around.

I don't intend to stop though. Mostly because, after years of crap, I would like to be able to look back on some good times one day. But I do have to write less. At least at home.

14.35 p.m. – At work

Emma has just rung to thank me for her flowers. She sounded quite emotional.

23.30 p.m. – At home

After a nice meal with Emma, we went to her local where we found Mike and Helena. Something which is becoming increasingly irritating. Not only because I'd rather be alone with Emma, but it seems that their relationship, if you can call it that, revolves around how many times they can have sex in a single evening. Great for them, but hugely embarrassing for us. And, truth to tell, a bit of a bastard for me. She's much too fit for the likes of him.

Friday 30 June

12.30 p.m. – At work

As the number two in the department, the entire morning has been spent with Julia going through the annual appraisals. An incredibly rewarding experience as it gives me the opportunity to gain revenge for all the shit things people have done to me this year. Nothing like an abuse of power to cleanse the soul.

13.50 p.m. – At work

Emma has just rung for a chat and told me that she's going out with some of her mates in Watford tonight. More importantly, I have been invited along. This should be fun. An evening in the company of a group of young nubile women all out on the pull.

And for some bizarre reason, she also called me 'sugar plum'. What the fuck's that about?

23.50 p.m. – At home

I learnt a lesson tonight. And it is one I will never forget. Over the years, I have seen loads of blokes drunk out of their skulls as poor women try in vain to get them home. They are embarrassed and humiliated but above all, they are angry. I have always wondered why these women don't just walk off and leave the arseholes because I always thought that if I were in their shoes, I would. But now I know better. Because Emma didn't just get drunk tonight, she got shit-faced.

Usually, nothing pisses me off more than a drunken woman. More often than not, they're loud, mouthy, crude and above all, bloody offensive. By ten o'clock, Emma was just like that. When she told the barmaid in O'Neill's that I was the best shag she'd ever had, I almost died on the spot.

But because it was Emma, and because she was having such a good time, I couldn't do anything but look after her. And watching her lolling about and dribbling in the back of a taxi on the way home didn't make me angry at all. In fact, it made me laugh. Because I know she had a good time.

And as I'm sitting here typing this, I've begun to realise that, despite all my reservations about her, I'm actually glad that she's lying in my bed in what I can only describe as a coma. Not because she's handy for sex, although that is a very important part. But because of all the other stuff as well. I've missed waking up next to someone and having a cuddle. I didn't really know it, but I have.

And if Emma's happy to be here, then I'm more than happy to have her here. I just hope she doesn't throw up.

Chapter 8

July

Saturday 1 July

11.30 a.m. – At home

I've just taken Emma home. Understandably after the amount she drank last night, she feels like shit and needs to have a soak and get changed.

At least she apologised for her behaviour, although it was pretty clear that this was more because she thought she should rather than because of what she can actually remember.

Sunday 2 July

23.50 p.m. – At home

After a quiet evening in last night to let Emma recover, we surprised Lou and Ray this morning by deciding at the last minute to take the kids off their hands and go to Southend for the day. Despite my fear of heights and hatred of queuing, it was brilliant. The kids loved it and Emma, now fully fit again, had a blast. But God knows how parents deal with their offspring twenty-four hours a day. Much as I love the little buggers, I was glad to hand them back. I am totally and utterly shagged out.

Monday 3 July

11.25 a.m. – At work

A strange morning. Having been forced to visit personnel by Julia, I was talking to the ugly bird when I suddenly realised that she's got a serious amount of facial hair. You could even call it a moustache.

It's nothing like my nan, or even Sue for that matter. It's very fine and blonde and, unless you get close, you can't really see it. But now I know it's there, it's going to drive me mad because every time I talk to her from now on, I'll end up staring at it. I know I will because that's what used to happen with my old English teacher Miss Saunders' breasts. It's the same thing. I was obsessed with them as well.

11.55 a.m. – At work

I've just spoken to Mike. He hasn't noticed ugly's moustache but has said he'll have a look and get back to me.

14.20 p.m. – At work

Great. We were in the pub at lunchtime when Mike told Kev about my facial hair fixation. He immediately got the arsehole and told me that I had no right to slag off his bird seeing as mine was a fat shortarse. When he said that, I lost the plot a bit and we ended up rolling around on the floor until a few of the others dragged us apart.

Now we've all been banned from the pub and I'm getting the blame because, according to lads' law, I shouldn't have had a pop at someone's bird behind their back. As a result, once again, no one is speaking to me. That is except for Mike. Not because he feels guilty for dropping me in it but because he knows full well that, if he causes problems for me, that could well have a knock-on effect with Helena. And he might be a twat and have a big mouth, but he's not stupid.

14.50 p.m. – At work

Brilliant. The events of lunchtime have obviously become the hot topic at work because now I've got Julia on my case for apparently dragging the name of the company through the mud by fighting in pubs. What a load of bollocks.

15.35 p.m. – At work

Emma has just called to make sure I'm all right. She actually sounds a bit upset so I'd best spend some time with her tonight.

Thinking about it now, I'm a bit surprised that I was so quick to jump to her defence at lunchtime. In all the time I've known her, although her weight has often been at the back of my mind, it's never really bothered me in so much as I've considered it a problem. Quite the opposite in fact. Over the last few weeks, I've started to think of her and her curves as being really sexy. Maybe I should tell her that.

16.15 p.m. – At work

Liz has rung to give me shit. She thinks that I've over-stepped the mark by taking the piss out of a female's facial hair. It is, by all accounts, a taboo subject and I now stand accused of sexual terrorism.

I can't get my head around that concept at all. If birds are that sensitive about facial hair, how can one of them spend hours staring in a mirror doing her makeup and not notice that she has a fucking moustache?

23.10 p.m. – At home

Although today was a poxy day, I managed to cheer Emma up on the way home and things took a sharp turn for the better when my arrival at home was greeted with a small pile of replies to my lonely hearts advert. I'd forgotten all about that.

Of the nine replies, three contained photos, although one was a nude picture of a fifty-year-old woman who, judging by the stretchmarks and saggy tits, must have had at least four children. The other two, although sadly fully clothed, looked quite decent. When I read the letters, I found out that one of them had a kid which ruled her out but the other was single. Diane of Moor Park, you are my girl. Or at least you would have been if I hadn't met Emma.

Tuesday 4 July

09.35 a.m. – At work

Emma seemed a bit fed up this morning so I've just e-mailed her to tell her that if she persists in calling me sugar plum rather than something slightly more masculine like butch, hunk or stud, I will have to think of a suitable response.

Although she's rung and told me to go ahead and do my worst, I've suddenly realised that this could be fraught with danger.

After all, a pet name is a reflection of how I see her, so unless I never want to have sex with her again, I best take my time and get it right.

09.50 a.m. – At work

I've just spent fifteen minutes trying to think of suitable names but all I've come up with so far is melons, tubby and piggy. All terms of endearment and affection as far as I'm concerned, but given yesterday's problems, hardly likely to win me anything other than grief.

Still no word from any of the lads. Not even Mike. They really are wankers.

10.05 a.m. – At work

Liz has just rung and asked me if I'd heard about what Kev did last night.

When I said no, she told me to meet her outside in about five minutes. Fuck me, this must be serious.

10.40 a.m. – At work

Holy fuck. By all accounts, Kev and ugly went out last night and they both got really pissed. But when he got back to her place, for some reason no one can work out, he waited until she was asleep, stuck a strip of Sellotape under her nose and ripped off her moustache.

When she woke up this morning, her lip was so red she had to call in sick. She's also given him the elbow and, because he's so gutted, he's also called a sickee. It's only the fact that she also has a mate who has a big mouth that anyone has found out.

Fuck knows how I'm going to fare here. But no doubt somewhere along the line it's all going to be my fault for bringing it up in the first place.

13.10 p.m. – At work

I have often used the expression 'that's the last thing I need' but I have never actually thought what the last thing I need would actually be. However, at least I now have a point of reference because it would be hard to imagine anything anyone would need less than receiving a bollocking in a packed-out café from a woman they hardly know.

All I was doing was standing there, waiting to pay for my sandwich, when one of the birds from personnel appears in front of me and starts giving me shit. According to her, I am somewhere between a pervert and scum. It was hard to tell exactly where because there were so many expletives included.

What is it about women that makes them adopt this air of solidarity every time some poor bloody male steps out of line? I mean it's not even as if I did anything. So why the bloody hell should this slapper have the hump with me?

It's not as if it's even any of her business. Not that she let a little point like that bother her. Oh no. She even involved the other women in the café. Now I'll never be able to go there again.

14.35 p.m. – At work

I've just had a call from Liz. Apparently, the bird who gave me shit at lunchtime thought I was Kev. However, when someone pointed out to her that I was the one who had got him all wound up about it, she at least claimed a partial victory. So that's all right then.

16.30 p.m. – At work

Bollocks. Julia wants me to go to Mitcham with her in the morning. Not what I wanted to hear at all. Can today get any fucking worse?

22.45 p.m. – At home

Emma has to do some stuff tonight so we stopped off for a quick drink before I went to the gym to work off my frustrations. Thankfully, she seems to think this is all really funny and we spent most of the time discussing the subject of her pet name. Cuddles seems favourite at the moment.

Luckily, Julia wasn't there. After the day I've had, I don't know if I could have dealt with that. Especially as I'm going to be stuck in a car with her for most of the day tomorrow. And judging by the look on her face this afternoon, I am not Mr Popular.

Wednesday 5 July

11.25 a.m. – At home

This morning, I've proved once and for all that I have no idea about women and what makes them tick. Because I didn't just fuck up, I fucked up big time.

When Julia picked me up at the flat, not only did she look stunning, but within about five minutes, she'd started going on about how warm it was. Then, she undid a button on her blouse revealing even more cleavage than she already had on show.

Of course, after everything that's gone on in the past, I started to think that she was after more than company on the journey. But to make sure, I casually mentioned that I was surprised she hadn't booked up for another spell on the beach by now. When she asked me what I meant, I replied that I'd have thought she'd rather be sunbathing somewhere hot than driving along the M1 in the rush hour with me.

I think I first suspected something was wrong when she did up the button on her blouse and pulled her skirt down a bit. But if I had any lingering doubts, they were swept aside when, after a minute or so of silence, she asked me straight out if I had, after all, looked at her holiday snaps. Like a total prick, rather than deny it, I said I had. At which point, she swerved on to the hard shoulder and launched into one of her tirades.

After accusing me of everything from sexual harassment to stalking, she leant across me, threw open the door and pushed me out before driving off and leaving me standing there like a prat. To make matters worse, I didn't even have any money with me as my wallet, and my phone, were hurtling down the motorway on the back seat of her Ford Focus.

As if that wasn't bad enough, and to put the perfect sealer on things, as I was standing there, the Old Bill pulls up and begins bollocking me for being on the hard shoulder without either a car or a good excuse. Still, at least they took me to a phone box so I could call a cab. Mind you, seeing the bastard's face as I handed over £15.30 in coppers from my change jar was almost worth the hassle.

The problem I've got now is, what the fuck am I going to do? I can't go to work. I'm supposed to be in Mitcham and my sudden appearance would almost certainly get people wondering. And if she goes in and starts ranting and raving about sexual harassment, it would be my word against hers and I'd lose. That'd mean the sack. More importantly, if Emma finds out, it'll be game over with her. And that means no more sex.

But I haven't even done anything. Well, except read the signals wrong this morning. That's hardly a hanging offence is it? Fucking women, if it's not one thing it's another.

12.10 p.m. – At home

Oh shit. Julia has just rung. She's cancelled her meeting in Mitcham and, having found all my stuff in the back of her car and tracked me down, will be here in five minutes. She also sounds quite angry which is not good. I wonder how she'll react to begging?

15.20 p.m. – At work

I guess all's well that ends well, but fuck me, that was a close call. When Julia turned up at the flat, she wasn't angry, but was actually quite calm.

After apologising for leaving me there, she said that, with hindsight, it was a bit stupid of her to have asked me to have her photographs developed, although she was a bit disappointed because she thought that as her deputy, she should be able to trust me. She then said that, as far as she was concerned, the matter is forgotten and we should get back to work and never mention it again. Something I was quite happy to agree to, which is why I'm sitting here rather than at home. My job may be boring as fuck, but it's better than the alternative.

I'm just glad she never found out I had a second set of prints made. I think the time has come for them to go.

15.35 p.m. – At work

I've just called Emma to tell her I'm at work and not in Surrey, but as soon as she spoke I suddenly started to feel seriously guilty.

Despite the fact that we've been going out together for a good few weeks, I was quite prepared to chase another bit of skirt this morning and I never even gave her a second thought. She deserves better than that. And really, I should be giving it to her. She's nice, pleasant and for some reason I still can't fathom, likes me a lot. And the more I think about it, the more I'm beginning to realise that I like her as well. I was stupid to put that at risk and it could have turned out really nasty. It's a mistake I don't intend to make again.

I just hope to fuck that Julia never tells anyone. I sure as shit won't.

16.00 p.m. – At work

I still feel bad about this morning, but I'm also starting to get the serious arsehole with Julia. I don't care what she said, she's been giving me the come-on for months and she knew exactly what she was doing when she gave me those photographs. Admittedly, that was all pre-Emma and I should have known better, but she can hardly get the hump when it all comes back to haunt her can she? Then again, maybe she realised that as she was driving away from me on the M1 this morning. Which could be why she came back, came clean and wants the whole thing forgotten.

Shit, this is all getting too complicated for me. I badly need a drink. But as the lads still aren't talking to me, it looks like it'll be a night out with Emma. Although I'm not exactly unhappy about that. Quite the opposite in fact.

22.40 p.m. – At home

Nice though it was to be with Emma, once we actually got in a pub I realised that I wasn't in the mood, so in the end told her I felt a bit ropy and came home.

To be honest, I was glad of the chance to get in and be by myself. Well, at least I was until I walked in and found that the second post had brought another six replies to my advert. None of which had photos in but all of which made me feel even more guilty.

And to top that off, as I was sitting in the bath, the old man rang and left a message on the machine. By all accounts, Lou's told him I have a female in my life and he wants to meet her on Friday night when he's taking us out. He also asked again that, for once, I try not to vomit. Apparently it's sending out mixed messages to his future wife.

Thursday 6 July

09.10 a.m. – At work

After a long and restless night struggling with my conscience, it was a blessed relief to meet Emma at Bushey. She does look increasingly attractive and, for once, when we stepped of the train and she slid her arm through mine, I actually felt quite relieved.

Sadly, when I told her that she'd be meeting my old man, she got quite excited. I guess having met both Lou and me, she thinks he's normal. Is she in for a shock. I just hope she doesn't wear anything low-cut.

09.50 a.m. – At work

Just been in with Julia. She seems a bit subdued and very professional this morning, which is most unlike her.

I must admit, I was tempted to say something to clear the air a bit but, knowing me, I'd only have made things worse so decided to keep quiet.

10.40 a.m. – At work

Bumped into Mike just now. At least he's speaking to me, even though all he did was moan about still being banned from the pub.

I'm beginning to wonder if keeping in with them is really worth all the hassle.

11.50 a.m. – At work

Rang Liz for a chat and, thankfully, at least as far as she's concerned, I have been totally forgiven for the stuff with Kev and the ugly bird.

Much as I like being with Emma, she hasn't been able to replace Liz in the gossiping stakes. To be honest, I wouldn't want her to. It's nice having someone else to talk to and I've missed spending time with her. Sadly, judging by the fact that she and Paul are still together, it's a sentiment she doesn't seem to share.

15.20 p.m. – At work

Out of the blue, as we ate our lunch, Emma broached the subject of holidays and told me that she thinks we should go away together. After almost losing her a few days ago, even though she doesn't know it, I have to say, I think that this is a top idea. Especially as I have a ton of time off due to me and if I don't use it soon, I'm going to lose it. Besides, a break from all of this will do me good.

The only decision we need to make is where and for how long? Something we shall decide tonight.

22.00 p.m. – At home

As soon as I mentioned that my mum lives in New York, the decision was made. Emma's never been before and I love the place so that's that. I'll check it with the old girl tomorrow, sort out the dates with work and then it's all systems go. I'm already getting quite excited.

Friday 7 July

16.10 p.m. – At work

Bless her heart, Emma has been on about going to New York all day. At lunchtime, she even dragged me to the travel agents and gathered up armfuls of brochures.

Checked with Mum, she's cool and so we fly out to the States at six o'clock in the morning on the twenty-first for ten whole days and back in time for the first game of the season. Fantastic.

Monday 10 July

10.10 a.m. – At work

A mixed bag of a weekend. Friday night with the old man wasn't as bad as I expected. He didn't mention Emma's chest once and my fledgling step-mum was actually quite nice. She has a warped sense of humour as well, which kind of explains why she's taken up with the old man. And despite the fact that we were in a packed restaurant, was more than happy to relate the tales of my barfing to my highly amused partner. As for Emma, she was great as always. Even the old man was charmed by her and, for once, he seems pleased that I'm actually happy. He even complimented me on my slimline frame which is a first.

Sadly, the rest of my weekend revolved around what is becoming an increasingly hated pastime, shopping. Emma has told me that she plans to spend a small fortune in New York, which means that some of the stuff she has in her flat will need to go. However, she still needs stuff to take out with her and what she has got isn't suitable. I'm sure that there's some kind of logic in there somewhere but if I think about it any more, I'll lose the will to live. The decision to just go with the flow was not hard to make.

14.55 p.m. – At work

After a few days' hesitation, I have bitten the bullet and shredded my photos of Julia. They were just too risky for me to hang on to and, while I will mourn their passing, having spent the last ten minutes gazing across the office at her bending over her desk, it is a comfort to know that the real things will never be far away.

I've said it before and will say it again; she might be a pain in the arse, but she's got great tits.

15.20 p.m. – At work

Emma has just rung and told me that she has to stay in tonight as Helena is going to help her perform major surgery on her wardrobe. That means either a night sorting out my flat or a night in the gym. Not the most difficult choice I've had today.

23.50 p.m. – At home

I finally crossed paths with Julia in the gym tonight. She'd obviously been there a while because, by the time I arrived, she was both hot and very sweaty. And she looked bloody awesome. So much so that for a second, the idea of trying it on again actually went through my mind. An idea which quickly vanished when I thought of myself standing on the hard shoulder of the M1.

After overcoming the inevitable, and very awkward, embarrassment, I grasped the initiative and told her that we needed to clear the air a bit. So we went for a coffee and did just that. Hopefully, now things can get back to normal.

I'm actually quite relieved. And not just because I don't need Julia as an enemy at work. Things seem to be going OK with Emma and I'm really starting to enjoy it. I even referred to her as my girlfriend today. Something I would never have done a few weeks or even days ago. Maybe Liz was right all along.

Two more replies on the mat tonight. One with a photo of an extremely fit blonde bird from Rickmansworth. Sorry love, I'm spoken for.

Tuesday 11 July

14.50 p.m. – At work

Shit. Emma told me at lunchtime that, as she's met my sister and my dad, and will soon meet my mum, it's about time I met her folks. This is bad. Coming face-to-face with fathers for the first time is my worst nightmare. Mostly because I know exactly what they're thinking. If I had a daughter, I'd be concerned about who was doing what to his little girl, and how often, as well.

Still, I guess it had to come sooner or later. I'll just have to make sure she briefs me first. I don't want a repeat of the slanging match I had with Maria's dad when I met him even though it wasn't my fault. If she'd told me her old man was a Scum Town supporter, I'd never have gone out with her in the first place.

Wednesday 12 July

09.40 a.m. – At work

Spent the evening in the pub with Emma last night pumping her for information about her folks. He's called Tom and she's called Janet. Common ground is that, like me, they eat meat, hate dogs, aren't religious and love Gaby Roslin. Dodgy ground is that, unlike me, they vote Labour, he doesn't drink and likes rugby while, for some strange reason, she has an intense dislike of Geri Halliwell. More worryingly, Emma has now broken the news that, although he now runs his own security company, he is actually an ex-copper. A detail which really should have been mentioned when we first started going out together.

The other important item of information is that they both hate football. So at least that's the biggest minefield out of the way. But I get the distinct impression that Emma's a bit of a daddy's girl, so I need to be wary. Best not drop anything about her astonishing sexual prowess into the conversation.

The one big bonus of course is that, when I do get to meet her mum, it should give me a good idea of what Emma will look like in thirty years' time. Blimey, there's a thought. What will Emma mean to me in thirty years? Will she be my beautiful wife and the mother of my children? Or will she simply be a distant memory dragged up when life is shit and I need to remember a moment of happiness? Who knows. I daren't think that far ahead or I'll go mad.

10.25 a.m. – At work

Liz has just called and told me that she's split with Paul. She sounds devastated and, without thinking, I offered to meet her after work. Oops.

14.30 p.m. – At work

Spoke to Emma at lunch and told her about my offer to provide a shoulder for Liz. Incredibly, given the response last time, she was fine and told me to ring her when I got home. Although touched by her trust, I sense a test of the 'forget and we're finished' variety.

22.15 p.m. – At home

As suspected, Liz is totally gutted. By all accounts, the dreaded 'L' word had been bandied about between Paul and her, and I know how hard it would have been for her to fall that hard for a bloke. To get it thrown back in her face is a serious knock-back.

I rang Emma on the way back from Liz's to be told that the meet with her folks is on Friday night. Just the news I needed on top of an evening of the blubbing female variety.

Thursday 13 July

10.50 a.m. – At work

As a result of some selfish bastard throwing himself under a train at Harrow, I had to go back home and drive into work. This meant that, not only was I late for work, but I missed meeting Emma on the way. And now I'm in a bad mood because I have to drive home, which is a bloody nightmare. Still, it could be worse: when I nipped in to see Emma, she told me that Liz has called in and taken a couple of days off. She must be in a bad way.

11.15 a.m. – At work

Just called Liz at home but no answer. Couldn't get anything on her mobile either.

12.00 p.m. – At work

As I am still avoiding personnel, I got Emma to check out Liz's next of kin. Luckily, they were listed as her folks and a quick call confirmed my suspicions that she has taken refuge at the porno villa.

I have to say, it was a relief to hear her voice, however shaky. After seeing the state she was in last night, I was getting quite worried.

Friday 14 July

09.40 a.m. – At work

Thanks to my wonderful Peugeot, last night I was able to drive us directly to the flat where we had a take-away, lots of sex and watched telly. Just what I needed after the last few days.

Then again, tonight could be just as traumatic in its own way.

14.50 p.m. – At work

Mike called earlier and told me that the ban from the pub has been lifted. Largely, I suspect, as a result of the dramatic fall in profits. He then told me that there was a mass invasion planned for lunchtime and everyone was going, including me.

Although a bit wary, it actually turned out all right although Kev still has the arse because the ugly bird isn't speaking to him at all now and the rest of the women at work hate him even more than they hate me. Something to be grateful for anyway. I still haven't forgiven him for slagging off Emma like that.

But I have missed being in the pub with the lads. I mean,

spending time with Emma is fantastic, but would she ever be able to tell me a joke about a cheese-flavoured condom? Not in a million years. I bloody hope she wouldn't anyway.

15.10 p.m. – At work

Just rung Emma and told her the joke about the cheese-flavoured condom. Not only did she not think it was funny, she made me promise under pain of castration not to tell it to her dad tonight.

17.30 p.m. – At home

Oh well, this is it. Washed, dressed and with my best manners fitted, it's time to leave for Northwood and the delights of Emma's folks. Once more unto the breach dear friends.

Monday 17 July

09.40 a.m. – At work

I'm living a bloody nightmare. And it's all down to Friday night. It wasn't that anything went wrong. In fact quite the opposite. They were OK and we seemed to get on, although I got the impression that if I'd have so much as laid a hand on her in his presence, her dad would have punched my lights out. And when after yet another Saturday spent traipsing around shops, Emma rang them to find out what they thought of me, her ex-copper of an old man somewhat predictably told her that he was sure he'd seen my photo in a briefing somewhere.

But I can live with all that, because it pales into insignificance beside the problem I now find myself facing. A poxy wedding.

As we sat down to eat, Emma's mum dropped the bombshell that her cousin, who is getting married in three weeks' time, has bowed to family pressure and changed her wedding plans from a small, intimate affair in a registry office to a full-bore church and marquee do in Surrey. As a result, Emma is now wanted as chief bridesmaid. An invitation she immediately accepted with great excitement and, tragically, on my behalf. I say tragically, because in three weeks' time, it's the first day of the football season. And having memorised the fixture list within hours of it coming out, I immediately knew that on the day Emma is at her cousin's wedding in deepest, darkest Surrey, I will be in deepest, darkest Yorkshire watching the Hornets beat Huddersfield. Even if I avoid the traditional piss-up and break every speed limit, I won't even get to the reception till after eight or nine.

Of course, I should've seen this coming. I only met Emma as last season finished and, as we have never really discussed this side of my life, she is clearly unaware that my attendance at every home game is obligatory as are the first and last away trips. Indeed, to avoid situations just like this one, weddings, christenings, illness and even funerals are all arranged so that they take place during the close season. Everyone knows that. Everyone, it seems, except Emma, her cousin and the sad excuse for a male she is marrying. After all, what kind of bloke is it that doesn't like football? God only knows what she's going to say when I tell her.

Still, at least her mum is a bit of a looker, which bodes well for the future. That's if we have a future after this.

11.30 a.m. – At work

Emma is driving me up the bloody wall. If it's not holidays, it's weddings. The latest is that she's taken the day off tomorrow and will be staying with her folks tonight so that they can take her to Surrey for her dress fitting in the morning.

On the plus side . . . shit. There isn't a plus side. At least not one that I can see.

20.50 p.m. – At home

Dropped Emma off at her folks' and headed for the gym. Luckily, Julia wasn't there so I was able to put myself through a severe workout while trying to think of the least painful way to drop the bad news.

Of course the best thing would have been to tell her straight away. Because now, not only is she going to have the right hump, but her folks, influenced as they undoubtedly are by a life of copperdom, are going to think I'm everything from unreliable to dishonest. Jesus, why is life so tough?

Tuesday 18 July

09.15 a.m. – At work

Called Liz this morning to see how she is. Everything seems OK, although she still sounds gutted. I don't know what this Paul geezer had but, whatever it was, he must have had a lot of it.

Not surprisingly, she told me that she's taking a couple of weeks off work to stay with her folks which means that I won't see her before we go on holiday. A bit of a bummer, but there you go. I'll bring her something nice back. From the two of us, naturally.

10.00 a.m. – At work

I've just had the strangest phone call. From, of all people, Barry the wanker. He wants me to help him stage a repeat of his now famous vegetable soup trick but, this time, with me as the stooge. He reckons that if he pretends to barf and I walk over and eat a few chunks, it could have a massive impact on whoever we choose as a victim. He was even talking in fainting terms.

He sounded quite gutted when I told him to piss off. I like the idea, but he's a twat of the first order. And besides, the thought of eating cold veggie soup at this time of the morning does not appeal.

I wouldn't mind seeing who he pulls it on though. Last time apparently, Lyndsy from accounts almost threw up when he popped the first chunk in his mouth.

10.25 a.m. – At work

Barry the wanker has just called again. He is desperate to do this but says that, if it's going to work, it has to involve someone no one else would suspect – me. If only he knew, the bastard.

10.50 a.m. – At work

Fuck me. He's rung again. Doesn't he ever give up?

14.15 p.m. – At work

Spent lunchtime in the pub with Mike and, after he'd discussed his sexual exploits with Helena, I mentioned my wedding-day plight. As I expected, his response wasn't what I would call sympathetic. Phrases such as 'What kind of a supporter are you?' and 'You can always get another bird, the first away game only happens once' made his position quite clear. If only it were that simple.

14.50 p.m. – At work

Mike has just rung and told me that he's spoken to some of the lads and they are now watching to see what I'm going to do. Apparently, even my status as a fair-weather fan hangs in the balance now. Cheeky bastards. Oh well, whatever happens, someone is going to get let down badly and, no matter who that is, I'm the one that'll suffer.

15.25 p.m. – At work

Yesssss! Once in a while, life is indeed sweet. As I suspected, there was more to the Barry the wanker calls than met the eye. He was running a double bluff.

The reason he wanted me to be the one to walk over and start eating the carrots was that he didn't want me as a stooge, he wanted me as the victim. Because instead of vegetable soup, he had brought in a bag of freshly barfed vomit obtained from his bulimic sister Andrea.

Sadly, the new lad in admin wasn't as switched on as me. And when Barry the wanker decided that, if I wouldn't play, he should at least get someone, the poor bastard, probably in a sad effort to establish himself as 'one of the lads', walked right into it.

As a result, he ended up becoming the second person to swallow that particular spoonful of Irish stew. Not, I would hazard a guess, a pleasant experience.

Tragically, as Barry was busily celebrating both his victory over the new lad and the sight of Sarah with the big tits heaving violently in the corner, his male victim made it known in the most obvious of ways that, while he might look like a skinny runt, he is in fact, a former Essex schoolboy Tae Kwon Do champion.

No doubt when Barry gets out of casualty later on tonight he'll see the funny side.

Wednesday 19 July

09.30 a.m. – At work

Spent last night with Emma and her folks. In between avoiding the glares from her old man and trying not to burst out laughing at the thought of Barry the wanker in casualty, I found out that the reason for the switch in wedding plans was because her entire extended family are very close and there are a fair few only children dotted around. Emma for one, her mum for another. They are also spread around a bit, and so anything like a wedding is a major social occasion. Hence a huge do rather than a small one.

Although glad I now have this important knowledge at my disposal, I can't help thinking of them all as selfish bastards.

10.15 a.m. – At work

Emma just called and told me that word in admin is that Barry the wanker has not only got a broken jaw and badly bruised ribs, but he's been suspended, again. Tragically, the new lad has been sacked and, if Barry decides to press charges, might even be charged by the Old Bill for assault.

A bit out of order really. Personally, I'd have promoted him.

14.25 p.m. – At work

I finally bit the bullet and broached the subject of the wedding with Emma at lunchtime. Even as I said 'because it's the first day of the football season' I knew exactly how pathetic it must have sounded.

To say she is not best pleased is, to put it mildly, an understatement.

23.30 p.m. – At home

Football, so often the cause of heartache and dismay in my life, is once again causing me problems. However, this time they really are serious and, what's more, they are personal. I've just spent the evening trying to explain, or rather justify, my love affair with the Hornets to Emma. Hard enough at the best of times but, to a recently obtained girlfriend who hates football and has a big day on the horizon, a potentially life-threatening experience.

Incredibly, for a short time I thought I'd pulled it off. After I'd said my piece, she quite calmly told me that she hasn't really got a problem coming to terms with the fact that a good part of our relationship will revolve around the exploits of eleven overpaid yobs (as she so delicately put it). But in a voice that was remarkably similar to the one my mum used to use whenever she caught me reading Dad's copies of *Fiesta*, she added that what she would not accept was that those same eleven overpaid yobs were more important to me than her. And the best way for me to prove that is to be at that wedding. The choice, apparently, is mine. Or rather, it isn't. Because as much as I love the Hornets, they can't give me the things that Emma can.

But I think I'll leave telling the lads about it until I get back from New York.

Thursday 20 July

09.20 a.m. – At work

My last day at work. Thank fuck. At least Emma is in a better mood, although I don't know if it's because her holiday is imminent or because she's enjoying the thrill of knowing that she's got her boyfriend exactly where she wants him.

10.10 a.m. – At work

Mike has just called and, in his most sarcastic tone, asked me if I'll be needing a ticket for Huddersfield. To avoid any ridicule, I told him to go ahead. At least if my prayers get answered and the wedding's called off, the day won't get wasted.

12.10 p.m. – At work

Just rung Liz for a last chat before my holiday. She told me to have a great time, spoil Emma rotten and bring her back something nice: George Clooney, if I can find him.

At least she sounds a lot more cheerful. Shame I couldn't get to see her.

17.00 p.m. – At work

Just been in to see Julia who, like Liz, told me to have a great holiday and bring her back something nice.

I said that I would. Not just to keep the peace, but because I want to. She's not so bad really. And she has got those tits after all.

17.45 p.m. – At work

Well, that's that then. No more work, no more lads and no more Julia for ten whole days. Instead, after an early night tonight, I'll be heading for Gatwick and then New York with a slightly domineering, but increasingly gorgeous bird in tow. I can't bloody wait.

Chapter 9

August

Thursday 3 August

03.10 a.m. – At home

We're back. Well, actually, we got back yesterday but, thanks to jet-lag, my body clock is all over the place which is why I'm sitting here wide awake at ten past three in the morning. Emma, however, seems to be immune to the effects of time zones because, as I'm writing this, she's in the bedroom fast asleep. Well, asleep isn't exactly true. I think she's in more of a coma judging by the hour I've just wasted trying to wake her up for a bout of horizontal combat.

As for the holiday, apart from the heat, it was brilliant. Emma had a blast and, like me, is now in love with the place. I'd hate to be there when she opens her credit card bill though. I had no idea one person could spend so much money with so little effort.

Although there were many great things that happened in New York, if I had to pick one to remember it by, I suppose it came when we were walking along one night and I suddenly realised that, for the first time in my life, I had a woman all to myself. No distractions, no complications, no work and no mates. Just me and her. It's not often you'll ever hear a bloke say it, but it was bloody romantic. And I know she felt the same. Because she told me.

We actually talked a lot while we were away, and most of that hinted at where we were going. Relationship-wise I mean. Well, to be honest, she did most of the talking, I just listened. Why do women know all this stuff and us blokes just stumble along?

I suppose what I'm trying to say is that, having been alone with her for two whole weeks, after what is only a relatively short time together, I've seriously begun to consider the possibility that maybe Liz was right all along and Emma and me really are suited. I certainly think the world of her and can't believe that we got on so well over there. Shit, I've got so used to being with her that I don't even want to think about what it would be like if she ever left.

Oh well, it's back to reality later. For me at least, Emma's well safe. Within an hour of touching down she'd rung work and told them she wouldn't be in until Monday because of the wedding. And of course, being women, they understood perfectly. When I called Julia, before I could say a word, she told me she wants to see me first thing this morning. Wonderful.

10.35 a.m. – At work

As I'm at work and Emma isn't, I brought in the seven lonely heart replies which came while I was away, and have just opened them. Sadly, none contained photos which is a bit of a bummer. Despite the nice letters, I wouldn't fancy getting in touch with someone I hadn't seen. She might be a right old tug.

15.30 p.m. – At work

Met Liz for lunch and gave her a huge box of jelly beans and a poster of George Clooney. She looks really well but she's not her old self. The old spark isn't there yet. That wanker certainly has something to answer for.

Sadly, despite the fact that she also got a carton of jelly beans, Julia has been on my case about targets all morning. I've also had to give Kev twenty quid for a ticket to a game I have no hope of going to. Not good, although at least he's speaking to me again.

Not much news though. Other than the fact that Barry the wanker is back at work and on a final written warning.

16.50 p.m. – At work

God almighty, I am shagged out. I need to get home badly. I'm so tired, even typing is an effort.

Friday 4 August

10.00 a.m. – At work

When I got home last night, Emma had just got up. As a result, when I collapsed into bed at about half nine, she was wide awake. But rather than be bored watching telly in the front room by herself, she decided it would be much better to watch it in bed with me. Better for her of course: for me, it was a pain in the arse.

First she got the hump because I asked her to turn it down, then I got the hump because she wouldn't stop fidgeting and then, because there was nothing on, she started getting all horny. And then, after I had satisfied her carnal desires and was finally on the point of returning to unconsciousness, she lifted herself up on one elbow and said 'What are you thinking about?'

Why do women ask that? Surely each and every female who has ever had sex must know by now that, as soon as the old baby juice has been dispensed, the male brain switches off sex and jumps to something entirely unrelated. We can't help it.

Of course, to keep her happy, I lied. And told her I was thinking about how wonderful she was and how lucky I am to have found her which was exactly what she wanted to hear. But the truth of the matter is that the only thing on my mind at that particular moment was how I'm going to tell the lads that I'm not going on Saturday.

And to be honest, it still is. And I still don't know.

12.05 p.m. – At work

I'm sure the lads can sense something. They keep asking me about tomorrow, but I haven't the bottle to own up to my weakness. Sean almost got it out of me by saying that he's got a mate desperate for a ticket, but when I told him I only had the one, he burst out laughing. Wanker.

The irony is, after spending a fortune in New York, the twenty quid would come in handy.

14.55 p.m. – At work

The deed is done. I told them in the pub at lunchtime that, unless a miracle happens and the wedding is called off before I leave for Surrey in the morning, I will not be travelling north with my fellow Hornets. As expected, the abuse was merciless. And richly deserved. I am weak.

All I can hope for now is that Yorkshire suffers an unseasonable snowfall over night. But given that it's been in the mid eighties all day, I'm not holding my breath.

Still, at least Mike offered to offload my ticket. Although he'll take his usual fifty per cent. Better something than nothing I suppose.

22.10 p.m. – At home

After falling asleep on the train and ending up in Berkhampstead, I got home late and, after a quick bite to eat with Emma – who judging by the pile of dishes in the sink, has done fuck-all all day – took her home so that she can sort herself out for tomorrow.

I'm dreading it already. Especially as she told me that her old man got the hump when she told him that it would be easier if she travelled down with me and not him. Just what I need on top of everything else. A day getting the evil eye from an ex-copper.

Saturday 5 August

09.10 a.m. – At home

I thought it would be bad, but I didn't know it would be this bad. This really is the worst day of my life. As Kev and the lads are heading up the M1 for the glories of Huddersfield and meat and potato pies, I'm sitting at home in my best suit waiting until I have to go and get Emma. I cannot believe that I'm missing the first game of the season. Not only that, but I'm missing it to go to the wedding of someone I've never met to a bloke I already dislike. I can't even begin to imagine what the lads are saying about me, but it must be bad. My ears are burning.

Thankfully, I've got a little radio which sits in my jacket pocket quite well, and if I use an earpiece, I should get to hear some of the game. Not in church of course, but outside when we're all hanging around.

I may not be there in body, but at least I'll hear what's going on.

11.45 a.m. – Café

After a nightmare journey down during which Emma moaned, or rather panicked, about everything from a brand new spot on her cheek to the size of her arse, I've just dropped her at her cousin's (huge) house and they've thrown me out. Never mind the fact that I don't know anyone, have no real idea where I am and am wearing my best suit. There are too many women in different states of undress, panic and make-up to allow an unfamiliar male to be present. So I have to go.

To be honest, it's a relief to get out of there. I could do with the peace and quiet. But I've still got over three bloody hours to kill and, as I can't be arsed to mix with any of the football-hating low-lives that were hanging around outside the (huge) house, I've adjourned to a local café with only my palmtop, a cup of tea and the *Sun* for company. I won't see Emma now until just before three thirty when she gets to the church. But if nothing else happens today, at least I know she'll look stunning.

Yet despite everything else, my thoughts are with the lads as they head up the M1. If I had even the slightest notion that they'd speak to me, I'd ring them up.

13.20 p.m. – Café

Bollocks! I can't receive Three Counties on my radio! Not even through the interference! I bloody hate coming this far south. Now I'll have to resort to Radio Five or Talk Sport in the hope that for once they'll give out the Watford score.

14.25 p.m. – Car

After a much-needed pint in a pub, I returned to the car to find that, joy of joys, I can just about hear Three Counties on the stereo. If I sit here until the very last moment, at least I'll get to hear the pre-match build-up and the first twenty or so minutes. I might even be able to sneak out during the service.

15.00 p.m. – Car

It's three o'clock. Kick-off time. Two hundred miles from where I'm sitting, my glorious lads are starting what will almost certainly turn out to be the best game of the season and they're doing it without me. Bastards, how selfish can you get? Why don't games get abandoned when you need them to?

15.20 p.m. – Car

Emma has arrived and, as I thought she would, she looks stunning. How can a woman who displays even the remotest sense of affection for me look so beautiful? Maybe I've made the right decision after all. The game sounds boring as shite.

16.35 p.m. – Car

I've been in trouble many times in my life, but I doubt that any of those come even close to the amount of excreta I will be swimming around in when Emma gets hold of me.

Everything was going so well. I was sitting right up at the back all on my own and had turned the radio right down until it was a strain even to hear it through the earpiece. The service was going great, everyone was happy and then what happens? Just as the vicar asks if anyone knew of any just cause why these two football-hating gits should not be joined in a life of tedium and nappies, Tom bloody Watt announces that Watford have just scored. And what do I do? Course I do.

I cannot even begin to describe how I felt at that precise moment, nor do I know how long the sound of my hissed 'Yes!'

echoed around the church. But I know one thing, I am dead.

Still, at least the lads are holding on.

17.05 p.m. – Car

As I predicted, Emma is furious with me, although for once I have had a stroke of luck and found an unlikely ally. The groom, far from being a football-hating low-life as I had first imagined, is in fact, a season ticket-holder at Arsenal. Leaving aside that obvious failing, he is at least speaking up for me, as are most of his mates who are also regulars at Highbury.

Of course, my immediate reaction was 'How could any footie fan get married during the season?' to which he replied rather smugly that as they are in the Premier League *their* season doesn't start for another week and if Watford were a half-decent side I wouldn't have been in this mess anyway. I have to admit, he's got a point.

Unfortunately, although their defence of me and my actions is sound and from the heart, Emma is far from accommodating. I have, apparently, heaped shame upon her and have also shown that Watford are more important to me than she is. I do believe grovelling of the highest order will be needed later.

On the plus side, she's had to travel to the reception with the bride's parents for some odd reason, which has left me to follow along on my own. And thanks to Mr Blaupunkt, I managed to hear a typically biased local radio report of a glorious Watford victory. At least something went well this afternoon.

Sunday 6 August

23.10 p.m. – At home

What a fucking weekend! Surely among the worst of my entire bastard life.

As if what happened in the church wasn't bad enough, things got even worse at the reception when the best man interrupted his speech to humiliate me all over again by asking me what the final score was. Then, just as I was on the point of leaving because no one, including Emma, would speak to me, I overheard some tosser say to his mate 'Who's the wanker with the fat bird?'

Well of course, I wasn't having that. So I walked over and smacked the cunt. And then, after a lot of pushing and shoving, I suddenly realised that they weren't talking about me and Emma at all. But even though I apologised, they still threw me out.

As I was trying to work out what to do next, Emma came storming out after me and went mental. And now she isn't even speaking to me at all. I've been trying to get in touch with her all day but as she's staying with her folks, it's been impossible. I've spoken to her old man though. And when I told him what happened and why, he seemed quite impressed that I had defended the honour of his daughter. I suppose that's something.

Monday 7 August

10.15 a.m. – At work

No Emma on the train this morning and I've just found out why. She's called in sick. On top of everything else, I've had an hour of various women ringing me up to find out what's wrong with her. So far, I've resisted the temptation to say 'How the fuck would I know?' because I think it might get the tongues wagging a bit more than I would like.

If there is a silver lining to my weekend cloud, it's the fact that Mike got full price for my ticket which means that, with his fifty per cent fee, I lost only a tenner. And because of my traumatic weekend, the lads have excused my absence. Apparently, despite the three points, mine was far more interesting.

11.30 a.m. – At work

Thanks to my trouble with Emma, I can't concentrate on anything. I've tried to call both her folks and her flat but keep getting answerphones.

12.10 p.m. – At work

Still no answer from Emma and, although I'm getting increasingly worried, I'm also starting to feel a bit pissed off.

After all, I was going to football long before I met her. Bloody decades before actually. And the fact that I was prepared to give up what has been an annual tradition to go to a wedding with her should count for something. Instead, she's got a strop on just because I wanted to know how my lads were getting on. And then, she gets even worse when I slap some bloke who I thought was giving her a bit of mouth. A few weeks ago when I did exactly the same thing, she was all over me.

Well, bollocks. If she wants to sulk, then she can get on with it. I'm fucked if I'm going to let it upset me any more.

14.10 p.m. – At work

Just had lunch with Liz and told her all about my weekend. She's astonished, although sadly, not at Emma's behaviour, but at mine.

First she called me a prick because I ruined one of the biggest weekends of Emma's life. And then she said that I should track her down tonight and do whatever it takes to get her back. If I don't, she thinks I'll lose her for good.

Why is it that if a woman digs her heels in with a bloke, no matter what the rights and wrongs, every other female on the planet stands right behind her? Why should I be the one to climb down?

18.30 p.m. – At home

Judging by the fifteen 'beeps' on Emma's machine, I think the tape must be full up by now. I didn't realise that it was possible to feel sorry, embarrassed, gutted, desperate and angry all at the same time.

I'm sure that things could be worse. But at this moment, it's hard to imagine how.

23.45 p.m. – At home

Oh my lord. To get rid of some of my frustration, I went to the gym tonight and, after a pounding on the rowing machines, headed for the jacuzzi only to walk through the door as Julia was climbing out. A sight which immediately took pride of place in my top ten erotic images. At least the real-life ones.

When she saw me, she came over and, somehow, we ended up sitting in the foaming water discussing my problem with Emma. A not unpleasant experience I have to say.

She might be a pain in the arse sometimes, but this time in the gym is working wonders on her. Especially when she's clad in a very tight and soaking wet black one-piece swimming costume.

Tuesday 8 August

09.15 a.m. – At work

No Emma again this morning and she's still not answering the phone at her flat so I've just rung her folks. Unfortunately, the person who answered was her mum who told me that Emma didn't want to speak to me and put the phone down. I'll bloody remember that.

To make matters worse, rumours have spread among the women that we have split up and they are now on my case. After all, using typical female logic, whatever has happened is naturally my fault. It has to be, I'm a bloke.

09.40 a.m. – At work

Liz has just rung and, when I told her I didn't go and see Emma last night, she gave me shit. I'm starting to get a bit pissed off with her as well now.

11.10 a.m. – At work

Fucking great. Liz has just called and told me that, unlike me, she has managed to speak to Emma and, by all accounts, she's totally devastated by what has happened so she hopes I'm pleased with myself.

As it happens, I'm not exactly thrilled about it either, but what can I do? She won't answer my calls and she certainly hasn't called me. And as hard as I'm trying, it's proving bloody impossible to get in touch by telepathy.

14.15 p.m. – At work

As expected, the lads are right behind me on this one. A point of principle has been established and they all say I should stick to my guns.

Although relieved to have a few people on my side at last, I'm starting to think that, unless I can get to speak to Emma soon, Liz might be right. It could be game over. To be honest, although I miss her, I'm not really sure how I feel about that at the moment. Is it really worth all this grief?

15.00 p.m. – At work

Bloody hell! Julia has just asked me how things are going with the Emma situation. When I said it was looking a bit grim, she told me that if I needed someone to talk to, let her know and we could have a drink or something after work.

God only knows what 'or something' means. But it sounds a damn sight better than 'or nothing'.

16.10 p.m. – At work

Liz is obviously trying to play the role of the United Nations. She's just called and told me that she's spoken to Emma again and has given her my side of the story. Despite this, she still doesn't want to speak to me and has now taken the rest of the week off. Apparently, to think things through.

And here's me thinking relationships were all about caring and sharing. When all the time they were about peace-keeping and diplomacy.

16.25 p.m. – At work

Hang on a fucking minute. What the bloody hell does she need to think through exactly? If she'd caught me in bed with Helena or found me wearing her underwear, I could understand it. But she didn't. All I did was one stupid and one not so stupid thing. And considering that less than a week ago we were in New York having the time of our lives, I'm a bit pissed off that she needs time for anything.

Shitty death, if she's like this now, what's she going to be like if I ever do something serious?

Wednesday 9 August

06.35 a.m. – At home

I can't believe what I almost did last night. In fact, I can't even work out if fate stepped in and saved me, or it jumped up and kicked me in the bollocks out of spite.

After unsuccessfully trying to get though to Emma for half an hour, I gave up, went to the gym and was sitting in the jacuzzi trying to decide whether or not I should just bite the bullet and go round to see her, when Julia walked in.

To cut a long story short, we ended up having a coffee, then a drink, and then another drink. And then we went back to her place for another, and another, and then another. And then we somehow ended up rolling around on her front-room floor with our hands all over each other.

I'd just got her top off and was finally about to get my hands on her magnificent tits when, out of the blue, my bastard mobile rang. And, for some reason, the theme song from *The Simpsons* reminded me not of Homer or Bart, but of Emma. Something which not only killed the moment, but which also made me feel incredibly guilty. The fact that, when I answered it, Liz was on the other end asking me if I'd made contact with her yet only made me feel worse. Something Julia obviously picked up on because, by the time I'd got rid of Liz, she was up, her top was back on and she was in the kitchen making coffee.

Thankfully, she was cool about it. In fact, she thought it was quite funny. But as I was leaving, she gave me a kiss on the cheek and said something which really got me thinking. She said that I have to go and see Emma and speak to her face to face. Because that's the only way I'll ever know what it is that I want.

And she's right. Although I would dearly love to have spent more time with Julia's body, the idea of any kind of relationship with her terrifies me. She's too hot and cold. Emma, on the other hand, may not be able to match Julia in physical terms, but she's got a thousand times more personality and, despite what's happened these last few days, is a lot more fun to be with. And the more I think about it, the more I'm starting to realise that's what really counts.

09.35 a.m. – At work

I've just been in to see Julia and apologise for last night. She just smiled and told me not to worry about it. But I can't help thinking that she sounded a bit down. Well, I actually kind of hope she is. After all, she almost had me.

09.55 a.m. – At work

I've just tried Emma again but can't get anything other than an answering machine either at her house or her flat.

10.30 a.m. – At work

Liz has just been down to see if there's been any developments. Much as I'd love to tell someone, anyone, about my close encounter of the Julia kind, I think that's something best kept to myself.

12.00 p.m. – At work

Julia never fails to amaze me. She's just been out and told me that she's given me the afternoon off to sort out my problems with Emma. Because if I don't, she's going to fire me for being a pain in the arse.

I have to say, I'm quite touched by her sentiment. Although I hope that somewhere in among it all is the hope that things don't work out and tonight the two of us will be back rolling around on her floor.

Thursday 10 August

09.15 a.m. – At work

Well that's that. It's all sorted. But not exactly back to normal.

When I left work, I headed home, picked up the car and went straight round to Emma's folks only to be told by her increasingly hostile mother that she was back at her flat and I was not to go anywhere near her. So obviously, I went straight round there and after a bit of persuasion through the letter box, got her to let me in. She looked bloody awful. But as soon as I started to speak, she burst out crying.

It took ages to calm her down but, eventually, she told me that it wasn't what happened in the church that had upset her, it was the trouble afterwards. Because the fact that I was so quick to jump to her defence proved the one thing that she'd secretly been worrying about ever since we first met – that I was embarrassed about her being fat.

Well I wasn't expecting that at all. And what was I supposed to say? If I'd have replied 'but you're not fat' she'd have said I was lying to make her feel better, and if I'd said 'but I don't mind' it would have devastated her. And of course, if I'd paused for too long, she'd have thought both those things and it really would have been all over.

So I did the only thing I could do. I gave her a cuddle, told her she was a silly cow and said that I didn't think she was fat, or plump, or tubby but what I did think was that she was beautiful.

And then I told her that she's the best thing that has ever happened to me and that if she's not careful, I'm going to fall in love with her. Not for what she looks like, because at the end of the day, fat, thin, tall or short, that doesn't matter, but for who she is and how she makes me feel.

And I meant every single bloody word. And now everything's cool again.

09.30 a.m. – At work

Julia has just asked me how I got on yesterday. When I told her it was sorted, she smiled and told me she was pleased for us two but more delighted for her. Because now I might actually do some work.

Cheeky cow. I hope she's not too disappointed though.

10.00 a.m. – At work

As a result of a call from Emma giving her all the gory details, Liz has just been down and given me one of her now famous full-bore smackers.

Of course, she had to have a pop at me by saying that, if I'd listened to her in the first place, things would have been a lot easier. And she's right, but I'll never tell her that. Besides, if I'd listened to her, I'd never have got my hands on Julia. Even if it was only for a few minutes . . .

14.50 p.m. – At work

Almost certainly thanks to Liz, news of the reconciliation and the use of the dreaded 'L' word has spread through the women at work like wildfire. It also seems to have had a major impact on the mood of the company. Whereas only recently I was one notch short of being a serial rapist, now every female in the company seems to think that I'm the dog's danglers, Emma's incredibly lucky and every other male is a worthless pig. Three ideals I have no problem with.

16.10 p.m. – At work

Emma has just phoned and told me that she's persuaded Helena to go out tonight and is cooking me a special celebratory meal. Pot noodles all round then.

Friday 11 August

09.40 a.m. – At work

Coming on the back of everything else that's happened recently, the last thing I needed was another degrading episode. But whether I needed one or not, last night I got one.

After a surprisingly nice meal and a bit of rolling around with a fantastically happy Emma, I was on my way home when I decided to stop off at a garage and stick in some fuel. As I was pumping in my tenner's worth of unleaded, I realised that, not only was the garage empty, but the sole person behind the counter was male. So I thought that it would be a good idea to make sure that the bodily fluids I was planning to use up over the coming weekend would be devoid of any unnecessary risks. And so, as I handed over a twenty-pound note, I asked him for some condoms.

And what happens? First the till roll runs out and by the time the pleb had managed to replace it, two other people, both women of course, were waiting behind me to get served. And then, of course, the bloody bar code machine at the counter breaks down. But to make matters even worse, the lone male attendant turns out not to be alone at all. His cry of 'Have you got a code for these condoms' brought not one but two females out of the office at a speed which would have made Sally Gunnell proud. Inevitably, both of them were pretty and under twenty and, clearly, neither could believe their luck.

Years of being abused and patronised by ignorant customers and, here it was, handed to them on a plate. Payback time. The drama, or should that be tragedy, that is my sex life, was ripped apart by two hyenas in women's clothing.

And what could I do? If I'd have told them not to bother, I would have been asking for that most final of nails 'But then you'd have to go without', and if I'd said they were for someone else, then I might have well just laid down and died right there. All I could do was to stand and wait while they dragged out the whole farce. Certain in the knowledge that my humiliation was not only making their shift a joy to work, but that it was also being captured on security video for them to relive when trade gets slow. My God, it could even end up on *Beadle's About*!

But my nightmare wasn't over. Oh no. Because having escaped that and driven home, I'd just made a coffee and was about to hit the sack when the police turned up at my front door and tried to arrest me. Because having just taken my change and stuffed it in my pocket, I hadn't realised that the dozy twats hadn't charged me for my petrol.

After I'd given them the laugh of their week by telling them what had actually happened, they took me back to the scene of my 'crime' and made me pay. Doubling my embarrassment at a stroke.

If there was a single crumb of comfort to be found, it's that the garage is one I don't usually use and will certainly never do so again. So at least it's unlikely that I'll ever see any of them again.

But why, when you can see naked women on the telly every night of the week, the newsagents are full of porn and the Internet is home to every kind of depravity imaginable, can't I buy a packet of bloody condoms without feeling like I should be wearing a raincoat? It's a responsible act! We're always being told to practise safe sex, but how can we do that if we're too embarrassed to buy a packet of three?

10.10 a.m. – At work

Emma has just rung to make sure that she hadn't poisoned me last night and so I told her, in an extremely hushed voice, what happened on the way home. Predictably, she thought it was hilarious. Women, as she happily informed me, have no such hang-ups about buying contraceptives. They just do it when they go shopping as if condoms are another commodity, because all females know that it's better to be prepared than pregnant and that men are crap about such things. Proof of this, as she was also quite happy to point out, comes from the fact that blokes, sex and responsibility are three words only ever used in the same sentence by the Child Support Agency.

Although initially miffed by this slur on my species, when I'd given it about a second's thought, I was grudgingly forced to agree. And it was nice to hear her laughing again.

10.35 a.m. – At work

Sean has just called to check I'm actually going to attend the game tomorrow. Cheeky bastard.

After what is almost certain to go down as the most complicated and stressful summer of all time, I can't wait to get back to the Red Lion and a bit of the old match-day routine. I hadn't realised how much I'd missed it until I actually began to give it some thought. And now I can't wait. OK, it's First Division and not the Premiership, but you can't have everything.

Mostly to avoid a repeat of the recent dramas, I've made sure that Emma is now well and truly aware that, if we are to have any kind of relationship, like it or not, there will always be someone else in my life and she lives at Vicarage Road. I go to see her about once a fortnight, usually on Saturdays but, thanks to the bastards at Sky TV, occasionally on the odd Friday or Sunday or Tuesday instead.

I've also given her a fixture list with all the games I plan to attend highlighted so that she knows well in advance. That way she can't spring anything on me at the last minute.

She's cool with it. And has said that she plans to spend footie days shopping with her mum. Which, if anything, is an added bonus for me because it means that no matter what happens on the pitch, for me at least, things could always be worse.

14.20 p.m. – At work

Spent lunchtime in the pub with the lads. Anticipation surrounds the return to our spiritual Saturday home and we're all like excited little kids. On top of that, Emma has called and suggested that we come back in to London tonight and hang out around the West End for a few hours. Something she knows I love doing. Mostly because, by the time we get home, we're totally relaxed and shagged out.

Life really is fantastic sometimes. I hope she brings some condoms.

Monday 14 August

09.45 a.m. – At work

A top weekend. Great night with Emma on Friday, a win for the lads and a nice day with her folks yesterday. Even her mum seems to have thawed out.

10.15 a.m. – At work

Liz has just called to see how I am and tell me that she met a new geezer at one of gay Darren's parties over the weekend.

She sounds really happy and, unlike the last time this happened, I'm actually chuffed to bits and told her that we'll all have to go out one night.

14.30 p.m. – At work

As we were having lunch, Emma, now firmly established back at work in admin, casually mentioned the possibility of us living together at some point. I am shocked. Although we seem to be closer than ever after our recent problems, we've still only really been together for about three months and this would be a huge step. Certainly for me. I've never lived with a bird before and I'm pretty sure that it's a lot more complex than having sex on tap seven nights a week. Appealing though that thought is.

This is going to need some serious thought. It's a bloody good job I'm not on piecework.

16.20 p.m. – At work

Not surprisingly, the idea of sharing my flat with Emma has dominated my thoughts all afternoon and I am actually warming to the idea.

Because as happy as I am living on my own, it's pretty obvious that I can't do it forever. And I don't really want to. The thought of cooking a Sunday roast for one when I'm hitting sixty does not hold much of an appeal. Not at all. And I would like to have kids of my own at some point – if not with Emma, with someone else. And I am thirty after all. So I guess if I don't want to be an oldie dad, time is running out.

So if she's willing to commit to us, then why not? I haven't got a problem with it really. After all, it's been nice having someone to wake up with at the weekends. Why not have it every day?

22.55 p.m. – At home

For some reason, Emma was feeling like shit tonight, but rather than leave her to get on with it and go down the gym, I went round to keep her company and watch the telly. And the strangest thing happened: she farted.

At first I actually thought that I had heard something else. But then I realised that she had actually lifted one cheek to do it. It was nothing earth-shattering, just a simple 'phut', but it was a fart nevertheless. And what's more, she never even said anything.

I have to say that I was shocked: I mean if it had been a bloke then my response would have been immediate, 'good arse' or some such comment. But what exactly should you do if a woman lets one go?

I suppose I could look upon this simple expulsion of air as a defining moment in our relationship. A sign that Emma is totally at ease with me. Then again, it could also be argued that it's her flat, she can do what she bloody well likes in it. But whatever it means, I feel strangely comforted by her show of domesticity. Though I doubt I will respond in kind. At least not for a while.

Tuesday 15 August

09.35 a.m. – At work

Emma seems to be back to normal. She even asked me if I'd thought about the two of us living together.

I told her that I liked the idea, but already we have hit a stumbling block. We both own our respective flats. And as I have no intention of leaving my place, especially not if it means sharing my living space full-time with a third party – even if it's the gorgeous Helena – and part-time with a fourth – especially if it's the irritating Mike – we are at an impasse. One which we will only get over when she decides to leave her flat and move in with me.

Wednesday 16 August

09.40 a.m. – At work

A little knowledge is, indeed, a dangerous thing. As we were sitting in the pub last night, Emma told me something in confidence that will shortly have a major effect on one of my best mates and now I don't know what to do.

Do I warn him in advance or do I simply keep quiet? Is it even any of my business? To be honest, do I care? Yes, I do. But what to do? If I do what I think I should, he will at least be forewarned but, then again, if Emma finds out I've told him, she could well go mental because she'll think I can't be trusted. I don't really need that at the moment. Best to sit tight and see what happens.

11.10 a.m. – At work

No need to worry. The secret is out. Mike just rang to tell me that he and Helena have split. He has apparently found out that she's been seeing her old boyfriend and so has given her the elbow. I gave my condolences of course. But my offer to meet for a quiet beer at lunchtime was declined. Mostly because I suspect he's a bit gutted but also because I know he's lying through his teeth.

Emma told me last night that the real reason they have split up has nothing to do with her old boyfriend at all. It is to do with the fact that Mike, a bloke I've known almost all my life, who I've laughed with, got drunk with and even had a fight with – a long time ago and it was an honourable draw because my dad pulled us apart – is, according to Helena, a crap shag.

Still, you can't help but feel sorry for the guy. He must feel like shit and there isn't a bloke alive who doesn't know what that feels like.

13.20 p.m. – At work

Women are bloody amazing! Emma has just rung and told me that Helena is indeed seeing her old boyfriend and all the stuff about Mike being a crap shag was bollocks. Of course, like all women, the fact that her friend lied to her seems to have been forgotten and now Emma is asking if it would be all right if we went out as a foursome on Friday! The fact that my mate is sitting at his desk totally gutted seems to be immaterial. And they say that women are caring, sharing types!

Still, if I don't go, there's always the chance that this bloke will have some oily tosser of a mate with him and he'll spend the evening sniffing around my bird. Trust her as I do, I don't trust anyone else so I suppose I'll have to go. Better not tell Mike though.

15.30 p.m. – At work

Mike just rang to tell me I'm an arsehole. God knows how, although I suspect it has something to do with Emma and Helena gabbing, but he has found out that I am planning to go on this foursome on Friday night and thinks that a real mate wouldn't do that. Before I could reply, he slammed the phone down and has now vanished so I can't put my side of the story.

Great. Once again I'm in the shit because of a woman and her big mouth.

19.25 p.m. – At home

As Emma was working late, I popped in for a pint when I finished to find that all the lads are united behind Mike who I have apparently let down in the worst possible way. And now, just for a change, no one is talking to me.

If I spend any more time in Coventry, I'll have to start paying the Council Tax.

22.10 p.m. – At home

I'm back at home early because Emma isn't talking to me either. I am, apparently, a shithead. I should have told her that Mike was devastated by Helena leaving him and then she wouldn't have said that we would go out with her. The fact that I did has clearly been forgotten.

I am now completely baffled by everything that is happening around me. How have I been dragged into all of this and why am I getting all the blame? The person who should be attracting all the flak is Helena. After all, she's the one who shafted her bloke and lied to her mate, not me.

22.50 p.m. – At home

I think I've worked it out. It's because I'm caught in the middle of a bird-feud.

Emma knows that Helena lied and deceived her but, as the real victim is one of the enemy, a bloke, then that's all right. However, because she has been wronged, Emma has to blame someone, and as women never do anything wrong, that someone is me. Mike, of course, has just got the arsehole and needs to sound off at someone. Also me.

It all makes perfect sense. And I'm going to just let them all get on with it because quite frankly, it's doing my bloody head in.

Thursday 17 August

09.50 a.m. – At work

As I expected, Emma was right as rain when I met her this morning. It was as if yesterday had never even happened. I wonder if I should get her to call the lads?

10.30 a.m. – At work

I've just been to see Mike and told him what actually happened yesterday – leaving out the most damaging bits of course.

As I suspected, he's also calmed down a bit and apologised for acting like a dickhead because he knows I'd never shaft him. So at least he's speaking to me again but he is a bit down. Bloody women.

14.25 p.m. – At work

Just called Liz to sort a night out with her and her geezer one night next week only to be told that she's given him the elbow. Apparently, he broke her golden rule and so he had to go.

When I asked what that was all about, she started laughing and hung up.

14.45 p.m. – At work

Just been up to see Liz who was still laughing and told me that her golden rule is never to go out with a bloke who's got a name for his knob.

Of course I had to ask and, incredibly, it was Bruno. Because it was big and thick. Although she started to tell me how she found out, I had to stop her. That really was more information than I really wanted.

16.20 p.m. – At work

Emma just called and asked me if Danny De Vito is coming out to play tonight. She can knock that on the head for a fucking start.

22.45 p.m. – At home

I have become a victim of my own domesticity. Sainsbury's, for a short time my favourite place in the whole world, has now become just another name on the list of places I have been embarrassed in. The episode with the condoms last week has come back to haunt me.

As we shopped tonight, Emma casually mentioned that 'we' needed some more condoms. Of course, it would have been simple to just bend down and pick up the ones we always use but this wasn't good enough. This time, there was a point to prove and she had clearly decided that this was one purchase that required thought and consideration. A process I was forced to take part in, even though I would rather have been standing naked in the fresh vegetable section. Something I think would have been only marginally less humiliating. And as we talked, and people looked, who should I spy at the end of the aisle but one of the girls from the garage. A member of the very duo who had started all of this. I tried to pretend I didn't recognise her, but her knowing smile bore through me like a laser beam. As she approached, my life flashed before my eyes. It was one of those terrible moments where you know that anything can happen but it is totally out of your control. Like a car crash or an unwanted erection. What would she say? And then what would Emma say? For a second, I thought about running for it, but even my legs let me down and I just stared, probably open-mouthed, I was too scared to notice. And then, as Emma studiously examined the details of the latest ribbed product, the girl from the garage looked me square in the eyes, smiled and winked. And then she was past and gone.

I could not get out of that shop fast enough. And I'll never go back. I couldn't, no wouldn't, go through that again for anything. That another human being could have that effect on me was just too much to bear.

Monday 21 August

10.30 a.m. – At work

The last few days have been hard work. Because on Friday morning, Emma's dad phoned to give her the bad news that her nan had passed on. Something which I don't suppose is nice at the best of times, but when you're the only child of an only child, as Emma and her mum both are, it must be devastating. Especially since it's less than a year since her granddad died.

Luckily, her dad had the presence of mind to ring me straight afterwards and ask me if I could get her home. And, thanks to Julia, I was able to borrow one of the reps' motors and get her there within the hour. Something which seemed to go down quite well although, not surprisingly, their place wasn't exactly a barrel of laughs. So rather than intrude, I saw her inside, told the old man that I'd wait for her to call me rather than the other way round, and left them to it.

She actually called me a couple of hours later and told me that she'd stop there until after the funeral on Wednesday. Perfectly understandable of course, but it's meant that I've been on my own all weekend and my time has been divided between home, gym and pub. Normally not a bad plan but, in this instance, a depressing one. Because with all four of my grandparents dying when I was tiny, I've never really known what it's like to have anyone close to me pass on. And having seen the impact it's had on Emma and her folks, it's not something I'm especially keen to experience.

But what it has done is to make me think about life. Or more importantly, my life. It might be a pain in the arse sometimes, but it's the only one I've got and I have to make the best of it. At the moment, that best is Emma. And so I've decided to make the most of every single second we have together.

Tuesday 22 August

09.25 a.m. – At work

Emma called last night and told me her parents would like me to be at the funeral. Although the very idea of it fills me with horror, I immediately accepted. Not just because I've missed her like mad, but because it's a further sign that I'm winning approval.

I hope the bloke I smacked isn't there though. That could be embarrassing.

15.15 p.m. – At work

Sean has just been down and casually mentioned that the vagaries of the early-season fixture list mean that Watford are at QPR tonight. Something I had completely forgotten. Although desperate to go, even his claim that 'It's what the old girl would have wanted' doesn't disguise the fact that it would be wrong. If nothing else, it would be disrespectful to Emma. Strangely, even Sean understands that.

16.25 p.m. – At work

I've just rung Emma to find out how she is. Although understandably still upset, she finally seems to be settling down a bit. Like me, I guess she'll be glad when tomorrow is over.

I did casually ask her what she was planning to do tonight but, sadly, after she'd told me they were sorting out the food and all that stuff, she didn't ask me what my plans were.

Although I know it's selfish and insensitive, it's clear that, at some point in our relationship, I'm going to have to educate her about the importance of football.

Thursday 24 August

10.10 a.m. – At work

Jesus. I hope I don't have to go through all that again in a hurry. Why are funerals so fucking depressing? I could have understood it if she was a kiddie, or even quite young, but she was eighty-seven for Christ's sake. Surely that's something to celebrate not whine about?

It would certainly have been better for Emma. I'd never have imagined I would see her so gutted. She looks shattered as well and, if I didn't know better, I'd think she'd lost weight. According to her mum, she's hardly slept or eaten anything all week. She's taken the rest of the week off as well. So what with the Bank Holiday, it'll be Tuesday before she has to come back, which is a good thing really. It gives her a bit more time to get herself together.

It's funny, I can't imagine anyone's death having that much of an effect on me. Well, apart from, God forbid, Joe or Katie. Or Lou. And Emma obviously. And possibly Luther Blissett. But family-wise, apart from the kids and my sister, there's not anyone. I'd be upset of course, even if it was the old man. But it wouldn't destroy me. I suppose that's a bit sad.

11.45 a.m. – At work

Emma has just called and told me that her mum and dad would like me to go over tonight. They think it'll do them all good to have someone else in the house. I suppose I should take that as a compliment.

Friday 25 August

09.20 a.m. – At work

Thanks to the Bank Holiday, it's an early finish today which means a serious session at lunchtime. Something which, after the month I've had, is much needed.

But sadly, the only humping I will be doing over the next few days will involve furniture rather than females. Last night, which wasn't actually that bad, I offered to go down to Pinner and help Emma's old man clear the old girl's house after the three of them have sorted through everything. Something they are doing today and tomorrow and at which my presence is not required. And if I'm honest, probably not wanted.

Thankfully, this pardon ensures that I will be present at Vicarage Road tomorrow. After a draw at QPR on Tuesday, the lads will be up for it. And so will I.

11.45 a.m. – At work

Just had a long chat with Liz. Despite the loss of Bruno, she seems to be back to her old, sparky self. And she looks fantastic.

I suggested that, as Emma is at her folks' tonight, we should give the pub a miss and go out on our own to catch up on old times. And so we are.

22.55 p.m. – At home

Spent most of the afternoon with Liz laughing and joking. Mostly about the times I've tried to pull her. She really is the most gorgeous bird and I still can't believe that she has so many problems with blokes.

Sadly, I had to decline her invite to one of gay Darren's parties. I wanted to get home in case Emma called and, like a twat, I'd left my mobile on the table this morning. Besides, I would have felt a bit awkward, knowing where Emma was and what she was doing.

But Emma hasn't called, and so I've ended up sitting here pissing about on FIFA 2000. Not that I mind, in fact it's actually been quite relaxing being on my own for a while.

Saturday 26 August

21.30 p.m. – At home

Just for a change, I'm in the shit. Only this time, it's serious and self-inflicted.

In the pub before the game today, we were talking about stupid things we'd done and I let slip that the April Fool toilet gag was down to me. Of course, no one believed I was capable of something so inventive and so, in typical fashion, I kept on and on until they were convinced. But while most of the lads were hugely impressed, Kev, who was one of the main victims and who, I suspect, has still not forgiven me for the stuff with ugly, was not.

Indeed, he has not only sworn revenge, he has promised to tell Barry the wanker first thing on Tuesday morning. That's not good. And to make matters worse, the Hornets lost.

Tuesday 29 August

10.15 a.m. – At work

Aside from Kev, who has decided that I will suffer far more if he doesn't tell Barry the wanker about April Fools' day but, instead, leaves me hanging on his every whim, the weekend didn't turn out half as bad as I expected.

Once we'd finished clearing the house, the mood at Emma's folks' place improved markedly and even the old man seems to be warming to me. He was quite pleasant, in fact. Well, as pleasant as an ex-copper can be.

Interestingly, as we were driving the van back to the rental company yesterday, he mentioned something about Emma's ex-boyfriend. By all accounts, although she thought the world of him, her parents clearly didn't. I even got the distinct impression that the old man had paid him a visit after the infamous Christmas split. And not to wish him all the best either. I'll have to remember that in future. Because I got the impression that he told me this as a thinly veiled warning. And even in his late fifties, if he wanted to, I have no doubt he could hurt me. Quite badly.

Still, at least Emma is back at work. I've missed her this last week. More than I thought was possible.

Wednesday 30 August

09.50 a.m. – At work

I made Emma bring over some clothes last night so that she could stay with me. Not because of any sexual motive, but because I thought she needed a bit of pampering and a bloody good sleep. And so we had something to eat, a bottle of wine and then went to bed where she slept like a log.

The result is that she's just about back to her old self. So much so that she was positively cheerful this morning. It's quite warming to know that little old me can have that effect on someone. But, as I thought, she's lost weight. There's a little bit less of her to cuddle.

11.25 a.m. – At work

Emma has phoned and told me that her dad's called and asked if we could go over tonight. Apparently, they have something to tell her.

That sounds interesting. I just hope he hasn't been speaking to his old police mates!

23.50 p.m. – At home

A night of mixed emotions tonight. Not for me, but for Emma. When we got to her folks, they sat her down and told her that her nan had left her the house in her will.

Although thrilled at this, it obviously brought back a few memories but, after a few tears, she was OK. God knows what she's going to do with it though. After all, while it might hold a lot of sentimental value, the fact is that her nan had lived there for over forty years and the decoration was strictly 1950s. It's like walking back in bloody time and would take thousands to get into shape. Emma doesn't have that. But I doubt she'd live there anyway. What with the memories and all.

Still, looking on the bright side, my bird's just inherited a four-bedroom house in a nice road in Pinner. And that has to be worth £175,000 of anyone's money. Probably more. Nice one!

Thursday 31 August

14.50 p.m. – At work

As expected, Emma told me over lunch that there's no way she could ever live in her nan's house. But she's also decided that she doesn't want to sell it either. Instead, she's going to rent it out. That way, no matter what happens in the future, she'll have money coming in and a nice bit of property to fall back on if anything happens.

Very sensible of her, although if it were me, I'd have thought 'Fuck it, what you've never had, you never miss' and blown the lot on a box at Watford and a nice motor.

She's also told me that I'm going to be spending tonight on my own. Having been all over the place for a while, she needs to stay at home and get the domestic side of her life back on track.

At least I'll be able to get to the gym. I've started to feel a bit lardy.

Chapter 10

September

Friday 1 September

15.10 p.m. – At work

After her girlie night in with Helena, Emma has announced out of the blue that she's going to capitalise on the weight she's lost and go on a diet. And of course, with typical female logic, the reason she has decided this is because, although I might not say anything, and despite what happened after the wedding, she still thinks that I'm unhappy with the way she looks and would prefer it if she were slimmer. After all, I'm a bloke, and blokes like skinny women, not tubby ones. It's a proven fact, everyone knows that.

Everyone except me, of course. Because I don't think she needs to lose weight at all. OK, she's a size sixteen, probably a bit less now, but I think she looks fantastic. She's what I suppose they used to call voluptuous.

And she knows I think that. Because I tell her all the bloody time. But of course, now that she's made up her mind, nothing I say will make the slightest bit of difference. Because, like most women who have a home truth to face, she has the ability to convince herself that, no matter what the circumstances, it's always someone else's fault. And the plain truth here is that she thinks she'll look better slimmer, not me. But if it's hard, well at least now she's got me to blame. Great. It'll be like permanent PMS.

Monday 4 September

10.25 a.m. – At work

The true consequences of Emma and her recent weight loss hit home on Saturday morning when she suddenly announced that her breasts have shrunk.

Although I've become increasingly familiar with them over the last few weeks, I can't honestly say I had noticed. They feel fine to me but, nevertheless, she assures me that they are smaller.

What this meant in real terms was that we spent an entire afternoon in Marks and Spencer buying her new bras. Not the most rewarding experience for a bloke it has to be said, although, in any other context, the thought of another woman fondling my girlie's breasts would be an extremely attractive one. But when it's a fifty-year-old housewife, it's not quite the same.

The rest of the weekend was spent chilling out and avoiding the subject of food. Although we did go to see Lou on Sunday where we found the old man and the rich widow. Incredibly, it seems that the fortunes of the whole Ellis family are on the up. Everyone seemed sickeningly happy.

13.40 p.m. – At work

Emma was busy at lunchtime and so I ended up in the pub with the lads. Thankfully, they reminded me that Watford have a game tomorrow night. Something I had totally forgotten about.

22.55 p.m. – At home

Bloody Emma almost gave me a heart attack tonight. When I reminded her I'd be going to football tomorrow, she casually said that maybe she should come along to see what all the fuss was about.

Of course, me not being enough of a proper man to simply reply 'Don't be silly love. Football's for geezers, not birds,' I minced about trying to think of a way to talk her out of it for almost half an hour before I realised she was taking the piss. Although slightly annoyed that she could mess about with something as serious as football, I have to admit, it was a good one.

Sadly, this was the only humorous interlude in what was an evening of misery. The effects of her being on a conscious diet, as opposed to a grief-induced one, are beginning to kick in.

Tuesday 5 September

10.00 a.m. – At work

Emma moaned from the second she got on the train this morning to the second we parted in the lift at work. That's almost fifty minutes of non-stop whining.

14.40 p.m. – At work

As I expected, she's now started to have digs at me for placing this pressure on her and, after a lunchtime of yet more griping, I've decided that I'm not having any more of it. Drastic action is called for.

15.10 p.m. – At work

Success. Thanks to the application of a large box of Thornton's very best and most irresistible chocolates, Emma and her diet have parted company.

Shit, I'm good. Although if she cracked that easy, she obviously has no will power at all.

Wednesday 6 September

09.35 a.m. – *At work*

Not a good night last night. After the game, which we lost, I stayed in the pub until closing time and arrived home, slightly the worse for wear it has to be said, at about eleven thirty to find Emma waiting for me.

But, as she happily pointed out, I would have known she'd be there had I bothered to switch on my mobile and listen to the messages she left me. So instead of a romantic, chocolate-fuelled romp, we had an argument about nothing and she went home in a taxi. Now she's got the arsehole.

Of course, now that I'm sober and thinking more clearly, I know that what I should have done, even though it wasn't really my fault, was tell her that I was sorry and grovelled. Because, as both Liz and *Woman's Own* taught me months ago, if a woman's moaning, the only sensible course of action for a bloke to take is to agree with every single word she says.

10.50 a.m. – *At work*

Emma has just told me that she's not speaking to me. But in between not speaking to me, she also managed to tell me that she really wanted to surprise me last night and, because I messed up, I let her down.

So, to recap. I go to football, and then have one or two Budweisers with the lads. She knows I'm doing this because I've told her about it on numerous occasions to avoid situations just like this one.

Yet, despite this, she decides to surprise me – which is fair enough – but even though she can't contact me to tell me, she decides to come over anyway. And because I'm not there, she gets the hump. And women wonder why men don't understand them.

11.35 a.m. – At work

Just rung Emma to see if she wants to have lunch, but she's still not speaking to me. Pub it is then.

14.10 p.m. – At work

For fuck's sake. Now she's rung and moaned at me for going to the pub. Apparently, I was supposed to go up and see her so that we could clear the air.

Is it me? Or do they really speak a different language?

14.25 p.m. – At work

I've just rung Liz to ask her if she can interpret for me. Because I haven't got a bloody clue what Emma is on about.

15.50 p.m. – At work

Liz has obviously talked to Emma who, in turn, seems to have finally realised that her boyfriend is freaking out. Either that, or she just feels horny.

Whatever it is, in a pathetic display of sexual cunning designed to win me over, she's just been down here on the pretext of offering me her last Thornton's chocolate. The fact that she had the top two buttons of her blouse undone and leant over my desk to give me a lengthy flash of her recently reduced, but still fairly ample, cleavage clearly shows that when it comes to getting what she wants, the woman has no shame.

It also proves that I don't have any will power either.

Thursday 7 September

10.05 a.m. – At work

A heavy night last night. But this time, a far more agreeable form of moaning was involved. Nuff said, I think.

15.45 p.m. – At work

I was planning a big night out tonight, but Emma has just rung and told me that her folks have called and want to know if we can go over there again tonight. They have something they want to discuss with her.

That sounds ominous. Last time she ended up with a house. Maybe they want to question me as a potential suitor? Bloody hell, now there's a thought. What are my prospects? Do I actually have any? I'd better ask Julia.

Friday 8 September

01.45 a.m. – At home

I can't sleep. Hardly surprising really. In view of the fact that my life has just about collapsed around my ears.

When we got to her folks', they sat her down and told her that, with the old girl no longer around, and his parents well catered for, the two of them have decided that, in a couple of years, when he hits sixty, they are going to retire, sell their house and go to live in France. It's what they've always dreamt of doing apparently.

But that means either selling his security firm or handing it on to Emma. And if it's the latter, unless she intends to bankrupt it, she has to learn the ropes. In short, they want her to quit her job and go and work for him.

Naturally, Emma was stunned. I mean, that's some career change: admin secretary to company director in the space of two minutes. And I don't know much about security, but I only have to look around their house to see that her old man's business must make a bloody fortune. Although I'm obviously pleased for her, I'd be lying if I said I wasn't worried about us. We're only just getting things together, and if she leaves work it's going to change everything. Which might be a bit of a bastard.

Still, he did say that he didn't want an answer straightaway but instead wanted her to think about it. But that's a lot to think about. And she hardly said a word on the way home.

09.40 a.m. – At work

Events of last night seem to have reawakened all my old insecurities. When Emma didn't appear on the train this morning, I began to imagine all sorts of things, none of which were good and all of which involved me being on my own again.

It was only when I got to work that I realised I'd left my bloody mobile switched off again. When I turned it on, I found three messages, all from Emma, moaning about my phone being off and telling me that she'd slept in, had missed the train and would see me later.

15.00 p.m. – At work

After a tough morning, where I got hardly anything done, it was an extremely cheerful Emma who met me for lunch. And as a result of what happened, I feel . . . well to be honest, I don't know how I feel.

After spending the night on her own, thinking about everything that her mum and dad had said, she told me that she'd come to a decision. As far as she's concerned, the most important thing in her life is the two of us. And while she'd love to go and work with her dad, she realises that, if she did, it might have a major effect on our relationship. And because she loves me, and loves the fact that we work together and everything that goes with it, she isn't prepared to risk that.

Hearing those words was an astonishing relief. But, even as she was speaking, I knew that it wasn't on. This is a huge opportunity and, probably, her parents' dream. If I let her pass on it, it would be for totally selfish reasons and I'd never be able to square it with myself. And I don't suppose her old man would be thrilled either.

So I told her that she had to do it. Because it was her future. And no matter what happened, we'd be OK because we're good together. And although she didn't say as much, I could see from the look in her eyes that I'd said exactly what she'd hoped I'd say. And now I'm going to lose her. I know it.

17.20 p.m. – At work

This afternoon has been the worst I can ever remember. It's like a huge cloud has appeared over my head and, any minute now, it's going to start pissing down.

Monday 11 September

10.25 a.m. – At work

This has been a hard, hard weekend. Friday night, we went back down to Emma's folks where she told them that she would indeed be handing in her notice and, hopefully, by the end of the month, will be working with him in Northwood.

Of course, they were all elated. And I pretended to be. But as each second passed, the only thing I could think of was that this was the beginning of the end. She's about to start drifting out of my life and there's fuck all I can do about it.

Not even a Watford win on Saturday cheered me up and, because Emma had planned a night out with Helena, I ended up getting bombed out of my brain on my own and didn't even see her until Sunday lunchtime.

At least seeing the kids in the afternoon cheered me up for a while. Although hearing them calling her Auntie Emma soon dragged me down again. And it made her quite tearful.

This is killing me already. How am I going to cope when she leaves?

14.15 p.m. – At work

Over a quiet lunch, Emma broke the news that she handed in her notice this morning. She leaves on the twenty-second. Shit. Now there's no going back.

15.20 p.m. – At work

Liz has just called to tell me that she's just spoken to Emma and is really thrilled. Not just for her, but for us.

Thankfully, she guessed from the tone of my voice that something is wrong and, rather than quiz me now, has made me promise to call her at home tonight.

Thank Christ I have her to talk to. Because, apart from Emma, there isn't anyone else.

Tuesday 12 September

10.25 a.m. – At work

All is well. In fact, it's better than well, it's fantastic. And it's all thanks to Liz.

I called her as soon as I got in last night and told her everything. About how I feel and what I'm worried about. But rather than tell me not to be a wanker, which is what I kind of expected, she told me to calm down and look at things rationally. And then she said that I had to talk to Emma. Because, as she pointed out, for all I knew, she might be worrying about exactly the same thing.

So when I got to Emma's, I took her out for a walk and did just that. And when I'd finished, she laughed, gave me a cuddle and then, just as Liz had guessed, she told me that she'd also been thinking about it. But unlike me, she's been a bit more practical and come up with what she thinks is the perfect solution. She wants to move in with me. Permanently.

And she's right. It's the obvious answer to everything. And as soon as she said it, I told her it was a great idea. And the black cloud that looked all set to destroy my life has finally fucked off. Hopefully, this time it's gone for good.

Wednesday 13 September

11.50 a.m. – At work

Although I'm chuffed to buggery about it, I've been giving some thought to what it's going to be like when she moves in. Because it's going to mean some massive changes. And I don't just mean in relationship terms either. I'm thinking about my flat.

Over the years, it's evolved into a bloke's home full of blokey things. And while Emma has been spending more and more time there, so far I've managed to resist her influence by putting back everything she moves around or hides away as soon as she goes home. But I can't do that if she's living there all the time, which means that her subtle changes will become permanent. And once she starts to see that, she'll almost certainly start to widen her net a bit. She's told me often enough how much she hates my football trophies being on the floor by the telly. And I've seen her looking around when she watches *Changing Rooms*, which probably means that visits to Homebase and Ikea are only weeks away. Thank God she hasn't moved the sofa yet. If she sees what's under there, she'll have a fit.

At least so far, Geri has escaped her attention. But I have a sneaky and worrying feeling that she's living on borrowed time.

14.30 p.m. – At work

Sean has just been down and told me that he and Kev have hit Barry the wanker with a major wind-up. Thanks to Sean's sister, they got hold of a security tag from a clothes shop and, having ripped off the plastic coating, inserted the magnetic strip into the lining of his jacket. At the last count, he'd been stopped and searched walking out of seven different shops and, although his mood currently borders on the rabid, he still hasn't sussed it.

Although thrilled to bits that once more my old foe is getting exactly what he deserves, it hasn't escaped my attention that, only a few short months ago, it would have been me on the receiving end rather than Barry. Which can only mean that, not only is Emma my bird and future flat-mate, but she also seems to have become a pretty effective deterrent.

16.15 p.m. – At work

Emma has just rung and told me that she's going to stay in tonight so that she can break the news to Helena that she's moving in with me. This is going to have a major effect on her as well, I suppose.

23.00 p.m. – At home

On the way to the gym tonight, for some reason I suddenly began to think about the number of things Emma has had to deal with over the last few weeks. Because while my domestic arrangements might be up for a sort-out, her whole life has been turned on its head.

She's not only lost her nan and gained a house, but she's about to change jobs and is leaving her home to move in with me. That's a lot for one person to handle and, although she's holding up brilliantly, I have a sneaky feeling that she's running on reserve. Sooner or later, I suspect a tear or two might be shed. I'll need to keep an eye on that.

Thursday 14 September

09.20 a.m. – At work

On the way to work, Emma told me that she's decided to hang on to her flat. Not because she thinks that she might need to escape from me at some point, but because it's been Helena's home for a few years now and she thinks she'll be able to get someone in to share quite easily.

I must say, I'm impressed. I've suddenly realised that Emma's got two properties, one mortgage and is going to be living with me rent free. Financially, that's a sweet move on her part. And one which, sooner or later, we'll need to discuss.

12.50 p.m. – At work

I've just had yet another shock in what is rapidly turning out to be the most stressful month of my life. Julia called me into her office to tell me that someone in aresehole town has been caught with their hands in the till and she has to go back to Mitcham to take over their sales and marketing department. And she needs to be there quickly. This coming Monday in fact.

Of course, I told her that I'll be sorry to see her go, but of more immediate concern to me is who takes over. All she could say is that she promised to put in a good word.

I have to be in the frame this time. And besides, I bloody deserve it. I've worked my bollocks off here and haven't even pulled any kind of a stunt since April Fools' day. Which reminds me, only Kev and the lads know about that and, rest assured, they'll be set right over lunch.

15.15 p.m. – At work

The lads have been set straight. They all know that this is serious and even Kev, still not totally grudge-free I suspect, has said he'll play the game and wished me luck.

Emma is, well, Emma. She's suddenly got this confident air about her and seems to be able to take everything in her stride. A kiss, a cuddle and a 'You can do it, Sugar Plum' was all it took to convince me that she's right. I can.

17.15 p.m. – At work

Frantic activity in Julia's office. Even the high-ups have made an appearance. Now that is rare!

Friday 15 September

09.20 a.m. – At work

Incredibly, as Emma and I were sat watching *EastEnders* last night, Julia called to tell me that I've got an interview for her job at ten o'clock this morning. According to her, if I do OK, it's already mine. No pressure there then. Yeah right, I'm shitting myself.

15.30 p.m. – At work

Well, the interview seemed to go OK. They were a bit worried about my being only thirty, but I pointed out that I'd done the job before, albeit on a temporary basis, and then gave them all the old bollocks about wanting to see through the good work that Julia has started.

After some discussion about my personal life, during which I threw in phrases such as 'long-term relationship' and 'totally committed', that was it. Game over. And now I have to wait.

17.30 p.m. – At work

The high-ups have just left but I haven't heard anything. Julia reckons I pissed it, but they did see two other blokes and a woman after me so who knows?

Now I've got a weekend of waiting. And after this last week, I'm suddenly absolutely shattered. All I want to do is have something to eat and climb into bed. Preferably with Emma.

The one thing I am a bit pissed off about is that I didn't get the chance to say goodbye to Julia. After my interview, she disappeared upstairs and I can't hang about. Still, I can always go round and see her over the weekend. It'd be nice to have one last look at those tits. If only for old times' sake.

Monday 18 September

09.40 a.m. – At work

As we were heading home on Friday, Emma told me that she had a surprise for me. After everything that's happened, she'd booked us into a hotel for the weekend so that we could get away, spend some time together, relax and unwind a bit.

But as we were on the way, my mobile rang and I received the calamitous news that I didn't get the job after all. Not only that, but to add insult to injury, they want me to fill the post until a 'suitable' replacement can be found.

I'm gutted. And after talking it through with Emma, who I have to say was fantastic about it all, I've decided that if, after all these years, they still don't think I'm suitable to run my own department, then they can stick their job up their arse.

I've just been down and handed the ugly bird in personnel my letter of resignation.

09.55 a.m. – At work

Just had two calls in very quick succession. One from Emma making sure I'd handed it in and the second from the managing director's PA informing me that he would love a brief chat at 3.00 p.m.

10.55 a.m. – At work

As expected, ugly has been working her little cotton socks off and news of my resignation has shot through the building. Inevitably, as if getting shafted for the third time after years of service isn't good enough, various rumours have sprung up to explain the 'real' reason for my sudden rebellion. These range from a lottery win on Saturday night to Emma finding me in bed with Julia last week. Something which also explains why she's leaving at such short notice.

Once again, I have to applaud the inventiveness of my

colleagues. Although the last one is a bit too close for comfort.

11.15 a.m. – At work

Mike has called to ask me what the fuck's been going on. Something which has suddenly made me realise that, when I leave, my day-to-day relationship with the lads will be over. No more lunchtimes and no more wind-ups. All we'll have is football. Bloody hell, now I feel a bit depressed.

12.00 p.m. – At work

At least the lads in the office have cheered up. But only because Liz has just been down to see me.

Unlike almost everyone else, she thinks I'm doing exactly the right thing. Not because she believes I should have got the job, but because she thinks a move will do me the world of good. She always did have a knack of saying the right thing. But now I've also realised that, when I leave, I'll see even less of her than I do now. And recently, that's been next to nothing. Now I feel a lot depressed.

14.20 p.m. – At work

Emma told me in the pub at lunch that, as she's now a property magnate and a prospective company director, if I want to stay at home and be a house-husband, she'll be more than happy to support me after we move in together. Although she would like to see my signature on a pre-nuptial agreement before she sets foot in my flat again.

After fishing out the lump of ice I dropped down her cleavage, she then said that if I really felt like I had to go out to work, she was thinking of taking on a chauffeur. The job's mine if I want it.

14.40 p.m. – At work

Shit, after all that's happened, I'd forgotten that this is Emma's last week. I hope to Christ they don't pull the same kind of stunts on her as we usually do when blokes leave.

16.10 p.m. – At work

My meeting with the main man did not go well. I was secretly hoping he would relent and offer me the promotion after all but instead, all he tried to do was get me to either change my mind or delay my departure. Neither of which is an option. In fact, our meeting backfired on him a bit because he reminded me that, while I have to work a month's notice, I have three weeks' holiday owing to me. And because they've shown no loyalty to me, I'm fucked if I'm going to show them any. And now, Emma won't be the only one walking out the door for the last time on Friday.

16.50 p.m. – At work

Of all the people I didn't expect to hear from, Julia was high on the list. But she's just called to tell me how gutted she is about me not getting the job despite all her efforts.

   If she was gutted about that, she was shocked when she found out I'd quit. Because without either a boss or a competent deputy, I have a sneaky feeling that she'll be back in this department before she knows it.

Tuesday 19 September

09.35 a.m. – At work

After the madness of yesterday, the plan last night was to do nothing but chill out with Emma and try to get my head around my impending unemployment.

   But when I went round to her place, I found out that Helena has already got someone wanting to move in. And so Emma has decided that, after a final few girlie nights in with her mate, if it's still OK with me, she'll be moving in over the coming weekend.

   That gives me less than a week to enjoy the solitude that is my flat. Well, at least the parts of it that are still mine. When I came home, she made me bring three boxes full of stuff back with me.

Most of which seems to have come from the Body Shop. Fuck knows what it's all for, but no doubt over the coming weeks, I will find out.

On the plus side, as the combined rent of Helena and her new flat-mate will also cover the mortgage, Emma will be quids in. I really must talk to her about that.

Wednesday 20 September

11.30 a.m. – At work

As I half expected, from Monday, Julia will be back at the helm for a while. However, what I didn't expect was to be told that Sean has been promoted and will be taking over my job when I leave.

Although a bit surprised, I'm actually chuffed. Better he gets it than someone else and now, after all these years, he'll get to know what it's like having obnoxious and stroppy twats working for him. I expect an apology for years of grief after about a week.

Sadly, news on the job front is not so bright for me. I've sent out about twenty CVs since Monday and not heard anything back. Mind you, it's only Wednesday.

16.45 p.m. – At work

What with everything going on at work, I've hardly seen Emma at all these last few days and, aside from the odd cuddle on the train, our relationship has been done over the phone. She seems perfectly happy though. I know she's having a giggle with Helena and I've heard that all kinds of things have been going on in admin as they get ready to send her off.

Speaking of which, aside from Sean, who has been welded to me all day in an effort to learn as much as he can about my job, I haven't really spent much time in the company of the lads since Friday. That's the longest we've ever been apart other than holidays. I wonder if they miss me?

Thursday 21 September

10.15 a.m. – At work

I met Emma on the way to work this morning and, after a much needed cuddle, she asked me if I knew what was being planned for her leaving do. I said I didn't, and now I'm terrified that something is being planned for me.

I don't really know if I could face another saggy-titted woman.

11.25 a.m. – At work

A quick call to Liz has revealed the worst. Not only are the women taking Emma out for a quiet meal straight from work tonight, but a joint pub crawl has been planned for the two of us after work tomorrow. She's also heard that some kind of 'o-gram' will make an appearance but she doesn't know when.

Shit. I hate things like that. I always have. Over the years I've worked here, I've seen more poor bastards than I care to remember, both men and women, totally humiliated by a succession of strippers, Tarzans, gorillas, firemen and even, on one occasion, Mickey Mouse. Although I think that was a bit of a cock-up.

And now I'm going to get hit again. I best make sure I've got clean pants on.

19.50 p.m. – At home

I was going to ask Liz if she fancied a night out tonight, but of course she's gone out with Emma and the others so I ended up having a few beers with some remarkably secretive lads and then coming home. Tomorrow is obviously going to be eventful.

Sadly, the only response on the job front has been a couple of 'No thanks' and this is really starting to worry me. At least I've got plenty of money to tide me over, but that's hardly the point. Maybe I should take up Emma's offer after all.

23.50 p.m. – At home

In my quieter moments, I've often wondered what it would be like to be a woman. Mostly because there are a number of things I envy them for. Breasts and the ability to retain their hair for the duration of their lives being the usual two. But I've always kind of fancied finding out how a woman feels when she has to deal with her other half making a complete prat of her. But I don't have to wonder about that any more, because now I know.

About two hours ago, I got a call from an obviously shitfaced Liz who told me that I had to come and take Emma home because she was too pissed to make it on her own. By the time I got there, she was sitting on the kerb, crying her eyes out and surrounded by vomit. And a very unattractive sight it was.

Of course, when she saw me, she started all that 'Billy, I love you, this is my bloke isn't he gorgeous' bollocks, but when I tried to get her to come home, she suddenly decided that she had to say goodbye to everyone so it took me almost half an hour to get her into the car. By that time, she was sobbing, all the girls were crying and a small audience of lads had gathered. Some of whom began abusing me for dragging her home when she was obviously having such a good time.

By the time I'd set them straight, she was fast asleep. And when I got back to Bushey, could I wake her up? Could I fuck. I literally had to drag her out of the car and up the stairs to her flat. At least Helena was in to help me. Thank Christ she was as well. I almost fucking crippled myself getting her into bed.

God knows how she'll feel in the morning. And to think that, as from tomorrow night, she'll be living with me. I still can't quite believe it. Mind you, after seeing her in that state, I don't know if I'm ready for it.

Friday 22 September

09.40 a.m. – At work

Somehow, Emma made it into work on time, but she looks like shit and has already shed a few tears. Not surprising really, because today is going to be hard for her. She's worked at this company for quite a time and a lot of the people in her office have become good mates.

I could say the same for me I guess. But I'm more frightened than upset. I don't trust my mates one little bit. And with bloody good reason if past performance is anything to go by. If I had the bottle, I'd do the off right now.

10.15 a.m. – At work

How sweet. Sue has just been over and given me two cards. One a goodbye one from the girls in the office and one from her wishing me good luck in my new home. Not strictly accurate, but I know what she means.

10.55 a.m. – At work

Kev has just been down and told me to be in the pub at lunchtime or else. That's bad.

He also told me that, because I will be unemployed, they don't want to sit with me at football tomorrow as I'll lower the tone. When I pointed out that this was a shame because I was planning on buying them all numerous beers for keeping quiet about my April Fools' stunt, he said that they'd meet me at the same place, same time, as usual.

11.35 a.m. – At work

Julia has just rung to wish me luck at whatever it is I end up doing. I am quite touched by this. Although it hasn't escaped my notice that, if she's going to be back in Watford, she'll probably be back in the gym. So at least I might get to see her once in a while. Which is nice.

12.00 p.m. – At work

Liz has just rung to make sure I will be in the pub at lunchtime. This is looking increasingly dodgy.

14.30 p.m. – At work

Thank fuck that's over. Although if I'm honest, it wasn't half bad.

For once, rather than indulge in their usual practice of humiliation, the lads had left everything to the girlies and the 'o-gram' wasn't a stripper, but a singing telegram. And it wasn't just for me, but for Emma as well. To celebrate the fact that we were moving in together rather than the fact that we were leaving. A bit soppy, but about a thousand times better than the things that had been running around my head.

We all got a bit pissed of course, and Liz has just told me that they're all sneaking off early this afternoon so tonight is going to be massive. Fuck knows where Sean is though.

15.25 p.m. – At work

Bastards. I knew it was too good to be true. Once again, I'm sitting at my desk covered in baby oil and sawdust after a close encounter with a stripper.

It's my own fault of course. When Sean rang to say that the lads were all in the basement having a clandestine farewell piss-up, I really should have twigged. Never mind, at least this one had nice tits. Although I could have done without having all the women down there urging her to get out my tackle. Emma was the bloody worst. As if she hasn't seen it enough.

16.25 p.m. – At work

Well, that's almost it. Our last day at work is just about over. In less than an hour, we'll be out on the piss, officially living together, she'll be working in Northwood and I'll be unemployed.

And although a bit worried about the job situation, I couldn't be more pleased. Because the simple fact is that, from now on, Emma is all that matters. She's beautiful, and funny, and I love her more than I could ever imagine it was possible for me to love anyone. And what's more, she loves me right back. To be honest, after everything that's happened to me these last few years, I just can't believe my luck.

Life is good.

Chapter 11

October

Tuesday 24 October

22.30 p.m. – At home

It's been a little over a month since I last wrote in this diary. But with a bit of time on my hands tonight, I thought that it would be nice to sit down and bring it up to date.

The reason I stopped was nothing to do with leaving work though. It was because, as I read though my last entry, even though I was covered in oil and sawdust, it suddenly struck me that, from that point on, my life was never going to be the same. And as I thought about that, and began to think about the other things that had been going on, the good things anyway, I suddenly realised that I couldn't imagine how things could get any better. I hoped they would of course, especially on the job front, but at that moment in time, I wasn't able to think how. And so, if I kept writing in my diary, all I'd probably end up doing was recording the decline of my life from that point on. And I didn't want to do that.

But as it happens, things have got better. Out of the blue, my old boss Dave got in touch and, having heard I'd left the old place, offered me a job working with him. It's less money and based in the West End which is a bastard. But I spend most of my time on the road and they've given me a company car which is great. It also gives me plenty of chance to speak to Liz as I'm driving around. Between us, I'm sure we could talk bollocks for England.

As for footie, well . . . that's not so great. But at least I get to see the lads, and on match days it's as if nothing has changed. Which suits me just fine.

As for Emma, it must be in the genes I suppose, but she's taken to the security game like a duck to water. Most mornings, she's champing at the bit to get to work and her dad is over the moon with her. She's even finally decided to learn to drive. In fact, as I'm typing this, she's on one of those seven-day intensive courses in Kent. I can't wait to see her face when she sees that her old man has got her a company car. She'll freak out.

She still hasn't lost any weight though. In fact, she's put on a few pounds and is back up to a proper sixteen again, although she finally seems to have come to terms with it. I don't mind: I think she looks great. But then I always did.

But the big difference has been here. At home. Because that's what it's become now, our home. It was hard at first though. Bloody hell, the first two weeks were murder. First she took over the spare bedroom and turned it into a walk-in wardrobe, then she infested my CD collection with everything from Boyzone to Steps. And as if that wasn't bad enough, the bathroom now resembles what is best described as a tart's palace.

We had loads of stupid arguments as well. Things like me leaving the toilet seat up, her leaving the toilet seat down and about how, whenever there's a game on, I can read a paper, watch Sky Sports, keep an eye on Teletext and listen to the radio all at the same time. Yet whenever she asks me to do anything, I never hear a word.

Then there's all the other stuff, the habits. Fuck me, she drives me mad sometimes. What is the point spending hours in front of a mirror plucking out your eyebrows only to colour them in again afterwards? And if there's a legitimate reason why she has to sing at the top of her voice all the time or play 'Angels' by Robbie bloody Williams over and over again, I wish someone would tell me what it is. But worst of all, how can anyone seriously think *Friends* is better than *Frasier*? Or for that matter, actually like *Brookside*?

And as I knew she would, she's started dragging me to Ikea and dropping hints about decorating although, so far, I've managed to resist. I did finally bow to pressure though and move Geri into the spare room. But only because Emma came home one day and told me that she wouldn't have sex in the front room until she was taken down. Still, she'll be all right in there. She's got Ricky Martin for company.

But at the end of the day, they're all little things and none of them really matter. Because we're happy as two pigs in shit. We laugh almost all the time and, if anything, I'd say we were closer now than we've ever been. We're certainly best mates. I suppose you could even say that we're soul mates.

I'm just glad we found each other. Even now, I still pinch myself every day because never in my wildest dreams did I ever hope things would be this good for me. And whether its down to fate, Liz or even Barry the wanker, I can honestly say that, for the first time ever, life is great. No, it's better than great.

Life is top.

If you enjoyed this book here is a selection of other bestselling sports titles from Headline

THE AUTOBIOGRAPHY	Gareth Edwards	£7.99	☐
THE AUTOBIOGRAPHY	John Barnes	£6.99	☐
ROPE BURNS	Ian Probert	£7.99	☐
FROM OUTBACK TO OUTFIELD	Justin Langer	£6.99	☐
BARMY ARMY	Dougie Brimson	£6.99	☐
VINNIE	Vinnie Jones	£6.99	☐
FORMULA ONE UNCOVERED	Derick Allsop	£7.99	☐
MANCHESTER UNITED RUINED MY LIFE	Colin Shindler	£5.99	☐
TEAR GAS AND TICKET TOUTS	Eddy Brimson	£6.99	☐
DARK TRADE	Donald McRae	£7.99	☐
A LOT OF HARD YAKKA	Simon Hughes	£6.99	☐
LEFT FOOT FORWARD	Garry Nelson	£6.99	☐

Headline books are available at your local bookshop or newsagent. Alternatively, books can be ordered direct from the publisher. Just tick the titles you want and fill in the form below. Prices and availability subject to change without notice.

Buy four books from the selection above and get free postage and packaging and delivery within 48 hours. Just send a cheque or postal order made payable to Bookpoint Ltd to the value of the total cover price of the four books. Alternatively, if you wish to buy fewer than four books the following postage and packaging applies:

UK and BFPO £4.30 for one book; £6.30 for two books; £8.30 for three books.

Overseas and Eire: £4.80 for one book; £7.10 for 2 or 3 books (surface mail).

Please enclose a cheque or postal order made payable to *Bookpoint Limited*, and send to: Headline Publishing Ltd, 39 Milton Park, Abingdon, OXON OX14 4TD, UK.
Email Address: orders@bookpoint.co.uk

If you would prefer to pay by credit card, our call team would be delighted to take your order by telephone. Our direct line is 01235 400 414 (lines open 9.00 am–6.00 pm Monday to Saturday 24 hour message answering service). Alternatively you can send a fax on 01235 400 454.

Name ....

Address ....

....

....

If you would prefer to pay by credit card, please complete:
Please debit my Visa/Access/Diner's Card/American Express (delete as applicable) card number:

Signature .... Expiry Date ....